The mountain was angry...

Crazy as the thought was, Mercy believed it. With the ground trembling beneath her, and the thunder rolling overhead in an endless, stunning wave of sound, she could only believe that Thunder Mountain was crying out in rage.

She pressed her face to her knees and tried to tell herself it was just an ordinary storm, just ordinary thunder. But she couldn't quite believe it.

"Mercy."

Lifting her head, she saw Gray Cloud crossing the pine-needle carpet with long, fluid strides.

"I want to get away from here," he said. "Then I will come back and hunt those who trespass on the sacred mountain."

Thunder roared furiously overhead, and Mercy realized with a chill trickling down her spine that she didn't know what Gray Cloud meant when he said *hunt.*

And she wasn't sure she wanted to know....

Rachel Lee wrote her first play in the third grade for a school assembly, and by the age of twelve she was hooked on writing. She's lived all over the United States, on both the East and West coasts, and now resides in Florida.

Having held jobs as a security officer, real estate agent and optician, she uses her background, as well as her natural flair for creativity, to write stories that are undeniably romantic. "After all, life is the biggest romantic adventure of all—and if you're open and aware, the most marvelous things are just waiting to be discovered."

THUNDER MOUNTAIN

RACHEL LEE

Silhouette Books

Published by Silhouette Books
America's Publisher of Contemporary Romance

For Margaret Cheney,
my dear Aussie friend,
whose letters bring joy to many a day.
And for Cris
[Always]

SILHOUETTE BOOKS

ISBN 0-373-51126-4

THUNDER MOUNTAIN

Visit Silhouette at www.eHarlequin.com

Printed in U.S.A.

CHAPTER ONE

Gray Cloud watched the woman toil up the rocky side of the mountain. She was foolhardy, coming here all alone, he thought. But *wasicu* women prided themselves on such courage these days, and this one displayed both courage and determination as she struggled up a steep slope over loose scree. Again and again she slipped and came down hard beneath the weight of her heavy pack. Time and again Gray Cloud held himself back. He would not aid her if she might be a threat. Nor would she appreciate his assistance.

The *wasicu* didn't trust him. They called him the Renegade of Thunder Mountain and thought he was dangerous. He didn't care about that, but he didn't wish to frighten this woman, who had come to do a task for her people. He, too, was here to perform a task, and that task did not include terrifying this woman—yet.

Standing back in the trees, he watched her painful progress and stood ready to intervene should she come to harm. But she did not. Scrambling upward on hands and knees over loose talus, she pushed on with dogged determination. At places she slipped back a foot for every two she advanced, but she never paused.

Gray Cloud felt a glimmer of admiration. Some people were strong of spirit, strong of heart, and it appeared this woman was one of them. She thought she was alone and unobserved, and yet she forged steadily ahead, refusing to give in or even slow down. Stubborn, Gray Cloud thought. Stubborn was good. Stubborn stuck when everything else fell away. That could be a problem for him. For the mountain.

He could have told her an easier way to go, but the woman and the mountain were settling things between them, so he simply watched it unfold. The mountain challenged her, and she accepted. The Stone People teased her with the sharp talus but didn't try to seriously harm her with a rock slide. Thunder Spirits grumbled and flickered in the dark clouds that always seemed to surround the very peak, but they didn't threaten her.

Gray Cloud and the mountain watched her progress.

The Indians called the mountain Thunder Mountain. It towered in rocky splendor and grim isolation over the surrounding peaks, a forbidding upthrust of granite and soil. It was a place of strong medicine, and it got its name from the thunder that often rolled down its stark sides into the valleys and plain below.

Wasicu scientists claimed to have explained the rock slides that rolled down the slopes with a roar of falling boulders that could be heard for miles.

Gray Cloud knew the white man's theory and dismissed it. The *wasicu* collected bits of information the way magpies collected little bits of straw and glass for their nests. They gathered all those small nuggets together, formed them into pretty patterns and called it knowledge.

Gray Cloud knew better. The mountain rumbled when the Stone People spoke. And *Wakinyan*, Thunder, dwelt in the air over the peak to bring enlightenment to those brave enough to seek visions on the mountain's shoulders. As a child he had come up here and had his first vision. All alone, in the dead of night, whipped by the wind as a storm raged around him, barely nine years old, he had stood on this very mountainside and spoken with the Thunder Beings. They had told him who he was and what he must do with his life, and ever since he had been different from other men.

They who spoke with the Thunder were set apart forever, charged with a task that might last a lifetime.

For Gray Cloud, it had *become* his life. There was, up above, a bowl-like depression in the mountain, a place called a cirque by white men. In that huge depression were multitudes of sticks bearing colored strips of cloth that the Lakota called *shina,* or robes. These robes marked the presence of all the people who had climbed Thunder Mountain to pray or cry for a vision. It was a holy site, and Gray Cloud's life was dedicated to protecting it from encroachment by miners and loggers, and by the curious. He was here to prevent the religious practice of his fellows from being turned into a spectacle, even thwarted entirely. And he would do whatever was necessary.

There were few enough holy places left to the red man. Gone were *Paho Sapa,* the Black Hills and heart of the world. Gone was Bear Butte, now crowded with tourists so that a man couldn't find silence in which to pray. A person needed solitude to pray or cry for a vision. Some ceremonies were meant to be publicly witnessed, but others were meant to be private, and prayer was meant to be a private conversation between the Earth People and the Creator.

Gray Cloud was dedicated to preserving the sanctity of Thunder Mountain.

But the woman climbing so steadily was not a threat to the sacred ground. At least, so he believed. She had come to study wolves, the first to come this far south in many years. The wolves dwelt in the caves on the western slope, away from the sacred ground of the cirque. The woman would study the wolves, and Gray Cloud would leave her in peace so long as she did nothing else. The wolves were strong spirits, after all, and could well take care of themselves when it came to a solitary woman. She would be no trouble.

As long as she didn't trespass.

When he saw that she had safely passed the most dangerous part of the climb, he drew back even farther into the concealment of the forest. Among the *wasicu* who had charged him with the murder of his sister's husband, he was believed to be a dangerous renegade. The woman would not be happy to know he was watching.

What was her name? he wondered idly. The spirits who had told him of her coming had not spoken of her name.

Tomorrow Woman.

The words whispered into his mind, carried by the wind. She was Tomorrow Woman. But she would not answer to the name. She would not know it. She would have a white man's name of some kind. But the spirits would not tell him that.

Tomorrow Woman. He wondered what it meant.

The mountain stirred, rousing a bit from its ancient dreams, aware of a trespasser on its slopes. Those who came to pray hardly caused a ripple in the mountain's awareness, hardly disturbed dreams that were almost as old as the planet. This trespasser didn't come to pray, and the mountain felt a dissonance.

The woman climbed steadily, never giving in. Her determination could be a problem. From everywhere, the mountain watched her and took her measure, and knew that she could not be ignored.

And then, elsewhere, the mountain felt a greater dissonance. A disruptive sense of invasion. There was another trespasser, one bent on destruction. One who would certainly cause harm.

The mountain shuddered a little, wakening further, and forgot the woman for now. There was danger on its slopes. A threat that could not be ignored.

Mercy Kendrick felt someone or something watching her as she struggled up the talus slope. The sensation was a prickle at the back of her neck, which she forced herself to ignore. It had to be a bird, or perhaps some small forest creature. Even a bear. Whatever it was, it was unlikely to bother her, so she refused to give in to the need to pause and look around.

It never entered her head that it might be the Renegade of Thunder Mountain who watched her. She quite simply didn't believe he existed, except as the product of overactive imaginations. Many Indians came up here to pray, and none of them was ever troubled. No doubt a combination of events and sights over the years had yielded the story of the Renegade, that desperate murderer who had never killed anybody on this mountain.

Oh, people died on this mountain. There was no question of that. The geological instability of the rocks made many places dangerous, and from time to time someone would be caught in a rock slide. Or struck by the fierce lightning that often played along the slopes.

The mountain seemed to create its own weather, and its very peak was usually shrouded in clouds. There was a place in Alaska like that, she seemed to remember, though she couldn't remember its name. Panting in the thinning atmosphere, struggling to climb on hands and knees, she didn't particularly care *what* mountain in Alaska made its own weather. Mountains everywhere impacted the weather, and when they were as big as this one…

She slipped and lost her footing, landing with a grunt on her stomach. Loose rocks tumbled away below her, the clatter loud in the natural silence. Then, from above, came the hollow boom of thunder, reminding her that at any moment the clouds could unleash a deluge, and then this slope would become slippery as ice. Gritting her teeth, she reached out with a leather-gloved hand and grabbed at a small bulge in the rock face. Tugging mightily, she pulled herself upward.

Rock climbing was easier than this, she thought. At least she wouldn't be struggling under a sixty-pound pack and sleeping bag. Nor had she expected this part of the climb to be so difficult. She had, in fact, expected it to be relatively easy, and she'd certainly climbed more difficult terrain in her time. But this mountain felt as if it were fighting her. Even El Capitan hadn't felt that way. El Capitan had been tolerant of her climb. Thunder Mountain didn't feel tolerant at all.

Exhaling, she blew her breath upward and shoved a strand of hair back. People would think she was crazy if they ever discovered that she believed mountains had personalities. That some were benevolent, some impatient, some evil. Well, maybe not evil. Thunder Mountain didn't feel evil, exactly. But it sure wasn't indifferent.

Oh, yeah! They would think she was crazy.

At last she reached the top of the rocky incline and was able to stand on a more level piece of ground. Turning, she looked back the way she had come and wondered if she were, in fact, losing her mind. The rock face she had just traversed looked a hell of a lot more dangerous from this perspective than it had from below. From below she hadn't even been tempted to give thought to finding another way. From here, she wondered how she had managed to climb it at all: smooth, without toeholds or handholds in its unmarked face, it was too steep. Steeper than she had originally imagined. Steep enough that she would certainly know better than to come back this way.

Now she could see, over the tops of the trees below, a breathtaking panoramic view of the ranches of Conard County, Wyoming. So much wide-open space, cut by the winding veins of draws and gullies, and all of it green with spring splendor right now.

Closer by, at the edges of the forest, colorful wildflowers bobbed their heads. Mercy gave herself a few moments to soak up the beauty, but she had promised herself that she absolutely would not stop until the light began to fail or the weather closed in. The sooner she reached the caves, the sooner she could verify the presence or absence of the wolf pack.

Turning, she shifted her backpack a little to resettle the load, then began to climb again. The terrain here was somewhat easier, and she was able to stay on her feet.

It would be a matter of considerable interest if there really were wolves on Thunder Mountain. In the first place, wolves hadn't been seen in this part of Wyoming for a couple of generations, at least. And it would be rare anywhere, even in wolf country, to find a pack at this altitude. Of course, it might be an adaptive feature of this particular pack. Certainly the higher country would be safer for them during breeding season.

But she was taking a serious career risk in coming up here on what might well be a wild-goose chase. The sightings of the wolves of Thunder Mountain were few: a hunter here and there who had wandered up the slopes after an elk; talk among the Indians who came up here to pray; sightings in the foothills among ranchers...who might well have mistaken a large coyote for a wolf at a distance. It wasn't as if wolves were an everyday sight, easily identifiable.

But the sightings and reports, scarce though they were, were enough to bring Mercy up the side of this treacherous mountain in the early spring. If there *were* indeed wolves up here, this would be the best time to locate them. During gestation and the first three weeks after the birth of a new litter, the pack tended to remain in one place. Thereafter they would move with increasing frequency. Long before that happened, if there were any wolves up here, she hoped to put electronic collars on at least a few of them so she could track their migrations.

But, of course, she might find nothing. That possibility weighed on her. Wolves had lately been reported in Yellowstone National Park, far to the north, but it wasn't yet certain if there were just a couple of strays or an actual pack, whether the wolves had really returned to the area, or some animal had ventured out on its own. Wolves were known to do that, too.

A lone wolf might be interesting to observe, but it would hardly have the impact on the field that she hoped to achieve. But a lone wolf would be infinitely better than none, because if she returned with word that there were no wolves at all on Thunder Mountain, the department chairman was going to have a field day at her expense. Dr. Lewis Clark Thomas wanted nothing more than to see Mercy Kendrick fall flat on her face. In his opinion, if she wanted to study anything, it ought to be apes. She was wasting her time on predators such as the vanishing wolf. No future in it, he said, and he would undoubtedly use a failure to find wolves here as another excuse to deny her tenure.

Future or not, she was inclined to think he was on her case because she was too independent to suit him. Instead of bowing to his authority and knowledge and just generally kissing up to him, she was prone to argue when she didn't agree. Oh, yes, he would love it if this proved to be a fool's errand. She would spend the next year hearing a daily "I told you so" from him. Smiling wryly now, she wondered if she would be able to endure it.

But wolves had all but vanished from the lower forty-eight states. There were some in Minnesota still, and reports of Canis rufus, the red wolf, in East Texas and Louisiana—although there was a great deal of disagreement about whether they were wolves or coyotes, or a mix of the two.

But none had been seen in this part of Wyoming for a long, long time. No, she couldn't pass up this opportunity. If the wolves were here, it would be a marvelous sign of resurgence, a banner marking the return of a species to its native habitat. It would be a small victory on the ecological battlefield.

Again she felt the prickling at the base of her skull. This time she halted and looked around, no longer quite so blithely certain that whatever was watching her was harmless. If it had followed her...

Shivering inwardly, she adjusted the straps of her pack and tried not to think about *what* might be following her up the slope of this mountain. A wildcat of some kind? A black bear? The thought of a sow with cubs made her scalp prickle. This far out, wild animals should still be wild animals, wary of humans. But with the Indians coming up here regularly to pray, perhaps the mountain's inhabitants were not entirely wild any longer. Perhaps they had lost their fear of men.

And that was when they became truly dangerous.

The slope steepened sharply, and for a little while the sense of being watched vanished. She was too busy trying to breathe, anyway. As she approached ten thousand feet in elevation, the air was thin enough to make heavy exertion uncomfortable. Reminding herself of the dangers to one who came from a lower altitude, she deliberately slowed her pace. Pulmonary edema could be deadly.

A little farther on, the mountain eased up on its challenge, giving her a fairly level run that allowed her to catch her breath and gave the backs of her legs a much-needed respite.

Heavy exertion always threw her deep into the well of reflection, so that minutes stretched into hours almost unnoticed. She really had little idea of how much time had passed or how much farther she had walked when she realized that the light had changed from an ordinary, almost colorless gray to an eerie, ghostly green.

Halting, she looked upward at the clouds and felt a sudden awareness of danger. These were no longer the familiar, leaden cumulonimbus of a thunderstorm. Instead they had become a writhing, seething mass of gray-green swirls that seemed to defy the very air currents on which they were borne.

A gust of wind suddenly swept down the side of the mountain and hit her hard, causing her to stagger sideways. Overhead, thunder cracked with deafening intensity, a warning she couldn't ignore. The air was chilly, and if she got drenched she would quickly become hypothermic. Her day's hike was over.

Gray Cloud watched the woman dig a trench so water would run around her, then climb into a sleeping bag between two layers of waterproof tarp. No tent. The wind would likely have blown down any nylon tent.

Another challenge to her, this time from the Cloud People and the wind. A small challenge, a minor testing of her mettle. She was handling it well, with no evidence of frustration or annoyance. Most *wasicu* perceived the weather as a nuisance unless it was sunny and mild. This woman betrayed none of that in her actions.

Nodding to himself, Gray Cloud settled down to await whatever might happen next.

During the night, the mountain and the elements ceased their teasing and challenged the woman in earnest. The wind snatched the tarp, scooping it up and away, exposing her to the deluge of the heavy thunderstorm. The rain lubricated the rocks above, and the thunder of a landslide added its roar to the thunder from the sky.

Mercy sat up, trapped in the wet sleeping bag, and tried

to see through a night as dark as pitch, where not even a glimmer of starlight pierced the clouds. Beneath her, she felt the trembling of the ground that announced the rock slide, felt it like giant footsteps. She couldn't tell, though, whether she was in danger—and if she was, there was no way she could move when she couldn't see an inch before her nose.

The sensation of impenetrable dark induced a panicky feeling of claustrophobia in her. The sense of being trapped was almost overwhelming, and she began to struggle against the confines of her soaked sleeping bag, needing desperately to feel as if she could flee, even if she might break her neck doing so.

Suddenly, stunning her with its unexpectedness, a heavy weight hurled itself out of the dark and flattened her to the ground, pinning her.

Oh, my God! Terror swamped her panic, and she began to struggle in earnest, convinced a bear was attacking her. And closer came the heavy, pounding footsteps of the rock slide. Some corner of her mind realized that death was imminent, that her life was now measured in mere seconds. The realization battered down the terror enough to let a rational thought through.

Don't move.

Almost as if echoing the thought in her mind, a voice growled in her ear, "Don't move!"

It wasn't a bear that was pinning her to the ground! It was a man!

For an instant relief swamped her. And then she remembered that a man could be as deadly as a bear. Remembered the tales she had dismissed about the Renegade of Thunder Mountain. Instinctively, she shoved at the weight crushing her.

"Don't move," he growled again. "The slide is coming this way!"

He was sheltering her with his body! "We should get out of the way," she heard herself argue with more presence of mind than she would have believed she had at that moment.

The man on top of her grunted sharply. It was here, she realized. The slide was here. The storm sounds were drowned in the deafening roar and clatter of the falling rocks. The world had gone insane, and there wasn't anything to be done except endure it.

The body sheltering hers jerked sharply, then they were free of the slide, the thunderous roar now below them on the slope. Moments passed as they lay there, still, waiting to be sure it was over.

A soft word escaped the man as he rolled off her. It sounded like an oath, but it wasn't English. After a moment Mercy dared to move, sitting up, still trapped inside her sleeping bag.

"Are you—" Her voice broke as she tried to peer through the dark at her rescuer. "Are you all right?"

"Mm." It was a short, affirmative grunt.

Her pack had been on the slope just above her head, and she reached for it now to get out her flashlight. As her hands touched the nylon, she realized just how much this man's body had sheltered hers. Her pack was covered with small stones, sharp pieces of splintered rock and one stone large enough to have killed if it had hit either of them. Shoving it aside, she pulled the pack toward her and felt around for the flashlight.

"We could have been killed," she said. A stupid, useless thing to say, but it was suddenly necessary to speak. Necessary to move. Necessary to do anything at all to hold at bay the realization that she might have been crushed to death under tons of rock. Or that she might have been buried alive.

Light. Oh, Lord, she needed light now. Light to shove

the walls of darkness back and assure her that she wasn't buried. Despite the raw wind that whipped her cheeks and blew her hair wildly about, despite the smell of forest growth and the feel of rain pouring onto her head, she still felt closed in by the night. Trapped.

At last her hand closed on the flashlight, and she fumbled with the switch. Suddenly the night jumped back, and the rain became a yellowish haze as it refracted the beam of the light. And the man sitting across from her looked like a vision carved from stone.

Gray Cloud. The Renegade of Thunder Mountain. There was no doubt in her mind that she was facing the man around whom the myths had grown. A man like this would draw uneasy attention wherever he appeared.

His Sioux ancestry was apparent in every plane of his dark face, in the dark eyes that stared unblinkingly at her, in the long jet hair that whipped wildly in the wind. He was dressed in ordinary enough fashion—jeans, boots and a zipped up jacket—but otherwise there wasn't an ordinary thing about him.

He was large—even when he was sitting cross-legged, that was apparent—and in the uncertain light the shadows added to an aura of danger and hardness that was almost terrifying. His hands were resting casually on his knees, and there was nothing at all threatening in his posture, but her mouth went dry, anyway. Dimly she heard herself make a small sound, something like a sighing moan.

"I am Gray Cloud," he said.

She swallowed hard. "I kind of…thought you might be. I'm, um, Mercy Kendrick."

"Mercy." He repeated her name as if accustoming his tongue and lips to the shape of the sound. "A name that sounds like the sigh of a sad heart." He turned his head, looking over his shoulder into the rainy night. "Come with me. There's a cave not far from here. I can build a fire there, to warm you."

Had she been in any major city in the country, or even any small town, she never would have gone anywhere with a stranger...and certainly not one with this man's reputation. But this was not any town or village; it was the isolated side of a mountain in the wilderness, and if Gray Cloud intended her any harm, he could do it here as easily as anywhere else. She was effectively his prisoner, caged by her isolation and the pitch-darkness of the cold, stormy night.

Sensing her agreement, he shouldered her pack and then waited while she struggled out of the sodden sleeping bag. When she was free, he scooped up the heavy bag as if it weighed nothing.

"Walk behind me," he said. "Hang on to my jacket or the backpack."

She handed him the flashlight, but he flicked it off as soon as she had a good grip on the waist of his jacket.

"How can you see?" she asked as they started off into the blackness. It was so dark that with each step she felt as if she were in danger of falling over a cliff edge. "You can't possibly see anything!"

"I can see." The flat statement was no answer at all, but as they moved forward through the darkness, she could not doubt that somehow he *was* able to see. Clearly. As clearly as if it were daylight. He moved forward surefootedly, and because she was right behind him, she encountered no obstacles that he didn't see first and warn her about.

The sound of the rain falling through the trees and striking the ground was a steady roar that drowned all other noises. It was, Mercy thought, like walking through a solid wall of sound, all her senses dead save hearing...and touch. The touch of her feet on the ground, the grip of her hand on his jacket.

Thunder boomed hollowly, echoing against the sides of the mountain, but no lightning was visible. Twice she was sure she felt something brush against her shoulders, something...batlike.

Then, ahead, she saw blue sparks, little dancing sparkles that seemed to appear out of nowhere and then vanish.

"What's that?" she asked, tugging on Gray Cloud's jacket. "That blue light. Do you see it?"

"Spirits," Gray Cloud said.

Spirits? Mercy felt her jaw dropping open, and only the slap of wind-borne rain reminded her to close it. Spirits. Every college-educated bone in her body rebelled at that unscientific answer, and she had to bite her tongue. This man came from a different culture, she reminded herself. Moreover, he was reputed to be some kind of crazy medicine man. Witch doctor. Whatever it was. So, naturally he would speak in terms of spirits.

And regardless of what they were, the blue lights continued to flicker here and there, in a Tinkerbell-like dance, the only things visible in the rain-darkened night.

Some kind of static discharge, she told herself. An electrical phenomenon, like the lightning. And when one brushed near her cheek as if it were a cobweb, she became convinced. The night was charged with electricity—any thunderstorm was—and they were practically in the clouds. This was just some strange kind of lightning.

But it was odd how it seemed to dance before them, as if lighting their way. Her natural curiosity surged, distracting her from her discomfort and the chill of the sodden night. Surely this was something never before studied?

But suddenly all the dancing blue sparkles were gone, and the rain was no longer pouring on them.

The cave. Here the wind was shut out, as was the downpour, the only detectable changes as they escaped the night's savagery.

"Here," Gray Cloud said. "Just settle down right here until I get the fire going."

Reluctantly, she let go of his jacket and settled cross-legged on the floor of the cave. The undisturbed darkness was disorienting, as was the echo of the rain off the cave walls. Only the solidity of rock beneath her assured her that she wasn't tumbling wildly through space.

Nor could she hear any sounds as Gray Cloud moved around in the cave. For all she could tell, he might have abandoned her. Well, if he had, he'd at least left her someplace dry and out of the wind. Turning her head slowly, she tried to penetrate the dark and wondered why there were no more blue sparkles.

Orange light flared suddenly, and gradually, from a small flame, a camp fire grew in the darkness. It was not enough light to reach the cave walls, so it still felt as if they were sitting on the edge of the world, but she could see Gray Cloud in the flickering light, along with the curtain of rain beyond the huge cave mouth.

"Come closer," he said. "You're wet, and you don't want to get a chill."

Almost as if his words had made her aware that she was soaked to the bone and that the night was cold, she began to shiver. Scooting quickly across the cave floor, she got as close to the blazing heat of the fire as she could and held out her hands in gratitude.

Gray Cloud settled on the far side of the fire, a choice that made it clear he offered no threat at the moment. The cave opening was behind her; she could run without obstruction. Or try to. She shivered again, realizing that even if she tried, she wouldn't get very far. He didn't have to guard her; there was no way she could escape him if he was determined to keep her.

After he sat down, he chanted something quietly. Some kind of prayer, Mercy thought, maintaining a cautious silence until he finished. When his black eyes opened and met hers unblinkingly across the fire, she found her voice.

"I heard about you before I came up here," she blurted. "I didn't think you were real."

His eyes never wavered, and his expression never changed. Nor did he answer. Well, of course not, she thought. What could anyone say to something like that, except to state the obvious? And this man didn't look like the kind who would often state the obvious about anything.

"You came to study the wolves," he said.

Mercy started. "How did you know that? I only told the sheriff!" And Sheriff Nate Tate was famous for not being a gossip.

Seconds ticked by, marked by the drip of water from outside. "I just know," Gray Cloud said finally. "You're *wasicu*. You wouldn't understand."

Wasicu. White. Mercy squelched a flare of irritation, thinking that it couldn't possibly be wise to annoy this man who was reputed to be a murderer…although Deputy Huskins, who had filled her in on all the wild rumors, had admitted that Gray Cloud had been acquitted of the crime. Not that that meant much; criminals were acquitted all the time, thanks to smart legal maneuvers.

"Well, why don't you try telling me, anyway," she said, unable to keep all her irritation out of her voice. "I don't want anyone to know what I'm doing up here." To protect the wolves, if they existed. Ranchers from the valleys below wouldn't hesitate to hunt down any wolves in the vicinity, whether the animals were a threat or not. Nor would they regard the fact that wolves were an endangered species. So were bald eagles, yet they were being killed all the time.

Another long silence. Gray Cloud, it appeared, could not be hurried into speech. That would make him a maddening companion, Mercy thought. Finally he spoke.

"*Tate* told me." He pronounced it *tah-day*.

"*Tate?*"

"You call it the wind. The wind spoke to me of you. *Wakinyan*, the Thunder Spirit, said you would come. The mountain has awaited you."

The wind spoke to me of you. The Thunder Spirit said you would come. The words caused a chill to trickle down her spine, an instinctive, primitive reaction of fear. Reminders that this man was of a different culture, with a different set of beliefs, didn't comfort her at all. In this dark cave, with no light save the camp fire, with Gray Cloud's intense dark eyes boring into her and the wild storm raging outside, reality seemed to have suspended its normal rules.

"I told you that you wouldn't understand," Gray Cloud said. He spoke as if it didn't matter to him one way or the other. "You're *wasicu*. You don't understand these things."

In fact, Mercy realized with another burst of irritation, he was speaking to her the way parents spoke to children who lacked knowledge...or had drawn erroneous conclusions from their observations. It was a gentle tone, almost kindly. Indulgent.

All her life long, because of her diminutive size and pretty face, she had had to fight to be taken seriously. She had been indulged, patronized and frankly dismissed simply because men tended to dismiss pretty women as fluff. Her instinct, as always, was to fight back. To argue. To prove she was *not* a bit of fluff.

But this man, the Renegade of Thunder Mountain, wasn't dismissing her because she was female or pretty. He wasn't even exactly dismissing her. He was stating in a kindly manner that cultural differences prevented understanding between them on this subject. It took her a minute to battle down her instinctive response to the tone, but when she had, she realized she was curious.

"Tell me what I don't understand," she heard herself say to him. "Please."

He continued to study her in silence, a moderately unnerving experience. She had to fight an urge to shift uneasily and look away. More than a minute passed, then he rose and disappeared into the shadows. When he returned, he carried a blanket. In silence he shook it open and draped it around her shoulders. Then he returned to his side of the fire.

"What you don't understand," he said finally, "would require years to explain."

She drew an exasperated breath, ready to argue, but he continued as if he were unaware of her reaction.

"You were raised in a world that separates man from his environment," Gray Cloud said quietly. "You don't understand that spirit is in everything. That *Skan,* the force that animates everything, is in every stone and rock, in every tree, in the breath of the wind. We speak of the Stone People, the Cloud People, the Four-leggeds.... It is as ordinary to me that I should hear a secret on the wind as it is to you to hear one from a friend."

"Animism," Mercy said. "I've heard of that."

"Animism." Gray Cloud repeated the word and shook his head. "You will label and define and separate and isolate...and all understanding is lost by so doing. There is a word your people have—*gestalt.* The whole that is greater than the sum of its parts. You are a gestalt, Mercy Kendrick. And if your scientists cut you into a million tiny pieces and label them all, they will still not define Mercy Kendrick."

He was right about that, she thought. Looking away, she watched how the rain just beyond the cave mouth glimmered in the firelight.

"So," she said presently, not looking at him, "did, um, the wind say it was okay for me to study the wolves?" If this man was going to obstruct her, she wanted to know it up front.

"The wolves will make that decision." Gray Cloud shifted, and the fire flared suddenly. Mercy turned her head swiftly, in time to see flames leap high, then fall back to a comforting glow.

"I mean them no harm," she said.

His black eyes bored into her. "No, you probably don't," he agreed. "Sleep here by the fire. I'll get you another blanket."

A few minutes later, with her back to the dancing flames, she watched the endless fall of rain, little flickers of orange and yellow, and felt sleep begin to steal over her.

And then she saw the dancing blue sparks again, just at the edge of her vision, as her eyes grew heavier and heavier.

Spirits, Gray Cloud had said. *Spirits.*

And as she drifted into sleep, Mercy realized that she had left the normal world behind and stepped into a place where the familiar rules no longer applied.

CHAPTER TWO

*T*he first gray tendrils of light touched the mountain's shoulders lightly, signaling a change of ascendancy among its inhabitants. Mice slipped into burrows; owls settled onto safe perches; bats returned to their caves. Birds welcomed the new day with chirps of song, and does led their fawns to streams to drink.

And the mountain awakened ever more, stretching and flexing powers long unused. The storm during the night had been a mere testing, the rock slide an exercise of atrophied muscles.

And neither had accomplished very much of purpose. The invaders were still on the mountain's slopes, unhindered, undeterred.

Deep inside, the mountain frowned. This was not good.

Mercy opened her eyes to a pale gray light and the sound of steadily falling rain. The wool blankets wrapped around her had kept her warm despite her wet clothes, but it was definitely a morning when she longed for a hot shower.

Sitting up, she discovered that she was alone in the cave. Seizing the opportunity, she struggled out of the blankets and pulled fresh clothes from her backpack. They were clammy, too, but not as sodden as the ones she had on. A minute later, dressed in fresh jeans, a wool sweater and relatively dry socks, she was willing to forego the shower. A granola bar made an easy breakfast.

The fire still burned in a pit hollowed out of the cave floor, and nearby was a stack of wood. Settling as close beside the flames as she could get, Mercy watched the

steady rainfall and considered the likelihood that people
had been seeking shelter in this cave for ten or twenty thousand years. The fire pit might have been hollowed out by
hands that had been dead for centuries. Had there been
more light, it would have been interesting to explore for
drawings on the cave walls.

Shivering in the cold, damp air, she inched closer to the
fire and wondered if Gray Cloud intended to return. She
told herself she didn't really need to fear him; had he been
a threat, surely she would have discovered it last night. But
offering herself such reassurances didn't really help. Not at
all.

He had saved her from the rock slide and brought her to
a dry cave for the night, but that didn't mean he was a safe
man. He was, after all, an accused murderer. He might have
killed once. If so, he could surely be capable of killing
again. She would have to be very cautious, very careful not
to arouse his ire in any way.

But she couldn't run. In the first place, she no longer had
any idea where on the mountain she was. Their long walk
through the rainy dark had left her utterly disoriented. If
she tried to find her way either up or down, she would
probably get lost. It wasn't as if Thunder Mountain was a
smooth pyramid where up was always up and down was
always down. No, the shoulders of this mountain were
ridged and rilled, and up and down could be utterly deceptive when it came to direction.

But there was also no point in running. Gray Cloud lived
on this mountain, and she was going to have to accept that
fact if she wanted to study the wolves. She couldn't drive
him off, and, renegade or not, he was no longer a wanted
man, so she couldn't ask for help from the Conard County
sheriff or the Forest Service. No, he had every right to be
here, and she was just going to have to get used to the fact

that her nearest neighbor for fifty miles might be a murderer.

The shiver that poured through her didn't come entirely from the chilly, damp air. Common sense kept arguing that she would be a fool not to leave this cave right now and head out of here. But common sense had also warned her not to go rock climbing, because it was dangerous. Mercy Kendrick never gave in to fear, and too often common sense was nothing but fear.

Gray Cloud might have killed someone, it was true. But no one had suggested that he had ever killed anyone else. The Conard County Sheriff's Department hadn't warned her that she shouldn't come up here because a mad killer was on the loose. When she had filed her plans with the Park Service, they hadn't advised her to stay clear because a murderer stalked the park. The slopes of Thunder Mountain weren't littered with the corpses of murder victims. Nowhere was there any evidence to imply that the man was a vicious repeat murderer or a serial killer. As long as she kept out of his way, she probably had nothing to fear.

And nothing was going to keep her from looking for these wolves. It was too important in too many ways.

The hypnotic sound of the falling rain mesmerized her, and she let it. There wasn't enough light to read or write by, so for once she was able to do absolutely nothing and not feel guilty for wasting time. Drawing her knees up, she wrapped her arms around her legs and stared dreamily out into the rain, watching how the water seemed to leach the color from the world, turning everything a misty gray.

Much as she enjoyed hot showers and the comforts of civilization, she had always been happiest when out in the wild like this, particularly in the mountains. Something about the outdoors soothed her soul in a way nothing else could. And when she listened to the rain and turned her thoughts inward, she could almost feel the power of the mountain beneath her, could almost hear voices in the steady patter of rain.

Inevitably her thoughts wandered back to the night before, to the strange man who had rescued her and spoken of Thunder Spirits and Cloud People. Well, Gray Cloud wouldn't laugh at the notion that mountains had personalities. Not the way Merle had.

Thinking about Merle Stockton soured her mood immediately. Ten years ago he'd been her climbing partner, a fellow graduate student and her best friend. Then he had wanted to be her lover. She still didn't understand what had dragged her back from the precipice at the last instant, but something had, and a good thing, too, because Merle had been engaged to another woman—a fact he had neglected to mention to her.

Just as he had neglected to mention that his father was primary shareholder in Stockton-Wells, Inc., one of the largest mining and lumbering concerns in the West. Not that Merle was responsible for the logging of the last of the primordial forest. In fact, Merle had, on a couple of occasions, been quite vociferous about the need to protect the old-growth forests. Still, when she had learned who his father was, she had felt deceived.

In retrospect, she wondered how she had ever believed he was a true friend. His deceits had been bad enough, but he had mocked some of the tenderest parts of her, such as her shyly confided feeling that mountains had personalities.

Unconsciously, she sighed and drew her knees closer to her chin. She had always been a little strange, feeling like an outsider looking in, but she had grown up strong and independent as a result. And being considered fey had led her to become fiercely intellectual…except for lowering her guard with Merle that one ill-fated time.

But last night Gray Cloud had spoken of things every bit as fey as any she had ever felt. Instinctively she had resisted what he was saying...but internally, part of her had heard him and understood him. What had he said? The force of life was in everything? Cloud People. Stone People...

Sighing again, she inched a little closer to the fire and wondered if he would return. Surely he must realize she had become lost during last night's trek. He couldn't just have abandoned her, could he?

Turning, she tried to scan the dark interior of the cave, hoping to see some sign that he would return. She could see nothing, however, except her own belongings, the fire and the woodpile. If he normally sheltered here, he had no extraneous possessions. Giving up, she returned her chin to her knees and stared out into the rain.

All of a sudden, as if it had happened while she blinked, a black wolf appeared at the mouth of the cave. Dark, almost blending with the rainy shadows behind him, he materialized as if from nowhere and stood utterly still, watching her with steady yellow eyes that reflected the firelight.

Mercy felt the hair on the back of her neck rise in a primitive reaction. The eyes that studied her were intelligent. Knowing. Eerie.

Then he was gone. As if she had imagined the entire thing. She'd heard that about wolves, that they could come and go like dark wraiths and move so fast you weren't sure you'd seen them. But that didn't prevent her neck from prickling with the uneasy feeling that she had just seen something supernatural.

Suddenly Gray Cloud filled the cave entrance, almost as if he had sprung right out of the ground or been formed from the wolf that had just vanished.

Mercy blinked quickly several times, wondering if she had been so hypnotized by the rain that she had fallen into some kind of trance...or dozed off. For a while he just stood there, silhouetted against the gray world behind him, an imposing figure in jeans, boots and jacket. A perfect male archetype.

Then he moved, shattering the almost dreamlike feeling of the past few moments, and came to squat beside the fire. He held out his hands to the heat, while water dripped from his long black hair.

"I saw a wolf," she said.

He turned his head and looked at her, his face revealing nothing. "Here?"

She nodded. "At the mouth of the cave. One minute he was there, and the next he was gone. It was incredible!"

"My people tell of how the wolves are so silent and stealthy that they can creep among a herd of horses in the dead of night and never disturb them."

Mercy felt herself nodding. "After what I just saw, I can believe it. But you were as silent yourself. Maybe the rain…" Her voice trailed off as he shook his head.

"We call the wolf *sunkmanitu tank,* which means essentially *spirit that looks like a dog.* Warriors have long tried to emulate his silence and stealth. You haven't been around wolves before?"

"In the wild? Not a lot." Actually, not since childhood, when a park ranger in Minnesota had introduced her to the wolves there and the wraithlike animals had stolen her heart, but she wasn't going to admit that. She'd already heard all she wanted to from her department chair about harebrained schemes. His obsidian eyes regarded her piercingly, as if he could see past her words to the truth in her mind, but he let her assertion pass.

"In the wild," he said after a moment, "wolves aren't at all the way your myths make them out to be. My father told me that, as a boy—when wolves were still plentiful— he and the others boys used to go out and dig up their dens and play with the pups."

Mercy drew a sharp breath. "Didn't the bitch object?"

He shook his head. "Wolves rarely attack humans. The female and her mate would watch from a distance but never threaten the boys. And when they were done, the boys put the pups back. In the wild, wolves are wary of humans. Wary and respectful. They could be a nuisance, of course, stealing food and killing the foals, but as a rule, the wolves had more to fear from man than man had to fear from them."

He shifted, settling cross-legged on the cave floor so that he faced her, with the fire beside him. "The wolves here are still wild. They won't give you any trouble, but they'll be shy of you. Observing them won't be easy."

"I really didn't expect it to be. But at this time of year they tend to stay close to their dens and not migrate as much. Mainly I want to ascertain whether there's a viable pack here."

His dark eyes bored into her. "Why?"

Mercy shifted, feeling suddenly uneasy, though she couldn't have said why exactly. "Because it's wonderful if the wolves are returning. And if they're here, we can protect them, make sure that no one hurts them."

His gaze never wavered. "The ecology of this continent was safe in the hands of the native peoples before the *wasicu* ever crossed the oceans. The wolves and the eagles abounded. The buffalo were like a black sea moving across the plains. We never cut down a tree without asking its forgiveness first. We lived in harmony and believed in balance.

"Now, less than two centuries after the white man first came to this part of the continent, it has become a matter of scientific interest that wolves have been sighted on the slopes of Thunder Mountain."

Mercy nodded, accepting the implied rebuke. There was no way to deny that the buffalo, the eagles and the wolves had been carelessly and needlessly slaughtered into near extinction.

"When you go down from here," he said after a moment, "you'll tell your people that there are wolves here. And the ranchers below will start to see wolves behind everything that happens to their cattle and sheep."

"Word is already getting around that there are wolves up here. That's how I heard about it."

"But no one was sure. You'll make them sure. And when that happens, traps will be set."

"Only on private property."

"You think the wolf knows the difference between private property and public domain? Do you think he cares? If he crosses a corner of the Bar C and gets his foot caught in a trap that Jeff Cumberland puts out because a calf has disappeared, do you think the wolf will know he has trespassed?"

"But if Mr. Cumberland's calves disappear, he's going to put out traps regardless. It could be bobcats, or coyotes or bears or..."

"Or stray dogs. Pet German shepherds have always been a greater danger to livestock than wolves. It wasn't so long ago a meat-packing company in Minnesota put a bounty on German shepherds because they were decimating the livestock in the area. The local farmers still went out and slaughtered wolves."

Mercy nodded, surprised that this isolated man had evidently studied the issue. She hadn't expected a renegade medicine man to be familiar with such things. In fact, she thought with an uncomfortable flushing of her cheeks, she hadn't even expected him to be literate, much less articulate and apparently educated.

"If a calf disappears," he continued, "the local ranchers are immediately going to assume the wolves are at fault. How are you going to protect them against being hunted?"

She looked down at her hands and considered the question, knowing full well that protected status for the species was no real protection at all. It certainly hadn't been for the bald eagle. "If they know the wolves aren't really a threat…"

"The information is available. They don't want to hear it. The assumptions are something they were raised with, and when men believe things to be a certain way, they become blind to other truths."

Well, she certainly had personal experience with the truth of that, Mercy found herself thinking. She had been blind to a few truths herself.

"What are you saying?" she asked finally. "That I shouldn't study the wolves?"

During the seconds that followed, she had the eeriest feeling of something brushing against the back of her neck, a chill, clammy touch that sent a shiver running down her spine. Instinctively she looked behind her, but there was nothing there. Just the wind, she told herself. *Tate,* Gray Cloud had called it.

Turning back, she found him staring at her with a steadiness that was unnerving. "No," he said when she met his gaze. "I'm just asking you to be careful what you do with the knowledge you gain."

But, she found herself thinking, if he felt she was endangering the wolves, he would probably do his level best to get her off this mountain. It didn't help to remember that he had been accused of murder. That even though he had been acquitted, his own people had cast him out. Whether or not it was murder, someone had died at this man's hands. Another chill trickled down her neck, but this one was purely psychological.

Just then a gust of wind swept a curtain of cold rain through the cave entrance and slapped it right against Mercy. Startled, she jumped and blinked.

"When the rain stops," Gray Cloud said, "I'll take you up the mountainside to where the den is."

"You know where it is?" She hadn't expected a boon like this, but had, in fact, expected to have to hunt for the den.

He nodded.

"Then you know how many there are? How long they've been here?"

Eyes like shards of obsidian stared back at her impassively. "I didn't count them, but there are more this year than last."

"Last year? How long have they been here?"

"Almost five years."

"And I never heard about it!" Mercy shook her head. "I'm surprised this place hasn't been crawling with wildlife biologists and conservation people."

"This place, as you call it, is sacred to my people. It had better not crawl with biologists and conservationists. Just leave it to the Indians, Ms. Kendrick. We'll take care of everything on Thunder Mountain, simply by letting it be."

Mercy returned his stare steadily for several seconds, then shook her head. "You know better than that, Gray Cloud. You know it won't be left alone. If I don't study the wolves, someone else will."

It was eerie, she thought, how he never moved a muscle, never blinked. Motionless, as if he had been carved from stone, he studied her. Just the way the wolf had earlier, she found herself remembering. With the same intent, focused regard.

At last he spoke, but on an entirely different subject. "The rain will stop shortly."

Mercy instinctively looked out of the cave, but she could see no sign that the steady downpour was abating, or that the day was lightening. "How do you know that?"

"I just know."

Slowly, she turned her head and looked at him again. Her impulse was to ask how he knew, but he would undoubtedly reply with something about the Cloud People or the wind, and she would be no wiser than she was right now.

"There's a cave that will make a good base camp for you," he said. "I'll show you where it is."

At least he hadn't changed his mind about taking her up there, she thought as she settled down to watch the rain. For a minute, when he had started talking about leaving the mountain to the Indians, she had begun to wonder.

By midmorning the rain had stopped, though the sky remained overcast and low clouds touched the peak of Thunder Mountain. The air was chilly, almost cold, but the wind had stopped, and the stillness took the bite out of it.

Every gorge and gully was filled with tumbling, rushing water, which made the journey difficult and sometimes dangerous. It wasn't long at all before Mercy was grateful for Gray Cloud's company. He knew the slopes of this mountain as intimately as most people knew their backyards, and he unquestionably saved her countless hours of retracing her steps to look for a passable route.

He had recovered her tarp from wherever it had blown to during the night, and he carried it for her now, along with her sodden sleeping bag. She wondered if that would ever dry out, then shrugged away the concern. She had her survival blankets, and Gray Cloud had insisted she take his wool ones, also, assuring her that he had more.

"Wolves don't usually venture this high," she remarked to him after one particularly rough climb up a steep, rocky slope.

Turning, he offered a hand and helped her over some loose rocks. "It's not safe for them to venture many other places anymore."

She glanced up at him, struck anew by the absolute midnight of his gaze. "You think they came here to be safe?"

"Perhaps." Releasing her hand, he turned and looked up the slope. "See the ravens?" He pointed to dark specks circling in the sky over some trees higher up. "That's where you'll find the wolves now. The birds are waiting for their turn at the kill."

Mercy nodded, wondering how he could tell that those specks were ravens. Must be the way they were flying, she decided. She had heard, of course, of the symbiotic relationship between the birds and wolves. The ravens were known to locate weak prey for the wolves, and then would feed on the kill when the wolves were done. Some researchers claimed the relationship was a close, social one. She would reserve judgment until she saw it with her own two eyes. She had more than once seen how easy it was to humanize behavior that had other adaptive explanations.

"This way." He headed them away from the circling birds, toward the more forbidding terrain to the north. "There is a harmony in nature," he told her. "What the wolves kill will feed many besides themselves. Nothing will be wasted."

And what about what he had killed? she wondered. Caution kept her from voicing a question that surely would have angered him, but she couldn't help wondering about the contrast between the man she had heard about and the man who was guiding her to the wolf den. "Do you...? Do you stay up here year-round?"

He glanced at her, then indicated the path with a jerk of his chin. "I live on this mountain."

"Why?" The question came automatically, out of her mouth before she could prevent it. When he halted and turned to face her, she wished the ground would open up and swallow her. Nosiness was inexcusable at any time, but when someone had secrets like this man's, it became more than inexcusable—it became dangerous.

"This mountain is sacred to my people," he said flatly. "Someone has to protect it for them."

That certainly wasn't the answer she had expected to hear. "Protect it from what?"

"From development. From timbering. These are public lands, Ms. Kendrick. That means a lot of people have a lot of ideas for using them. And most of those ideas are incompatible with the needs of my people."

"But surely you could come to some kind of compromise?"

For a moment he didn't move, not even the slightest little bit. When he spoke, his voice was dry. "Of course we can reach a compromise. When the *wasicu* allow us to use their churches and cathedrals for our secular needs. Maybe we can hold a powwow in the nave on Sunday morning."

Under other circumstances, Mercy would have found the image amusing, but this man didn't intend it to be funny. And he was right, she admitted. Holy places should be treated with respect, and she seriously doubted that hordes of tourists and developers would treat the mountain that way.

He resumed their upward trek, leading the way across another rushing torrent with a familiarity that said he knew this mountain and its moods intimately. Mercy longed to ask him how long he'd been up here and what he thought he could possibly do to prevent timbering or development if the weight of the Forest Service and corporate America ever got behind it.

The ideas that occurred to her—sabotage and murder—were so unsavory that she left the question unspoken. If this man was as dangerous as his reputation led one to believe, she didn't want to know it. She much preferred to think the tales were exaggerated. Besides, he had taken care of her in more than one way since last night's rock slide. He had placed his own body between her and danger. For now she would give him the benefit of the doubt—and hope that she wasn't making a disastrous mistake.

A finger of cold air snaked down inside her sweater, and she shivered. The clouds appeared to be thickening again, and the air was heavy with moisture. A low rumble of thunder sounded in the distance, and she wondered if they would reach their destination before another storm was unleashed on them.

Ahead of her, Gray Cloud suddenly halted and squatted. From where she stood, Mercy was treated without warning to the sight of powerful thighs and hard buttocks stretching old denim tight. Uncomfortable with her response and with the fact that she was all alone in the middle of nowhere with an incredibly virile man, she dragged her gaze upward and tried to focus on his hawkish profile.

"Something wrong?" she asked.

"Footprints."

She edged closer and peered over his shoulder. There, in mud left by the rain, were the unmistakable prints of heavy hiking boots. "Don't a lot of people come up here?"

"No." He lifted his head and looked ahead. "We get a few hunters in the fall, but not many. And hikers usually keep to the lower slopes." He pointed to the boot prints that were visible all the way across the shallow depression ahead of them before vanishing into a stand of pine trees. "I didn't know anyone at all was up here except you."

Mercy opened her mouth to ask him how he could possibly know that about a mountain this big, then caught herself. He would probably say the wind told him. "Well, it's public land," she said after a moment.

But he remained squatting, studying the prints. "Someone walked through here in the last couple of hours. As heavy as the rain was, it would have washed out these prints pretty fast." After a couple of moments, he straightened and looked down at her. "I don't think you should stay alone out here until we find out about this guy."

The absurdity of the idea struck her, but she managed to turn her head swiftly and bite her lip before she could remind him that she was already out here alone with a strange man, and, what was more, a man who had been accused of murder.

"Just what do you expect me to do?" she was able to ask finally. "I'm here to study the wolves, not hide out. And there's no reason to think anyone would want to harm me, anyway. Or that we'd even run into each other on a mountain this size."

She half expected him to argue with her, if only because he seemed like the type of alpha male who wouldn't care to have his dominance questioned. He said nothing, though. Whatever he thought, he kept it to himself.

But she couldn't fail to notice his increased alertness, the way he intently scanned the ground ahead of them, the way he frequently cocked his head as he tried to identify sounds. Not even a birdsong escaped scrutiny.

And gradually it began to dawn on her that this man, renegade or not, was a far better judge of what was worrisome on this mountain. If he thought the presence of someone else in this location at this time of year was worth worrying about, she might well be wise to listen.

"Not much farther now," he told her when they paused for a break during the early afternoon. "The cave I'm thinking of isn't too far from the den, but not so close that your presence would disturb the wolves."

"I really appreciate this, you know. Last night. You taking me up here."

He looked straight at her for the first time in hours. "You mean well. I have no quarrel with you."

As if to say that he would, if her intentions changed. As

if to say he might, with someone else. It sounded suspiciously like a threat, and Mercy felt the back of her neck prickle. The silence between them suddenly seemed strained, uneasy, and she needed desperately to fill it.

"Do you stay up here all the time?" she asked him, since the question had never truly been answered before.

He nodded once, briefly.

"But—" She caught herself again, before impulsively asking if he didn't miss other people, didn't miss the comforts of civilization. Stupid questions, she scolded herself. Why should he miss other people? And maybe he couldn't afford any of those comforts, anyway.

Almost as if he read her thoughts, something in his face shifted, easing the harshness there just a little. "Some people are complete in themselves, Ms. Kendrick. Needing others is a weakness."

"Or a strength," she said impulsively. "What kind of world would we live in if no one needed anyone else?"

She fully expected him to retort, but he stiffened just then, and stared into the space beyond her.

"What's wrong?" she asked.

"Shh."

Looking around behind her, she could see nothing, so she strained her ears to hear. Beyond the omnipresent sound of rushing water, she couldn't hear a thing.

"Let's get going," Gray Cloud said abruptly.

She turned to him. "What happened? Did you hear something? See something?"

"I heard a couple of gunshots."

"Somebody signaling for help?"

"Maybe. Come on. Let's check it out."

She wasn't at all keen on checking out gunshots, but she couldn't in good conscience object. If there was any possibility at all that someone was hurt, they *had* to go to his aid. She didn't approve of guns, though, and generally didn't much care for the uses to which people put them.

Gray Cloud quickened their pace considerably now, out of concern that someone might be in serious trouble. Mercy couldn't imagine how he had heard the shots over the roar of running water that seemed to fill the entire forest, but there was no doubting that he'd heard something, and that he was making a beeline in the direction he thought it had come from.

Maybe he hadn't heard anything at all. The thought twisted sinuously into her mind as if whispered into her ear. Why would he pretend to hear something? But how *could* he hear anything over the rushing water? Why hadn't she heard it, too?

Because he was better attuned to the forest sounds from living here all the time. Because an unusual sound, however faint, would probably catch his attention faster than it would hers.

Struggling upward behind him, breathing heavily from exertion and the thin air, she tried to argue with her growing uneasiness. From the moment he had shielded her with his body last night, he had taken good care of her. There was absolutely no reason to think he had a hidden agenda of any kind.

After all, she told herself, if he wanted her off this mountain, there was no reason to drag her all over it. Instead he could have scared her away with very little effort at all. She wasn't so dedicated to studying these wolves that she would have withstood a serious threat.

Panting, she neared the top of a steep climb and gladly accepted Gray Cloud's hand when he turned and leaned down to offer it to her. In that instant, as she watched her small pale hand disappear into his huge dark one, she became aware of him as a man.

Awareness caught her between one breath and the next,

hitting her like a blow to the solar plexus. Gasping again, this time with the shock of it, she felt him lift her with one hand, pulling her up the slope as if she weighed no more than a feather.

No, she thought as her feet settled firmly on the ground once again. No. Of all things, not that. She didn't need or want sexual attraction in her life ever again. It was too painful, too distracting. She was here to work. Period.

"Stay behind me now," he said in a low voice. "It can't be much farther."

"How can you be sure of that?" she asked, keeping her own voice at a level barely audible over the rushing water. "How can you even be sure we're headed in the right direction?"

"There were two shots. The second gave me the chance to locate the direction it came from. As for the distance…" He gave a little shake of his head. "Sound can't travel very far under these conditions and still be distinct."

He was right, she guessed, as she followed close behind him into the shadowy depths of a thick stand of pines. Just as she was drawing a breath to ask him how he had learned such things, he stopped abruptly and held out an arm, silencing her.

His nostrils flared as he lifted his head and tested the air. "Blood," he whispered. "Stay here while I check it out."

She didn't feel the least urge to argue with him. He moved as silently as a wraith, she thought as she watched him slip away farther into the shadows beneath the trees.

Under the sheltering boughs of the trees, the shadows were deep, almost nightlike. As she waited, the wind kicked up a new waterfall of sound as it whispered through the treetops. Cold air trickled down the neck of her jacket, and she tugged at the collar, trying to close the gap opened by the pack on her back.

Blood. That could mean so many things. Someone seriously hurt. An animal killed by a poacher. An animal killed by another animal. Maybe a predator had brought down prey of some kind, and someone had shot at it. A lynx, maybe.

Or a cougar? Suddenly she couldn't remember if there were still any cougars in these parts. Uneasy, she looked around at the shadows, which seemed to be darkening and deepening visibly as she stood there, and thought of all the animals that *could* present a danger. Bears. Grizzlies. Not every predator was as harmless to humans as wolves. Some, like grizzlies, wouldn't hesitate to attack.

Shivering a little, she hugged herself and shifted from one foot to the other.

It was dark in here, under these trees. Darker than just a few minutes ago. Thunder rumbled hollowly, and some of the taller trees groaned as the wind caught their tops and made them sway. What was taking Gray Cloud so long?

Shivering again, she turned around slowly, trying to shake the crawling sense that the day was turning sinister, that the entire mood of the mountain was growing threatening. Silly, she told herself. It was just that the clouds were thickening and dimming the light. Mountains might have moods, but that was just her interpretation of the difficulty of their slopes, not a real manifestation of feelings. Not something that could change and alter as a person's moods could.

Certainly not.

But the feeling was inescapable, and as her uneasiness grew, so did her impatience. What could possibly be taking Gray Cloud so long? If someone were seriously hurt...

If someone were seriously hurt, he would have to do what he could for them before coming back for her. Simple as that. And it might take an appreciable amount of time. The weight of the backpack on her shoulders seemed to be growing more onerous with each passing second, and finally she shrugged it off and leaned it against the trunk of a tree.

Overhead, the quickening wind sighed through the tops of the pines like a soul in torment. A drop of rain found its way through the maze of branches and needles and struck her icily on the cheek. Slowly, she tipped her head back and looked up at a patch of dark sky. The gray of the clouds had taken on a darker, greenish cast, and the clouds themselves, from what little she could see, seemed to be moving with terrible swiftness.

Thunder rumbled suddenly, loud enough to make the ground beneath her feet tremble like a drum skin. It seemed to go on forever, strengthening, fading a little, then reaching a deafening crescendo. Instinctively she squatted, making a smaller target of herself, hoping that none of the trees would become a lightning rod.

The mountain was angry. Something had happened to anger the mountain, and, crazy as the thought was, she believed it. At this moment, with the ground trembling beneath her and the thunder rolling over her head in an endless, stunning wave of sound, she could only believe that Thunder Mountain was crying out in rage.

Clapping her hands over her ears, she pressed her face to her knees and tried to tell herself it was just an ordinary storm, just ordinary thunder, no more threatening than any other natural fury she had endured in her life. But she couldn't quite believe it.

"Mercy."

Gray Cloud's deep voice pierced the comparative silence when the thunder's growl died away. Lifting her head, she saw him crossing the pine-needle carpet with long, fluid strides. At once she straightened, feeling foolish at being found huddled like a child in a dark closet.

"Did you find someone?" she asked.

He shook his head, a brief negative. "A poacher shot a doe and fawn."

"Oh, no!"

Bending, he lifted her pack and indicated she should turn so he could help her into it. "I want to get you up to the cave," he said. "Away from here. Then I'll come back and look for the killer."

"Why don't you look for him now? He might get away if you wait." The straps of the backpack settled onto her weary shoulders, and she nearly winced from the bruised feeling.

"I can hunt better alone."

The thought of the murdered deer caused her lips to part, her lungs to draw air, her mind to frame an argument. But then thunder roared furiously overhead, and the green light filtering through the trees darkened even more.

He was right, she thought. The deer were already dead, and the mountain was enraged.

Besides, she realized with another chill trickling down her spine, she didn't know what Gray Cloud meant when he said *hunt*. And she wasn't at all sure she wanted to know.

CHAPTER THREE

*T*hunder Mountain felt the death of the doe and fawn all the way to its root in the heart of the Earth. Needless death. Needless destruction. Violation of the sanctity of life. The doe and her fawn had not been killed for food, but for pleasure. For the sake of killing.

The mountain knew humans. For more than ten thousand years men had climbed its slopes, seeking the powers of the universe, seeking answers to questions and visions to guide them. And then had come the invaders from the east. Only a short time ago, as the mountain felt. Only a little while ago had come the hordes from the east, men who killed for sport and enjoyment. Men who had nearly exterminated the buffalo and the wolves and the eagles. Men who respected nothing and never dreamed that they were trespassing on old and ancient powers, that they were breaking covenants that had existed since the dawn of time.

Puny little mortals, yet so destructive.

The mountain shrugged, and its shoulders trembled. The invaders must be driven out. The threat must be removed. Thunder Mountain had to protect its denizens, from the smallest lichen to the oldest owl.

Wanton killing could not be tolerated.

The mountain reached out for Gray Cloud, the mortal who was the servant of Thunder. Gray Cloud could be counted on to help.

The cave where Gray Cloud left Mercy was little more than a chamber scooped out of the side of the mountain. It provided shelter from the rain and wind, and had only one tunnel leading deeper into the mountain. After a few moments' study, she decided that the mouth of the tunnel and the passageway behind it were too small to allow casual human exploration. Satisfied that she needn't fear poachers or bears coming from that direction, she dismissed it.

And there was wood. Though he'd said nothing about it, the presence of the woodpile meant either that he sheltered here himself often, or that he had prepared for her arrival. She would have thanked him for it, and for guiding her here, except that he never gave her the chance.

He'd stared at her long and hard, a look that cleaved her tongue to the roof of her mouth, and said, "I'll be back by morning to take you to the wolves." And then he was gone, as if he had never been. Slipping away into the rainy forest as swiftly and silently as the wolf had done earlier.

It was, Mercy found herself thinking as she shivered in the chilly air, a good thing his eyes were dark and not tawny. If he had looked at her with a wolf's golden gaze, she would have begun to believe in werewolves right there and then.

But his gaze was as dark as obsidian, and just as hard. It chilled her and challenged her all at once, just as his masculinity kept frightening her and challenging her with an awareness she didn't want. He was a killer, she reminded herself. Maybe not a murderer, but there seemed little doubt he had killed someone. Maybe the killing had been justified. Maybe that was why he had been acquitted.

And maybe she should have paid more attention and learned more about the situation before she had come up here. It was a little late now to be worrying about what Gray Cloud was capable of.

The first thing she did was build a fire in the pit hollowed out in the rock floor of the cave. Again she wondered how many generations had built fires here, wondered if mammoth hunters from long ago had camped in this very cave and sat on the floor right here as the fire caught and began to burn.

She could almost imagine their weather-wizened faces gathered around the flames as she spread out her soaked sleeping bag in the hope that it might dry sometime in the next month or so.

Thunder rumbled again, but the cave walls deadened the sound a little, making it less threatening. The day had darkened until it was almost nightlike. Flickers of lightning could be seen now through the cave opening. Thunder Mountain was certainly aptly named, she told herself when at last she settled close to the fire and tried to warm her nearly numb hands.

All of a sudden another deafening crack shook the ground with earthquakelike ferocity. On and on it rolled, causing the ground to tremble as if heavy trucks were rolling by. Wrapping her arms around her knees, she stared out through the cave mouth and watched as pitchforks of lightning sizzled through the air, blinding in their intensity.

The mountain is angry. This time she didn't even argue with the thought. It was as good an explanation as any for this terrifying display of the power of the elements. Safe and dry in her little niche, she thought of Gray Cloud tracking the poacher. Surely he couldn't even be attempting it in the midst of this violence?

It was easy, as she huddled by the fire, to understand why this mountain was believed to be sacred. Short of a tornado she had survived as a child, short of a force-five hurricane, she had never seen nature unleash such ferocity. Thunder had begun to rumble almost continuously, and lightning flashed and flared over and over, bringing a brighter-than-daylight brilliance to the waning afternoon. Nothing would be afoot in this. Any creature with sense would have hunkered down to wait out this wrath.

And unbidden came the memory of the blue sparkles she

had seen last night, the dancing blue lights that Gray Cloud had called spirits. Some kind of electrical activity, certainly. It had to be. No other explanation was acceptable in a rational world.

But this was not a rational world, whispered a voice in the back of her mind. Not on this mountain. Somewhere during her climb up the rugged lower slopes she had left behind the world she knew. This was the world of sentient nature, of shamans and spirits and powers beyond imagining.

Shivering again as that strange chill trickled down her neck, she inched closer to the fire until the skin of her cheeks tightened from the heat, and still she felt cold and her back felt exposed. For the first time since she had conceived of this trip, it occurred to her that it might not be a simple matter of camping out and watching wolves. Other things might be involved. Other forces.

What had Gray Cloud called the wolves? *Shunk*-something. Spirit that looks like a dog. She shivered again, remembering the eerie golden eyes of the wolf she had seen earlier. Eyes that had seemed too intelligent. Too knowing. Too human. Not the big, sad brown eyes of a dog at all. It was easy to understand why wolves had received so much bad press over the years, but even knowledge of the true nature of the beast didn't prevent the atavistic response to an animal with eyes that were too knowing.

Suddenly her breath locked in her throat, and every thought flew from her head. Standing in the mouth of the cave was a black wolf. The same one she had seen this morning at the other cave. And he was looking at her with those incredible glowing eyes, looking at her with recognition, as if he, too, remembered their earlier meeting.

Those golden eyes transfixed her, preventing her from looking away, preventing her, it seemed, from even thinking. They seemed to absorb her, drawing her into the heart of the fire that lay between them, drawing her into whirling mysteries of blue lights and golden eyes.

And then, just as she sucked a ragged breath of air into her lungs, the wolf released her by the simple expedient of closing his eyes slowly. Lazily. Almost drowsily. Then, turning, he sat on his haunches with his back to her and stared out at the wildness of the storm.

As if he were standing guard.

The sound of her tattered breaths was smothered by the fury of the storm without. Even the crackle of the fire was almost inaudible. Reaching out, never taking her eyes from the wolf, she felt around for her pack. From it she pulled a pen and pad, then, by the light of the fire, she wrote down all her impressions of the creature who sat in calm and complete disdain of her presence. It was as if, she found herself thinking, the wolf had measured her and judged her to be no threat to him.

Thunder hammered at the sky again, and lightning danced from cloud to cloud and then zig-zagged to the ground. The wolf's ears pricked, turning a little this way and that, but otherwise he was undisturbed by nature's violence.

When she had written down everything she could think of, Mercy dropped her chin to her knees and just watched the wolf across the top of the fire, the heat giving the scene a wavery, dreamlike effect. Such a beautiful creature, with a nobility and edge that few dogs had. And such big feet...

Suddenly the wolf rose onto all fours, crouched, hackles rising. A low growl filled the cave, along with the sound of the coming storm's fury.

It could be anything, Mercy told herself as her heart started to hammer. A rabbit. A squirrel. Just some strange smell borne on the wind.

And then, with shocking suddenness, the downpour began as the heavens unloaded a heavy, concealing curtain of rain. The wolf stayed tense for a short while, then slowly settled back on its haunches in a pose of alert relaxation. Mercy released the breath she had been holding and relaxed, too, albeit more slowly.

Inevitably she wondered if the wolf had somehow sensed the coming rain and decided to shelter here from it. Well, of course the wolf hadn't *decided,* she amended silently. Not in the way a human being would make such a decision. The animal had simply learned through experience that he could keep dry here.

Almost as if he'd read her mind, the wolf turned his shaggy head and looked at her over his shoulder with those uncanny, intelligent eyes. Looking into that unblinking gaze, Mercy found it dangerously easy to believe this animal could have made a decision, could indeed have reasoned, in the human sense of the word.

Oh, Lord, all this talk of spirits and Cloud People was getting to her. What did it matter what had brought the wolf to this cave? Regardless, she had an incredible opportunity to observe one closely and the even more incredible experience of feeling protected by him. For surely, if anything threatened the wolf, the animal would protect her as a consequence of protecting himself.

Suddenly aware of how close to the fire she was sitting and that her cheeks were beginning to feel like singed paper, she scooted back a little. Once again the wolf looked at her over his shoulder, then resumed his watch over the rain-soaked mountainside.

And suddenly, in the oddest way, she became acutely aware of just how isolated she was, of just how high up this mountainside in the middle of nowhere she was sitting. She could scream her lungs out, and no one would hear but that wolf and a few other forest creatures. If she died, they might not find her bones for years.

It was as if she rose above herself and with an eagle's

eye saw the little speck that was herself surrounded by the vast untamed wilderness of the mountain. Had she been insane to come up here alone?

Once again the wolf looked at her with eyes that were too knowing. Too intelligent for any beast. The last time she'd had the feeling she was looking into an eye as intelligent as her own had been with a humpback whale she had been studying off Australia. She had believed then that whales could think. She was beginning to believe that this wolf could, too.

And the feeling didn't make her comfortable at all.

The wolf was still with her when night fell, but shortly after total dark blanketed the world he rose suddenly, raised his nose to the wind and let out a long, long howl that made the hair on Mercy's neck stand on end. He was answered from out of the night by other howls, and for the first time in her life Mercy heard the famous harmony of a wolf pack, each animal picking a different run of notes, with the result that three or four wolves could sound like a dozen or more.

Then her companion gave her one last, long look and disappeared from the cave into the rainy, windy night. Shivering, Mercy reached for her notebook and bent to the fire to scribble her impressions of what had just happened.

All of a sudden she was aware of not being alone. Her scalp prickled as she slowly, reluctantly raised her head.

Breath left her in a rush as she recognized Gray Cloud. "Lord, you scared me!"

"Sorry." He stayed where he was, just inside the cave mouth, regarding her with eyes that, despite the difference in color, reminded her of the wolf's.

"You didn't catch the poacher?"

"There was a slight wrinkle."

She tipped her head back a little farther to better see him. "What kind of wrinkle?"

"There are more than one of them. And two of them, at least, were headed up this way when it started to rain."

"Headed this way? You mean to *here?*"

He gave a brief nod.

Pushing herself to her feet, she crossed to the cave mouth and stood beside him, looking out at the pitch-dark, rainy night. "They can't move in this."

"I did."

She glanced at him, noting that once again he was soaked, but apparently oblivious of it. *You're not an ordinary man.* The words rose to her lips, but she bit them back. And then she remembered.

"There was a wolf here earlier."

"Again?" For an instant, an instant so brief she wasn't sure she saw it, one corner of his mouth quirked upward. "They like you."

She shook her head, not prepared to consider any such possibility. "I could have sworn it was the same one that turned up this morning. But that's not the point."

"It isn't?" He turned so that he faced her. "Wolves approach you twice in one day, and you don't consider it significant?"

"I didn't say that! But I'm trying to make a point here, if you'll just let me finish!"

He made an inviting gesture with one hand.

"The point is, the wolf came and sat here at the cave mouth for several hours, and once he acted as if something disturbed him. Growled, raised his hackles. Maybe somebody was out there."

"Could be." He moved another quarter turn so that he, too, looked out into the rain-soaked night. "Well, you're not alone now. As for the wolves—lady, you need a change in your perspective."

She felt her hands clench into fists but managed to speak evenly. "What does that mean?"

"Wild animals have approached you twice in one day. Think about it. The wolf honors you. Appreciate it."

Adopting a different perspective was something like running head-on into a brick wall, Mercy thought. She had been aware that seeing the wolf twice was exciting, unique, but she hadn't thought of it as being honored. And yet...

Staring out into the night, she considered what he had said. Considered what it might indicate. "You think he sought me out deliberately?"

"Once might be chance. Twice is something more."

Something in her was inclined to agree. Something purely unscientific, of course. Something that...could see spirits. "That implies that wolves think," she argued, instinctively reaching for her ivory tower of objectivity.

"Are you so sure they can't?" The question was asked mildly enough. Almost casually. "Open your mind."

That stung her. "My mind *is* open." The very nature of scientific inquiry required it.

But Gray Cloud shook his head ever so slightly. "Within your preconceived limits, your mind is open. You equate the wolf with the domestic dog. Your ability to perceive the intelligence of other species is limited by your notion that man's intelligence is at the top of a pyramid in lonely splendor. That no other species approaches it."

Before she could marshal a response, he held out one hand, cupping his palm as if to receive something. Instantly a light appeared there, a sparkle of electric blue. "You see it," he said. "What do you call it? The *wasicu* have no name for it. No definition. Most of them couldn't even see it, because it doesn't exist within their accepted framework. *You* see it. You perceive many things beyond the fringe of your knowledge, but you try to hide them even from yourself, because they don't fit."

He held his palm out a little more, as if offering it to her. She folded her arms tightly across her breasts, refusing the invitation, barely managing to keep herself from stepping back.

"Call it magic, if you will," he said after a moment. Slowly he closed his palm, and the light vanished. "But it's as real as you are. As I am."

"What do *you* call it?" she asked.

He shook his head. "It doesn't matter what I call it. You're merely looking for a reason to dismiss it."

The realization that he was right was discomfiting. If he called it anything—anything at all—she would have a starting point from which to dismiss it. And that wasn't very scientific, was it?

But it was, she realized with a queasy sinking sensation in her stomach. It was exactly the scientific frame of mind. If you couldn't label it and put it in a laboratory, it didn't exist. There was a certain perverted security in dismissing anything that couldn't be precisely quantified. Or in dismissing anything that could be reproduced through quackery. Like that group of scientists who insisted on dismissing paranormal phenomena because the effects could be reproduced by a magician...never realizing that being able to produce those effects didn't necessarily mean they had found the *only* means by which they could be produced. That was like saying a full-spectrum light bulb produced light the same way the sun did simply because both produced the entire spectrum.

When had science become so perverted? she found herself wondering. When had it stopped recognizing that it was a search for the real causes behind observable effects, that it was not in the business of dismissing effects because the cause was not apparent?

Well, she thought uneasily, that wasn't true of everyone, of course. Or of all fields. But it seemed to be rife in some, and she had evidently fallen prey to that way of thinking. She ought to be excitedly questioning the man beside her, trying to learn about that blue light. She ought to accept the evidence of her own eyes and set about finding out all she could. Instead...instead she was standing here trying to dismiss it as a magician's trick of some kind.

And that was dishonest. Horribly, frighteningly dishonest.

Slowly she lifted her gaze to his and saw a kind of patient understanding. "What...what is it?" she asked.

He cupped his palm again, and the blue light reappeared. "The life force," he said. "It's in everything. All around us. Hold out your hand."

Slowly, shaking internally, she held her hand out almost reluctantly, palm cupped upward in imitation of his. She half expected him to place the blue light into her hand, but he didn't. Instead, he reached out with his other hand and touched her palm gently with his forefinger.

"Here," he said. "Don't you feel it?"

What she felt was a sudden, shocking, totally unexpected surge of sexual awareness that zinged like lightning along her nerve endings straight to her core. Instinctively, she leapt back as if she'd been burned and immediately turned away, afraid he might see her reaction on her face.

He should have questioned her, but he didn't. Finally, surprised that he said nothing at all, she dared to dart a look in his direction. He was staring out into the night as if nothing at all had happened.

What a strange, strange man, she thought, wrapping her arms around herself, wishing away the ache he had awakened. What a very strange man.

Thunder continued to grumble into the night. Gray Cloud settled himself before the mouth of the cave, leaning back against the wall with his long legs stretched out before him.

A completely self-sufficient man, Mercy thought as she curled up in blankets and watched him across the fire. He needed no one, nothing. And that meant he was utterly free, didn't he?

Sighing, she let her eyelids droop. And slowly, slowly, she felt sleep stealing over her. As her mind began to drift into dreams, she saw Gray Cloud rise and come to her side, felt him reach down and touch her cheek with gentle fingertips. Dreamily, she watched as he lay down beside her, felt herself sink happily into his embrace as he drew her against him, as his lips began to scorch a path across her cheek, toward her mouth.

It was as if some long-held tension inside her let go. With a long sigh of blessed relief, she arched her neck, begging for the warmth of his mouth on the sensitive skin there. A gasp escaped her when he obliged, covering the hollow of her throat with his hot mouth. Little by little his tongue and lips trailed upward and to the side, closer and closer to her ear....

Sharp pleasure speared through her as his mouth found the sensitive spot behind her ear. Warm waves of aching arousal surged through her, causing her to press against him, silently begging him to come closer.

Closer...

His tongue in her ear, warm, wet, provocative. A shimmery shiver of delight ran down her neck from her ear...soft caress of fingertips along her throat...quicksilver thrills dancing down her side...clothes slipping easily away...

She turned her head to watch his hand trail toward her breast, and saw blood on his fingers....

A frisson of shock brought her jolting awake. Sitting up abruptly, she unleashed a ragged breath as she realized the cave was nearly dark, the fire merely embers. A dream. It had been a dream. Gray Cloud was still on the other side of the cave.

He watched her with eyes that seemed to guess what she had been dreaming. But there was no way he could know, she told herself a little hysterically. No way he could realize her body was still aching with a desire that had been born in the fog of a dream. That her flesh remembered touches that had never happened.

"Shh," he said softly. "Be silent. Someone is out there."

Fear trickled through her veins, banishing the last of the passionate glow left by the dream. Quickly she tossed the blankets aside, ignoring the cold night air, and reached for her hiking boots. Her breath made little clouds of ice crystals as she struggled to pull the boots on and lace them with fingers that were quickly growing numb. Lord, it was cold! The dying fire provided almost no heat and very little illumination.

At last, boots on, she crawled quietly to Gray Cloud's side. Beyond the entrance the night was still, silent except for the whisper of the wind in the pines. Clouds scudded across a gibbous moon, and the cold, eerie light seemed only to heighten the darkness of the shadows beneath the trees.

"How do you know?" she whispered finally. "Did you see something?"

He shook his head and laid a finger to her lips in a gentle remonstrance. He barely glanced at her before he resumed his study of the world outside.

He wasn't crouched as if he expected trouble, Mercy realized. But he was watchful, alert to any sound or movement from the woods. How could he be sure that it wasn't just some animal moving about in the dark? There were many creatures who stirred only in the shadows. But he seemed convinced that whatever was out there was some kind of threat, and if he believed it was an animal—a grizzly, say—he would want them to make as much noise as they could to scare it away.

Therefore he believed the threat was human.

Shivering, this time more from fear than the late hour or the frigid air, she instinctively inched closer to Gray Cloud. He offered the only safety and protection on this dark, cold night. The strength of sinew and bone was little enough against some terrors, but it was all there was right now.

"Look." He whispered the word, a mere breath of sound instantly lost in the forlorn sighing of the wind. A jerk of his chin indicated the woods to the right, where the deepest shadows lurked.

Mercy stared until she thought her eyes were going to come out of her head, until the shadows themselves seemed to become twisting, sinister shapes. Exhaling a soft, frustrated breath, she closed her eyes and rested them for a moment, then opened them again.

She gasped as she saw what Gray Cloud was talking about. There beneath the trees she could see fox fire, the soft bioluminescence of decaying wood. And against it she could see something dark moving, an incomplete silhouette mostly swallowed by the shadows.

She wanted to believe that it was an animal, but Gray Cloud had said someone was out there, and after a moment she realized the shadow had two legs. Only two legs. Who would be out there in the dark moving around?

And why?

Whoever it was could unquestionably see the glow of the fire in the cave, too, for the dying embers in the pit were at least as bright as the fox fire, and maybe more so. Had she gone behind the fire to reach Gray Cloud, her shadow would have been as visible to the man below as he was to them.

Shivering again, she leaned closer to her companion and

drew a quick breath when he astonished her by draping his arm around her shoulders and holding her to his side. The embrace was in no way intimate; it was the kind of casual action any friend would take under the circumstances, but Mercy's reaction to the touch was not at all casual.

Her breath tangled in her throat, as if uncertain whether she meant to inhale or exhale, and her heart skipped a beat. And just as swiftly, her mind rebelled at her reaction, reminding her that she didn't need this attraction, nor did she want it. Nor was it appropriate, she told herself sternly. Someone was out in the woods below the cave, possibly intending harm, and this most definitely wasn't the time to get distracted.

But no argument could keep her insides from turning into molasses when the arm around her shoulders tightened a little, bringing her closer still to his warm, hard side. She ought to be running as if all the hounds of hell were at her very heels, but she knew with distressing clarity that even if she tried, her body wouldn't obey her command.

What it wanted—*all* it wanted—was to sink deeper into this man's embrace. In defiance of common sense, in defiance of the threat in the dark woods, her body cast aside every instinct for self-preservation.

Tilting her head a little, she looked at the shadowy profile of the man who held her and wondered wildly if he hadn't somehow managed to cast a spell over her.

Just then a sharp crack of sound pierced the murmuring of the wind. The next thing Mercy knew, she was lying flat beneath Gray Cloud.

"Gunshot!" he whispered sharply in her ear. "Don't move."

A moment passed before understanding penetrated her shock, but when it did, she froze. A few seconds later, Gray Cloud eased off her and inched back toward the cave entrance.

The uneasiness she had felt just moments ago didn't hold a candle to the fear she felt right now.

Easing around a little, she was able to see his shadow as he stood in the mouth of the cave. Silhouetted against the slightly lighter gray of the clouds, he appeared huge, threatening. She hoped whoever had fired the shot couldn't see him from out there.

Who could possibly be shooting in the dead of night? she wondered. Shooting in the dark showed appalling carelessness. A person who would do that didn't much care what he hit.

The night grew hushed as the wind suddenly stilled. Then a blue pinprick of light appeared in the air beside Gray Cloud. Mercy caught her breath in amazement and watched as the blue light slowly expanded until it was the size of a golf ball. It made no sound that she could detect, and its light barely illuminated the side of Gray Cloud's face.

In an instant it winked out. There was a moment of absolute silence and stillness, as if the night, too, held its breath; then the wind unleashed a tree-rustling sigh, and the world returned to normal. In the distance, a low, irritable growl of thunder could be heard.

Gray Cloud turned, a looming monolithic shadow in the darkness. "He's gone."

Mercy sat up immediately. "Gone? You mean the person who shot at us? How can you know that?"

As soon as she asked, she wished the words unsaid. She was in no mood to hear that the wind had told him, or the spirits had whispered secrets to him. But he didn't say anything at all. Maybe he considered it pointless to answer her because she wouldn't understand.

And that made her feel stupid. She didn't like to feel stupid. She was a biologist, not an ethnologist, and she had no background from which to understand this man's beliefs, his perspective. That was not stupidity!

But perhaps it was mulishness, she found herself thinking. Since yesterday she had been feeling that there was something beyond normal ken on this mountain. That the usual rules of reality were different here. Just take that cold, cobwebby brush she had felt on her neck several times. No breeze, however chilly, had ever felt like that. And what about the blue lights? Was she going to deny seeing them?

Tilting her head back, she looked up at Gray Cloud. He was a man; he had two arms and two legs. But he was more, she realized. He spoke to the wind and heard the voice of the Thunder Spirits, and he lived in a world populated by Stone People and Cloud People. In the palm of his hand, blue light danced.

If she acknowledged these things, then she acknowledged that he might know that the person with the gun was gone. The question was, was she going to believe it?

A shiver ripped through her, born of something other than the chilly night air. If the usual rules of reality didn't apply, then what rules did? Rules that allowed spirits to communicate with mortals might also allow invisible things to do harm.

She shivered again, and suddenly Gray Cloud was squatting beside her, touching her cheek with gentle fingertips. "You're cold," he said, and moments later he had her cocooned in the warmth of wool blankets.

An unusual man, she found herself thinking as she shivered again and yet again. He had given her his blankets last night to replace her sodden sleeping bag, and now he wrapped her in them because she shivered. He had cared for her every single moment since he had placed his body between her and the rock slide.

A cold-blooded murderer? No way. He might have

killed, but it seemed impossible that he could have done so in cold blood. Not a man as protective as he was.

She turned her head and tried to see him, but the darkness, hardly lightened by the faintest red glow from the fire pit, kept its secrets. He remained nothing but a powerful shadow. "Do you think that person was shooting at us?"

A moment passed, then another. When he spoke, his voice was low, intense. "The wind whispers of fear, not death."

"Which means?"

"That someone was trying to scare one or both of us off this mountain."

She shivered again, contemplating the possibility while her heart began to beat in an uncomfortable rhythm. Scaring someone could get nasty. Very nasty. "But why?" she asked after a moment. "Why would anybody want to do that?"

He had been squatting beside her, but now he lowered himself to the ground and sat cross-legged beside her, facing out toward the restless night.

"You'd better get some sleep," he said.

She could have spluttered in frustration, even though she knew there was no answer to her question. He could have speculated, but what good would it have done?

"Just one more thing," she said. "Could you tell what he was shooting at?"

In the dark she saw him turn his head slowly and look straight at her. Stray starlight caught his eyes and made them gleam eerily. "He was shooting at me."

CHAPTER FOUR

Again an act of abomination. One of the man-things had attempted to harm Gray Cloud, he who was keeper of sacred trusts, he who was guardian of the holy places.

The mountain stirred, deeply troubled.

Slumbers as old as time had been disturbed, sacred trusts had been broken, and now the sanctified peace of the mountain's slopes was threatened.

Some things could not be tolerated.

After the gunshot, Mercy gave up all attempts to sleep. However she looked at it, there was a very real and very human threat on the slopes of this mountain. Shooting into the dark like that went far beyond an act of incaution. Whoever had done that really didn't give a damn who got hurt. He was willing to hurt anyone and anything to achieve his purpose.

She shivered inwardly, horrified that anyone could be so uncaring. So callous.

Yet someone evidently was, and that someone was stalking these woods with a gun.

She shivered again and wrapped the blanket tighter around her shoulders, wishing morning would hurry up and get there. Not being able to see made everything so much worse.

"Gray Cloud?"

In the darkness she could dimly see his shadow move as he turned toward her. "Yes?"

"Why would anyone be trying to kill you?"

"Who can fathom the mind of a *wasicu* killer?"

Exasperated, Mercy sat up and glared at him in the dark. "Damn it, don't go all inscrutable Indian on me!"

"Why not?" He sounded faintly amused. "That's what I *am*."

"Oh, stuff it! You must have *some* idea why someone would want to kill you! Even crazed *wasicu* killers generally have some kind of motive!"

A low, quiet sound filled the cavern. It was a moment before Mercy realized that Gray Cloud was chuckling. *Chuckling!* "I'm glad you find this so amusing!"

In an instant his laughter died, and when he spoke, there was no hint of it in his voice. "I don't find it amusing at all."

"Well, good! Now suppose you tell me why you *think* somebody might want to kill you."

For a long time, it seemed, there was no sound but the forlorn moaning of the wind through the trees and the lonely sound of an owl.

"This mountain," Gray Cloud said finally, "could make many people very wealthy. There's a fortune in timber alone, and the mineral wealth has been estimated in the billions. Apart from that, the resort potential is phenomenal."

"None of that explains why anyone would want to shoot you."

Despite the dark, she felt his gaze on her, no less intense for being invisible. It was as palpable as a touch in the dark.

"All of that explains why someone would wish me dead," he said levelly. "I'm dedicated to preventing the rape of Thunder Mountain."

"But how would anyone *know* that?"

"I've made no secret of it. I've warned developers away before."

Slowly Mercy lay back against the rolled-up blanket she was using as a pillow. "Warned them away how?"

He didn't answer.

She didn't like that. What could he be hiding? she wondered. Maybe there was more to fear on this mountain than one fool with a gun. Maybe Gray Cloud was as dangerous as rumor had painted him. Maybe she was a fool to trust him at all.

Yet, she reminded herself, he hadn't hurt her. Not one little bit, and he'd had ample opportunity to kill her or terrorize her, if he wanted to. None of which answered the question of how he had warned developers away.

Shivering again, she burrowed deeper into the blankets and thought longingly of her warm, soft water bed at home, of the calm predictability of academic life. Why had she ever thought she wanted to climb the side of a mountain to study wolves?

"So you think the gunman has something to do with developers?" she asked.

"Very likely."

"But why should they go to such extremes? Why should one man be so important that they think it's necessary to kill him?"

Again he was silent for a long while before he answered. "I have dedicated my life to preserving the sanctity of Thunder Mountain. I will die to protect this place for my people. A man who will die for his belief is dangerous."

"There are other ways to remove you."

"None that would silence me. And your wolves are a threat, too, Mercy Kendrick. A very big threat. Every bit as big a threat as I am, if word of their presence on this mountain becomes widespread. Any development effort would be tied up for years by environmentalists determined to protect the wolves."

"Any development effort would be tied up for years by

environmentalists anyway. Removing the wolves would hardly change that.''

"Removing them would make it easier."

Mercy sat up again, disturbed and deeply chilled. "They couldn't possibly—"

"Why not? If the wolves are wiped out right now, and if I'm removed, who's to ever say that the wolves were here? Preservation of an endangered species will become moot. And ordinary environmental considerations are not enough to prevent timbering and mining."

Mercy drew her knees up to her chin and wrapped her arms tightly around them, hugging herself. She didn't like the sound of this at all. If someone really were after the wolves, they would be after her, too, just as soon as she verified the existence of the pack. Never had she imagined that being a wildlife biologist could set her up for murder.

Another shiver passed through her. "I don't like the sound of this."

He gave a grunt of agreement.

"Why—why have you dedicated your life to protecting the mountain. Isn't that unusual?"

"*Wakinyan* spoke to me, and I was given this vision for my life. A vision must be fulfilled."

A vision must be fulfilled. Mercy's scalp prickled a little with the realization that what drove this man was far beyond her understanding. Forces she had heard mentioned, but never really believed existed, drove him. Imagine a life-long dedication to fulfilling a vision. Imagine feeling bound to expend your last breath in defense of a place.

"What is the extent of your vision?"

"To have Thunder Mountain protected by white law as a holy place of my people. To have your people acknowledge the right of mine to this place."

"How can you possibly hope to accomplish that?"

"The opportunity will come." He spoke with absolute

conviction, and Mercy could only nod her head; there was no way one could argue with conviction.

All of a sudden she felt the ground beneath her tremble slightly, a faint vibration as if a heavy truck were rolling by—only there were no trucks on this mountain.

Thunder, she thought. It had to be thunder, a growl so deep and low that it was beneath the threshold of hearing. But then the tremor came again, a slow shaking of the ground beneath her.

And the mountain groaned.

Earth sounds. The moan came from deep within the heart of Thunder Mountain, an eerie, inhuman groan that rose from the bowels of the earth.

"What's that?"

Gray Cloud's answer was casual. "The mountain."

"The mountain? Mountains don't make noise!"

"They do when they move. Thunder Mountain is angry."

Because it was dark, she couldn't see anything but his shadow against the slightly lighter night beyond the cavern mouth. Right then, though, she wished desperately that she could see him. Even though there would be nothing on his face to read, it would have helped her to be able to see him. "Why?"

"Because the doe and fawn were murdered. Because there are people on the mountain who respect nothing at all. Because they intend harm to all that the mountain protects."

She had always believed that mountains had personalities, and she could even believe they had moods—certainly she'd felt those moods when she'd been caught on the side of a mountain in a sudden storm or had seen the changing faces of the peaks as sunlight dappled them. But the concept of a mountain actually reacting to events on its slopes...

Well, why not? she asked herself. Hadn't she felt that El Capitan welcomed her climb? Another rumble, barely felt, passed through the ground beneath her, accompanied by a low moan that made the hair on her neck stand up. A thinking, reacting mountain. A living mountain. An entity of rock and earth rising nearly fourteen thousand feet.

Suddenly realizing that she was holding her breath, she expelled it on a long sigh. She was surrounded by the mountain. Here in this cave she was surrounded by rock and earth, held in the loose embrace of Thunder Mountain.

Sitting in the dark with nothing to distract her, it was easy to imagine she could feel vast power surrounding her, easy to think of all the ways a mountain might exercise that power. Rock slides, earthquakes…

Another shudder passed through her, this time her own, as she considered just what powers a sentient mountain might have. Man believed himself to be in control of his environment, but the truth was that the elements were more powerful than man, as they proved time and again with floods and tornadoes. But the earth… Unless one lived at the foot of a volcano, the powers of the earth itself weren't usually apparent. But sitting here in the dark, surrounded by the rocky arms of the mountain, Mercy had no illusions about its power. She could feel it thrumming in some subtle way, could sense it somehow, almost the same way she could feel a static charge when the hair on her arms stood up.

"Why?" she heard herself ask Gray Cloud. "Why should the mountain care?"

"Why does a mother care about her babies?"

"Oh, come on! A mountain that thinks is already difficult to accept, but one that cares about a deer? One that cares about what some puny man is doing? If a mountain can think and feel, it has to have a very different perspective from ours. A human lifespan would have to be a mere blink of an eye to it. How could it possibly care about what mortals are doing?''

"It cares," he said presently. "It cares. And if I were you, Mercy Kendrick, I'd be hoping that Thunder Mountain doesn't decide I'm a threat.''

She shivered again and told herself it was from the chilly night air. In fact, it was from the uneasy awareness that she and Gray Cloud were *not* alone in this cave—that the rock arms that sheltered them belonged to a being that might well be listening.

Like sitting in the stomach of a whale, Mercy thought uncomfortably. Devoured by stone.

And the mountain could, she realized unhappily, do just that in an instant. It would take no longer than that for a rock slide to seal this cave off and trap her forever in the maw of the mountain.

I mean you no harm. She caught herself thinking the words, trying to communicate that simple reassurance to the mountain. *I mean you no harm.*

And she just had to hope that the mountain perceived it that way. That the mountain believed her.

Because it could surely destroy her.

Morning slunk into the cave with watery gray light and a distant growl of thunder. More of the same, Mercy thought as her eyes fluttered open and her body shifted stiffly on the hard cave floor. Another rainy, stormy day on Thunder Mountain. Did the sun ever shine up here?

Turning her head, she sought Gray Cloud with her eyes and saw that he was gone. Instead the black wolf sat at the cave entrance, watching her with his strange golden eyes, unblinking golden eyes. Eyes that were far too intelligent.

And she was feeling just disconnected enough, just crazy enough, this morning to think that that wolf had to be Gray

Cloud's alter ego. It only came when Gray Cloud was gone and always vanished just before he returned.

Shapeshifter.

In an instant she remembered old tales of the powers of shamans, tales that spoke of men who turned into beasts to hunt and kill their enemies. Tales of men who could become any animal to accomplish their purpose. Were Native American shamans capable of shape-shifting?

She had no idea, and not for the first time she cursed her lack of knowledge of the subject. She had come up this mountain expecting to observe wolves, not to deal with a totally alien culture or a sentient mountain.

Or a wolf that might really be an Indian medicine man.

God, was she losing her mind? These thoughts were insane! She shouldn't even be wondering about such things. In reality, no one shape-shifted, werewolves were merely the inventions of fiction and...

And wolves didn't come in from a rain-soaked day to keep company with a human in a cave.

Although, why not? she wondered. All over the world there were tales of wolves nursing human infants. Romulus and Remus were merely legendary members of a small but widespread fraternity of children who had been raised by wolves. If wolves would nurse human children, why wouldn't they come into a cave with a human? And hadn't her readings told her that wolves accepted the dominance of humans?

But that didn't really explain why this wolf kept showing up to watch her as if *she* were the subject of a scientific study. Or why he would then turn and assume a position very like that of a guardian.

Why should a wolf want to protect her?

Why should a mountain moan in anger?

Had she somehow slipped into another reality during her climb up the side of Thunder Mountain?

The wolf blinked slowly, offering no answers to her questions. Those strange golden eyes that seemed to see through and beyond her, that seemed to see into the dustiest corners of her soul, offered no solutions.

Where had Gray Cloud gone? He was supposed to take her to the den this morning. But perhaps he was scouting for information about the man who had shot at him last night. The man who had killed the doe and fawn.

The thought made her shudder again.

The wolf edged farther into the cavern, almost as if he wanted to approach her. Mercy found herself holding her breath in hopeful anticipation. It never even entered her head that perhaps she should fear the animal. Not once. All she felt was a sense of awe that the wolf didn't seem to fear her.

Releasing her pent-up breath silently, she waited. The wolf eased closer, moving in a slightly crouched position, almost as if stalking, yet without the appearance of threat. More of a cautious approach. And his eyes never once left her.

So beautiful, she thought. So beautiful and perfect with his big feet, his eyes more widely separated than a dog's, his long, slender legs. Wolves were beautiful creatures.

Just then the ground trembled again, and a deep, hollow groan, just barely audible, rose from the rocks beneath. The mountain was angry. Mercy was suddenly as sure of it as Gray Cloud had been last night. And today the thought terrified her.

Thunder cracked, a deafening gunshot of sound that reverberated within the cavern and caused Mercy to cover her ears. The wolf's hackles rose, and he turned swiftly to stare out into the gray morning. Wind tossed the treetops, causing a rush of sound like a huge waterfall. Thunder rumbled again, a deep-throated grumbling that seemed to shake the ground.

The earth shook again, and some instinct impelled Mercy to scramble to her feet and dart toward the cave entrance. Just as she reached it, a rain of rocks broke loose from the ceiling of the cavern—mostly sharp, jagged little pieces that might have cut her but would not have seriously harmed her.

A sudden, ominous silence blanketed the world, as if the universe was holding its breath. Then, with a shocking crack of sound, a large piece of rock broke loose from above and crashed to the floor of the cave.

Right where Mercy had been sitting.

The wolf tilted back his head and howled, an eerie, lonely sound. From the distance came an answering howl, and the animal took off, moving so swiftly he was but a blur as he slipped past Mercy into the rainy morning.

Mercy hardly noticed. Horror made her skin crawl as she stared at the piece of rock that could have killed her. *Would* have killed her if some instinct hadn't driven her to move.

The mountain was angry, and it seemed it was angry at her.

"What happened?"

Whirling around, Mercy came face-to-face with Gray Cloud. He was wet again, soaked from the rain and appearing not to notice…or care. He was one with the elements as surely as were the trees towering around them. He knew what had happened, Mercy found herself thinking. He *had* to know. The conviction made her skin crawl even more.

"The mountain tried to kill me." The bald statement hung shockingly in the stormy air. Part of her mind rebelled, refusing to believe such a thing, refusing to accept that a mountain could be sentient, let alone that it could try to kill. But in her heart, in her chilled blood and stunned mind, she knew it was the truth. The mountain had tried to kill her.

Gray Cloud didn't speak. He stepped past her and peered into the cave, which was little more than a dark maw in the side of the mountain. The day was darkly gray, and the cave seemed to swallow what little light there was.

But Gray Cloud saw. She knew it in the way his back stiffened as he stared at the boulder lying right where she would have been. The boulder that would have crushed her as easily as a man would have crushed a fly.

He backed up a step before he turned his head and looked at her. "You'd better leave."

Leave? "Why? Why the hell should I!" Fright was replaced in a violent rush by anger. She hadn't succeeded as a rock climber because she was afraid of a moody mountain.

And as anger cleared away the last of the fear, she looked at the fallen boulder and told herself that it had been a random occurrence. The rock had probably been loose for centuries, and the vibration caused by the deafening peals of thunder had simply caused it to fall at last. It was merely coincidence that it had fallen where she had been sitting moments before. There was nothing more sinister in it than that. Nothing.

It was all that talk Gray Cloud had spouted about the mountain, as if it were a fully aware being, that had made a natural occurrence appear to be so menacing. The truth of the matter was that nothing unnatural was occurring here at all, and that it was simply suggestion that was making it all so ominous. Just a little thunderstorm and a tremor, and she was turning it into a Hollywood horror concoction!

"No," she said to Gray Cloud. "I'm not leaving." She half expected him to argue with her, to warn her away, but he didn't.

And that was perhaps the most ominous thing of all, the

way he simply looked at her as if her decision to remain mattered not at all, as if she were too insignificant to worry about.

She looked from him to the boulder in the shadowy cavern and wondered if she were being utterly foolhardy. Yes, she thought uneasily, she probably was. But she hadn't let the forbidding faces of Devil's Tower and El Capitan deter her from climbing them, and she wasn't going to let a fallen rock prevent her from studying the wolves. Wolves that she knew beyond a shadow of a doubt were here, reestablishing themselves in the country they had once roamed freely. No, a rockfall wasn't going to drive her away.

Nor was she going to allow herself to become unnerved by Gray Cloud's mystical attitude toward this mountain. Yes, Thunder Mountain had personality and moods—all mountains did—but it wasn't capable of striking out against individuals on its slopes. No way. Let Gray Cloud view it however he chose, but she was *not* going to allow herself to be drawn into some insane belief that this mountain was as much an actor on this stage as she was.

Absolutely not.

She faced Gray Cloud squarely. "You said you would show me the dens."

He nodded his head once, regarding her impassively from obsidian eyes. Water dripped from the ends of his long black hair, and a drop clung to the tip of his hawkish nose.

"We'll have to climb another five hundred feet, and it's difficult terrain. Bring whatever you'll need, because you won't want to come back here until the end of the day."

He was right, she thought a little while later. The climb was really rough. It would have been easier to go straight up a rock face than it was to climb up and down the ravines he led her across while traveling ever higher into thinner air.

Worse, because conversation was out of the question; she had ample time to think about all that he had told her, all that he hadn't said. Time to think about what was really going on on this mountain, and why anyone should want to kill someone else over it. After all, she had only Gray Cloud's word that a doe and her fawn had been killed, or that the gunshot last night had been directed at him. Only his word that anyone was actually trying to hurt anything at all on this mountain.

He'd lived up here for a long time. All by himself, devoted to a mystical purpose in what might actually be a form of insanity. Even as the thought slithered across her mind, she felt guilty for having it. It was wrong to judge the manifestation of a different culture as some kind of insanity; even a wildlife biologist knew that. But she couldn't help wondering if his preoccupation with protecting this mountain wasn't a little extreme, even in his own cultural terms.

A fanatic. Yes, he probably was a fanatic. And who could say exactly what a fanatic might do in attempting to achieve his goal? He certainly might attempt to terrify a lone wildlife biologist into vacating the mountain. He might be willing to out-and-out lie about things like the doe being shot. He would surely be capable of fabricating things he told her in an attempt to scare her.

Well, she wasn't that easily scared. But she *was* uneasy about being alone on this mountain with a fanatic who might be capable of anything at all in pursuit of his ends.

Sliding down the side of a ravine, struggling to keep her balance on loose dirt and gravel, she wondered if she was insane to be following this man higher up the mountain. True, he had done nothing overtly threatening, had in fact protected her, but...

But he really didn't need to lead her farther up the mountain if he wanted to get rid of her. They'd been completely isolated since their first encounter. He could have killed her at any time and left her body for the scavengers. A search party would have found only bones, and probably not for months or even years. This mountain was so vast and dangerous that if she disappeared up here, no one would even suspect foul play.

So he didn't have to lead her higher if getting rid of her was his goal. Which meant that he didn't want to hurt her. Didn't it?

Logically, it made sense to her that he was trying to be helpful, not obstructive, but emotionally she wasn't quite so ready to believe it. Not when he kept trying to frighten her with tales of sentient mountains and gunmen. Pausing at the foot of the ravine, she drew a deep breath and then embarked on an upward climb with Gray Cloud just ahead of her and to one side.

Thunder, which had been growling steadily like an angry beast at bay, suddenly shattered the air with a deafening crack. At the same instant a rock on the slope above her broke free and began to roll straight at her. She saw it coming toward her in a horrifying freeze-frame of instant awareness that she was about to die.

Gray Cloud saw it, too. Turning swiftly, he braced his feet and bent, grabbing her forearm in an iron grip. With one powerful yank he tugged her out of harm's way. The momentum of his movement threw them both in the same direction, causing them to fall and slip downward on the slope as the boulder rolled by.

Mercy came to an abrupt halt wedged against a rock, and Gray Cloud half slid over her before he could stay his motion. Stunned, she lay gasping, unable even to open her eyes. But finally she did look up at him, and the world spun away.

Gazing into his dark eyes was like staring up into the night sky. The darkness seemed to swallow everything,

seemed to be a bottomless pool into which she was falling.
So black, so deep. Endless night.

Mesmerizing.

His eyes seemed to contain entire worlds, she thought
hazily. If she could only manage to see far enough into
them, she was sure she would find the answers to ancient
questions.

And the answers to newer ones, such as why was her
heart beating so hard and so loudly? Why did everything
within her feel as if it were turning to warm molasses? Why
did her eyelids feel so heavy and droopy, and why, oh why,
was she breathing so deeply, like a sprinter at the end of a
race?

And why was she wishing, hoping against hope, that
Gray Cloud would come closer, that his firm lips would
part a little and that he would lean down and would...

Kiss her.

His pupils dilated suddenly, as if he'd had the same
thought at the same instant, and then his mouth was on
hers, answering all her questions with the warmth of his
touch and the weight of the powerful body that half covered
hers. Some recognition deep in her soul was unleashed as
lips touched lips. *Yes.*

An aching flood of need washed through her so rapidly
that she was swamped instantly. Hungers she had heard
about but only dimly felt in the past were suddenly vivid
and overwhelming. Her entire being yearned upward to the
man whose mouth touched hers. Deep inside she felt a
swelling, a pulsing, as everything slipped away except the
moment and the man.

A deafening blast of thunder shocked them both back to
awareness. The wind suddenly rushed down the gully, tugging at Gray Cloud's hair and whipping it around. They
jerked apart, and some corner of Mercy's mind wondered
why the mountain had gotten so angry over a little kiss.

For a long moment, ignoring the threatening thunder and scolding wind, Gray Cloud stared down at her. And then, as if shaking himself out of a dream, he pulled away and stood. Before she could start to rise, he reached down, grasped her hands and lifted her to her feet.

"Are you hurt?" he asked.

She shook her head quickly, feeling embarrassed. "No. A few bruises. Nothing important."

"Let's get going, then."

The kiss had never happened, she found herself thinking as she followed him up the side of the ravine. A meeting of lips that had been so brief and fleeting it had never occurred. Not really. Not where it mattered. Not in the heart or soul.

At least not in Gray Cloud's heart and soul, because it had been an earthquake in hers. The man was...irresistible. And that terrified her as much as anything.

If he turned to her right now and reached for her, she would go to him. She would do what she had always steadfastly refused to do: allow herself to be used. Because that brief contact had made her want him so badly that she doubted even her very strong instinct for emotional self-preservation would be enough to save her now.

She had tasted the forbidden fruit, she found herself thinking. Had tasted it so briefly and found it so very sweet.

She was all alone on a vast mountain with a reputed killer...and she wanted to make love with him.

"I am crazy!"

She spoke aloud without intending to, but the sound of her words penetrated the natural sounds of the wind and thunder in the most jarring way imaginable. Too late to snatch the words back, she could only scowl as Gray Cloud turned his head and looked down at her from a little higher up the slope.

"That makes two of us," he said.

Mercy didn't find that thought at all comforting.

The climb that had seemed to take forever had, in fact, taken only forty-five minutes. Not too far to climb every morning. Her base camp at the cave was not so close to the wolves that it would trouble them. She gave Gray Cloud high marks for his site selection.

The den was on a rocky slope; a small ledge protruded over the hole that had been burrowed into the hillside, and on the ledge slept a large gray wolf. It stirred a little as they approached, lifting its head to fix them with golden eyes. Mercy halted and hunkered down, trying to be quiet as she tugged the lens caps off her binoculars and raised them to her eyes.

A moment later she had the wolf in focus. "The alpha female," she whispered to Gray Cloud. The wolf was clearly pregnant, and in a wolf pack, usually only the alpha female ever bore young. Some researchers held that only the alpha male and alpha female ever mated; others had observed interference behavior that had the effect of limiting the mating of the other wolves in the pack, though not always eliminating it entirely.

The bitch stared at Mercy, tawny eyes blinking very slowly, measuring and gauging the potential threat. Gray Cloud hunkered down, too, and waited in perfect stillness as the moments ticked by.

"So beautiful," Mercy whispered on the merest breath. "So beautiful."

"She'll whelp soon," Gray Cloud murmured back. "Not much longer."

Mercy wished with all her heart that she could witness the event when it happened. It would *have* to be very soon, as Gray Cloud said. The wolf had remained at the den because she sensed the closeness of her own time, so the rest of the pack had gone hunting without her, in all likelihood, and would bring her back some of their kill.

Gradually the female relaxed and lowered her head to her paws once more. For a while after that she continued to stare steadily at the intruders, but finally her eyes began to droop closed, and she looked as contented and relaxed as if she were sunning on a warm summer day, instead of lying in the cold, stormy air halfway up a mountain.

And it *was* cold today. As soon as Mercy cooled off from the climb, she had to zip her jacket to the throat, and before long she was wishing for a hat of some kind to cover her ears. Instead she had to be content with hunching her shoulders up and promising herself that she would bring her stocking cap tomorrow.

The den was in a small, rocky clearing, a place that seemed to have carved out a peacefulness for itself. Here the storm didn't seem quite so threatening somehow, nor did the wind bite quite so hard. Perhaps, Mercy found herself thinking, the mountain and wolves were happy together here, and that was what affected the mood.

Because it was a mood. The clearing had an unmistakable aura of serenity to it, a feeling of rightness. Here the mountain was content.

When her arms began to ache, Mercy reluctantly lowered the binoculars and glanced at Gray Cloud. He was sitting cross-legged beside her, his eyes closed and his head tilted back, looking relaxed and meditative.

In his own way he looked as much a part of the scene as the wolf did. And that left Mercy feeling like an intruder. Like someone the mountain *would* want to push away.

Uneasy, she tore her gaze from Gray Cloud and told herself that she would not succumb to the crazy thoughts that kept flitting through her head, thoughts about not being welcomed by the mountain, thoughts of how much she wanted to touch Gray Cloud, how much she wished he would touch her.

Something was definitely wrong with her brain circuits, she thought. Definitely something screwy in the way she kept thinking about the man beside her rather than her task here. Screwy in the way she kept falling into thoughts of the mountain as a being. The altitude had to be affecting her. Hypoxia, maybe? Wasn't that the term for lack of oxygen?

She was clutching at straws, and she knew it. Trying to find some way to explain strange events and her strange companion—and her even stranger reaction to him.

As she sat there telling herself not to look at Gray Cloud but to concentrate on the wolves, her attention strayed upward to the sky above.

Her breath caught in her throat. The clouds no longer looked like gray storm clouds as they scraped the treetops. They had turned green and swirled malignantly, as if they had a life of their own. The hollow rumble of thunder continued at a distance, as if it came from elsewhere and bore no relation to the clouds overhead.

"Oh my God," she whispered as her hair began to stand on end. Her skin prickled all over, as if a million tiny bugs were dancing across it. The small silver friendship ring she wore on her right hand began to feel warmer than skin temperature. What was going on?

"Lie down."

She turned her head toward Gray Cloud in astonishment. "What?"

"Lie down," he demanded roughly. Even as he spoke, he was stretching out flat on the ground and tugging at her arm. "Lightning's going to strike."

It took a moment, just a moment, to click. And then she realized why her skin was prickling and her ring felt warm.

A huge potential electrical charge was building right here, and at any moment...

She lay down as flat as she could get on her stomach and had the presence of mind to set the binoculars aside. Her ring. It was growing warmer still, and she yanked it from her hand, afraid she would get burned.

The ground hummed, as if the rocks were vibrating with the building power of the electrical charge. It was an eerie sound, almost like the whine of an electrical transformer, but it was coming from the ground, and all the more frightening for its origin.

Cheek on the cold, hard ground, she looked at Gray Cloud and saw his black hair spreading and standing on its own as the growing charge caused each strand to try to get as far from the others as it could.

The crawling sensation on her skin intensified, and she began to feel as if there were cobwebs all over her face.

I'm going to die. The thought was stark, clear. Lightning was going to strike this very spot, and if it didn't kill her, she was going to wish it had.

The humming sound grew until it seemed to fill the universe. The wolf howled, a lonely, eerie protest.

And then, with the suddenness of a thunderclap, there came the crack of a gunshot.

CHAPTER FIVE

*The intruders intended harm. Evil emanations filled the
air as the one with the tiny thunderstick moved toward the
quiet clearing. Anger thrummed in the mountain, and it
gathered itself to deal with this abomination. Power grew
and focused, building until the mountain hummed its rage.*

As soon as the sound of the shot faded, Mercy instinctively started to lift her head, but Gray Cloud shot out a
hand and held her down. "Don't!" he snapped sharply.

Of course. She would make a target of herself. And the
building charge in the ground... Her ring, which she had
dropped on the dirt before her face, was vibrating visibly.
The ground thrummed and hummed, a growing threat.

Another gunshot.

And then the world disappeared in a flash of white light
so intense that it hurt Mercy's eyes as it washed away all
color and contrast. The crack of the accompanying thunder
was so loud that the concussion was more felt than heard.
She saw Gray Cloud's lips move briefly, but she couldn't
hear him.

After a few moments she realized that the humming of
the earth had lessened slightly but hadn't entirely quit. Gray
Cloud's hand was still resting on the side of her head, and
his dark eyes warned her to keep down.

Her heart was hammering so hard that she couldn't catch
her breath. Worst of all, though—worse than the terror of
both lightning and the person with the gun—was the sense
of hopelessness. Helplessness. There was nothing at all she
could do but lie here and await the outcome of events.

She hated that feeling. Hated it so much that she twisted her head a little, trying to see anything at all besides dirt and Gray Cloud.

The humming was growing again, she realized, and the cobwebby feeling was intensifying. More lightning. She wondered if the man with the gun was lying down, too. And if Thunder Mountain was trying to kill him. Or her. Or all of them.

A wolf howled, probably the female, and then lightning snapped to the ground again, blindingly bright. Almost immediately there was another, and then another, and one of them struck so close that Mercy felt its heat sear the back of her neck.

Then the sky opened its floodgates and released a deluge that soaked them to the skin almost immediately.

But the terrible humming of the ground was gone, and the cobwebby feeling had vanished. Mercy dug her fingers into the earth and gave a huge sob of relief as she realized that she was safe from the lightning at least.

But that left the person with the gun.

"Don't move," Gray Cloud said quietly. "I'm going to circle around to check for the gunman."

Concerned, she reached out and caught his hand, staying him. "No!" she whispered sharply. "You could get hurt."

He silenced her with a shake of his head. "We need to know if he's still here. I'll be careful."

Moments later he was slinking away into the gray mist of rain in complete silence.

Leaving Mercy to lie on the ground and wonder why she didn't just go home and forget this insanity.

Just then the wolf howled again. A beckoning, beautifully lonesome sound. A moment later another howl answered her, and then another, and another, until Mercy couldn't tell how many voices responded as the harmonies built.

Grabbing the binoculars, she wiped the damp lenses on her sleeve and put them to her eyes. The alpha female was crouched before the den, her head tilted back so she could give her full-voiced cry. And it looked—oh, God, it looked as if she were bleeding. Had she been shot?

Without thinking, Mercy started to rise but caught herself before she got to her knees. The gunman might still be out there, and he might be inclined to shoot anything that moved…except that he wasn't shooting at the wolf right now.

Again she started to rise, needing to help in any way possible. Just then Gray Cloud entered the clearing, walking upright, and headed straight for the wolf. The female crouched, hackles rising, but she didn't flee, nor did she bare her fangs.

Even over the steady rush of the falling rain Mercy could hear Gray Cloud talking softly, a soothing singsong chant of some kind as he approached the wary wolf.

The female hunkered even lower but remained where she was, not even backing up as the man drew closer and closer.

When he reached her, Gray Cloud knelt beside her and began to gently check her side. As if sensing that he meant to help, the wolf relaxed her posture and rolled onto her side, giving the man access to her wound.

Mercy wanted to charge up there and help, but she held herself back, realizing that she would only frighten the wolf and disturb the tentative trust that had formed between man and beast. Best to stay back.

Taking care to keep quiet, she pulled a notebook out of her pocket, bent over it to keep the rain off it and began to hastily scribble her impression of all that she was seeing: the den, the wolf, the man, the interaction between them.

At some point she realized that pairs of tawny eyes were looking into the clearing from the edges of the forest all around. The pack had gathered and was staying back while Gray Cloud was with the female.

Moving slowly, careful not to startle, Mercy tried to count the wolves in the pack and find a distinctive marking on each one by which to identify them. Packs could grow to as many as thirty members, though they seldom did. This one, unless she had miscounted or had failed to see some of the wolves, numbered six, including the alpha female, a typical size.

A soft sound beside her alerted her, and she turned her head to see the black wolf that had twice visited her standing a few feet away, staring straight at her. She was sure it was him because of the light-dark markings over his eyes, unlike the other wolves of the pack.

And he had come to her again. The awe she had felt before became something almost reverent as she realized she was developing some kind of bond with this wolf.

And his tail was up, she realized. Only the alpha male and alpha female carried their tails straight up.

Oh, how she wanted to reach out and touch him, just to be sure he was real. But as soon as the thought crossed her mind, the wolf turned and vanished into the rain. Moments later she heard his howl, then heard it answered by the rest of the pack.

Turning, she saw all the tawny eyes vanish as the wolves pulled back from the clearing. Only the alpha female remained, lying docilely beneath the reassuring touch of Gray Cloud's hand. A minute or so later he rose and turned, walking away from the wolf as steadily and calmly as he had approached. Behind him, the female rolled onto her belly and watched his departure.

"Is she all right?" Mercy asked when Gray Cloud reached her.

"Seems to be. She's got a small score in her side. I can't tell if it was a bullet graze or something else."

"You think the gunman was shooting at her?"

He shook his head. "I don't know. Probably. I don't think you ought to come up here by yourself."

Mercy couldn't have agreed more, but that presented a serious problem. "There's no reason to think he'd hurt me."

"We've covered this ground—" He broke off abruptly, tilting his head and closing his eyes as if he heard something. Long seconds ticked by, and then he said, "All right."

Mercy waited for explanation and, when none was forthcoming, asked, "All right what?"

His eyes snapped open. "The wind says to let you do as you wish, Tomorrow Woman. That you must do as you intend for it all to come out as it has been ordained."

Mercy gaped at him, astonished past speech. When she could manage to speak, all she could ask was "Who's Tomorrow Woman? And what's been ordained?"

"You are Tomorrow Woman. Thus the wind has named you. As for what has been ordained..." He gave a noncommittal shrug. "We'll find that out, I guess."

Mercy looked away, not sure how to react to this. She wasn't sure which was harder to accept—that the wind had named her or that events were ordained. She was an avid believer in self-determination, and she was a long way from believing the wind spoke, let alone named things.

Doubt me not, Tomorrow Woman.

The whisper seemed to come from the trees, and as soon as she heard it, Mercy felt ice run down her spine. She was imagining things! She had to be! It was just the power of suggestion, after hearing Gray Cloud speak with such conviction about what the wind was saying.

Lie to yourself, Tomorrow Woman. The truth will triumph.

Ice touched the base of her skull as a new kind of terror

took her. Could she really be losing her mind? Hearing voices was the sign of the worst kind of insanity. If she thought the wind was talking to her...

Shivering, she shook herself mentally. No. She had to concentrate on the wolves. Concentrate on what had *actually* happened in the real world. Her mind was just playing tricks on her, that was all. Not enough sleep. Too much tension because of the gunshot and the lightning. Overload.

This time no voice responded to her thoughts, and she allowed herself a brief sense of relief. All she had to do was focus on the task at hand...and figure out how to avoid trouble with the gunman.

She turned to Gray Cloud. "We need to tell the rangers that someone is shooting up here. You can't shoot in a National Forest, can you?"

"A person who shoots at an endangered species hardly cares about the rules."

"That isn't what I meant. I was thinking the rangers would do something about it."

Gray Cloud looked impassively at her, indicating nothing at all.

Yeah, right, Mercy found herself thinking. What *would* the rangers do about it? Looking for one man—or even a couple of men—on this mountain would be extremely difficult. But still, they ought to know.

The problem was, she didn't want to go down the mountain now to tell them. She would miss the birth of the wolf pups if she did, and as a consequence would miss an important part of her study of this pack's existence and behavior.

But if the gunman roamed unhindered here, he would have more opportunities to harm the wolves.

She turned toward Gray Cloud. "We have to do something to stop them."

He tipped his head just a fraction of an inch but never took his eyes from her.

"We can't let them hurt the wolves, Gray Cloud! We need to do something to prevent it!"

Even as she spoke, it struck her that perhaps it was ridiculous to align herself with Gray Cloud this way. What did she have as a basis for trusting him, apart from his assertion that he was here to protect the mountain, and apart from the way he seemed to be taking care of her? It wasn't much...but perhaps it was enough.

Just then a long, low moan drew their attention back to the pregnant wolf. She had risen to a squatting position, and even at this distance she appeared to be agitated and breathing hard. Mercy snatched up her binoculars again and peered through them.

"She's whelping!" This was the last thing Mercy had expected to see in the open. She had expected the wolf to retreat to her den.

The bitch stopped moaning as soon as she saw her first pup, almost as if once she understood what was happening, her contractions no longer bothered her. Instead she settled down to licking each newly arrived pup, washing away the placenta, and then tucking the newborn to her teats until the next delivery began. Seven pups in all were born during the next four hours. At some point the alpha male had returned and paced a patrol as his mate produced the litter.

During a pause in the delivery, Mercy was struck by a thought and looked at Gray Cloud. "What happened to the gunman? Why would he take one shot at the wolf and then disappear?"

"The mountain drove him away."

She was tempted to let that pass, because she knew she wasn't going to like the answers to any questions she asked. Curiosity, however, wouldn't let her ignore it. "How?"

"The lightning. You felt the power of the mountain."

Sometimes in life a fundamental shift in perception occurred. One of those shifts struck her now, with all the force of an earthquake. All her attempts to rationalize away her feelings came to an abrupt halt. As if she had abruptly been hurled hundreds of feet into the air to look down on her place in the world, she suddenly saw all that had been happening from a different perspective.

She was the mountain. Massive, towering above everything around, trees furring her slopes, sheltering animals so small they were nearly invisible. And she saw the intruders, troublesome as lice, threatening the natural order.

Yes, she thought, the mountain could take action, but whatever action it took would be on its own scale, destroying much more than its target. Rock slides, once set in motion, would carry away trees and animals, as well as the intruder. The lightning would strike in the area where the charge had built, but within that area were potential victims other than the intruders. The wolf, for example, could be hurt.

So the mountain restrained itself and took action only reluctantly. But when it acted...

Mercy shivered and was suddenly back in her own time and place, perceiving things from her own perspective. She couldn't possibly have really touched upon the mountain's consciousness, could she?

Gray Cloud regarded her steadily from enigmatic eyes.

The mountain drove him away. She found herself believing that it was possible. The lightning would certainly have been a good tool for that, yet not precise enough to avoid doing other damage by accident. Which meant she could have been hurt. Gray Cloud could have been hurt. The wolf could have been hurt.

And somehow the understanding of how those forces worked was even more terrifying than blaming it all on natural occurrences. She looked at Gray Cloud again and found herself sinking into his obsidian gaze. This time, though, she felt as if his eyes were a window, and she was gazing into the black heart of the mountain.

Beware, Tomorrow Woman. Beware. All is not what it seems.

The fire burned brightly, orange and yellow flames leaping in the pit in the cave floor. The night was chilly and damp, and the endless thunder rumbled angrily. The night was alive with threat, and Mercy couldn't deny it any longer. All her scientific training had gone by the wayside, leaving her facing a stark reality in a world that was alien to everything she had believed.

Aware now, whether she wanted to be or not, she could feel the vitality of the mountain around her. It was a cold vitality, far removed from the swift, hot responses of humankind. The anger it felt was not swift and thoughtless but righteous and measured, a growing determination not to tolerate desecration.

And in that awareness she found another awareness of the ecosystem. She found herself reaching out with all her senses to embrace the world around her, the world of Thunder Mountain, from the smallest insect to the tallest tree. It was a perfect world, each creature serving a purpose in an endless cycle of life, death and rebirth.

Until mankind had arrived. Mankind interrupted that cycle and disturbed the balance. And disturbing the balance had awakened the slumbering mountain to its role as guardian. The mountain would protect its inhabitants.

What if the mountain misinterpreted *her* presence here and perceived her as a threat? Gray Cloud hadn't answered her when she'd asked him that, and then he had vanished somewhere into the night to do whatever it was he did when he left her.

The feeling of being watched, which had never quite left

her, seemed more ominous now than before. The mountain was watching her. How could she possibly escape being watched as long as she stayed here? And how could she do anything else when it seemed clear that someone was up to no good?

She couldn't leave the wolves unprotected, particularly the pups. And the wolves themselves wouldn't do anything to protect them from men. She wasn't even sure, at this point, if she dared leave the wolves unprotected long enough to hike down to park headquarters and alert the rangers. So that left her and Gray Cloud—if he was what he said he was.

But her quandary merely raised the question of *how* she could protect the wolves. This man might not be deterred by the presence of witnesses. In fact, he might just kill the witnesses.

What she needed to know, she thought, was the goal of the person or persons with a gun. What did they really hope to accomplish, and at what price? But how could she possibly learn that unless she could question someone? And who would she question?

Ask the mountain. Ask the wind.

The thought twisted sinuously into her mind, rattling her with a sense that she had been invaded somehow. Something *other* was able to get into her head, to say things to her. The mountain watched her, the wind whispered to her, and the night was full of threat.

Drawing her knees up to her chin, she wrapped her arms around them and stared into the fire, trying to shake the clammy sense of foreboding that clung to her, trying to sort out all her mixed feelings about today's events.

And wishing Gray Cloud would return. No matter how her mind wanted to distrust him, her emotions trusted him implicitly. And since that brief almost-kiss earlier, part of her just plain couldn't stop thinking about how much she wanted him to take her into his arms, how much she wanted him to take her on a journey to the end of the rainbow.

That was dangerous. If her mind was clouded with desire for him, how could she correctly evaluate him and what he was doing? For heaven's sake, the man had been accused of murder. He lived as a recluse on the side of a mountain and spoke to the wind and thunder. Was this a man she wanted to give her heart to?

Her mind said no. Her heart said...maybe. Damn, couldn't she pick someone better than that? Someone with an unclouded past and a bright future? This man had nothing except his dedication to this mountain and his vision. Even if he wasn't the killer he was reputed to be, it was still a recipe for grief!

Hormones, she told herself grimly. That was all it was. She wasn't really interested in him as a person; she was merely responding to his masculinity. And he *was* masculine. A slow, secret smile curved her mouth as, for a brief time, she forgot all her worries and thought about Gray Cloud. Very masculine. And so completely different from the academics she was accustomed to spending time with.

He moved with none of the flat-footedness of the street dweller, none of the constrictedness of someone who was used to being hemmed in. He moved instead with a fluid, confident grace. And he was truly a beautiful man. Not handsome, not pretty, just...quintessentially masculine. Incredibly appealing.

But not someone to let herself get involved with.

With a stern mental shake, she forced herself to stop thinking about Gray Cloud and start thinking about the wolves. The seven pups wouldn't even open their eyes for another eleven or twelve days. Until then they would be able to do little but whine, eat and crawl short distances by pulling themselves along with their forelegs. They certainly wouldn't be able to leave the den.

In her research she had come across records of wolves who had been observed to move their litters from den to den during the critical first three months, but the earliest moves recorded had been about three weeks after birth. It was likely, then, that the wolves and the pups were pretty well tied to this particular den at least until then—which made them extremely vulnerable to anyone who wished to harm them.

And that meant she and Gray Cloud *had* to do something. But what? It would take days to hike down to park headquarters to report the gunman. It wouldn't take that long to kill all the wolves, particularly with the pups so helpless.

But anything she could think of doing to protect the animals would also interfere with them. They were wild animals, not meant to be penned in or shadowed everywhere. Continued human protection could create problems, too.

Sighing, she closed her eyes and wished Gray Cloud would return. What if the gunman came back here? She shivered again and tightened her arms around her knees.

If she had an ounce of sense she would head home and leave the whole mess to the park rangers. But she'd never in her life turned tail from anything except emotional involvement, and she wasn't going to start now. The mere thought of abandoning those wolves made her stomach turn sour.

"Mercy."

As soundlessly as a wraith, Gray Cloud stepped out of the wind-tossed night and into the cave. Mercy looked up and lowered her knees, feeling a mixture of relief and apprehension at the sight of him. He squatted beside the fire, taking care to keep it between himself and the cave mouth, and warmed his hands.

"Did you find out anything useful?" she asked.

"There's more than one *wasicu* on this mountain, and they're all working together."

"How...? How did you discover that?" She almost hadn't asked, then resigned herself to the answer.

"The spirits told me," he replied levelly. "Men, hired guns. They're here to clear the mountain of problems. The wolves. Me. You."

"Me?" Mercy gasped the word. "Me? Why me?"

"You know about the wolves. You're with me." He shrugged a shoulder. "What does it matter? They see you as a problem. They were hired to remove any obstacles to the goals of their employer."

"Who hired them?"

Gray Cloud shook his head slightly. "I wasn't able to learn that. Just how many and what their purpose is."

"We need to do something!"

He lowered himself to the ground and sat cross-legged. His dark eyes, looking like bottomless pits, stared at her over the flames. "I tried to persuade the wolves to move. The pups are too young, but..." He shrugged again.

Mercy felt an icy tendril of panic grip her stomach, but she couldn't tell what caused it, whether it was the horrible situation or the man who faced her across the fire. "Umm...how did you try to persuade the wolves?"

He didn't answer, but his gaze never wavered.

Mercy looked away, her heart beating with uncomfortable rapidity. The world she knew kept slipping away, and it was getting harder and harder to get it back. She was sliding slowly into a place where men talked to wolves, blue fire danced in the air, and the wind whispered secrets. And it was getting more and more difficult to tell herself that these things weren't real.

The power of the mountain seemed to surround her, and the wind had spoken to her. She had seen the blue light that Gray Cloud called the life force. Was she going to doubt her own senses in favor of a lifetime of beliefs? Or was she going to accept the evidence of those same senses in the face of all that she had believed throughout her life?

"I take it," she heard herself say, "that the wolves aren't going to move."

"Not just yet."

"What are you going to do about it?"

He cocked his head, still staring steadily at her, as if she were an interesting puzzle.

"You *are* going to do something?" she insisted.

"What would you have me do?"

"There must be something! If they want to kill the wolves, it would be so easy right now, with the pups helpless and the pack tied to that one den."

"In the way of wolves, the pack will move on if something happens to the pups. They won't risk themselves needlessly to save the litter. You know that."

She *did* know that. The adults would move on and leave the pups to their fate. It made evolutionary sense, survival sense, but it appalled her nonetheless.

"You're viewing the wolves in human terms."

She was; she admitted it to herself. It was a little shocking to her to have to be reminded of that by a man who—to her way of thinking, anyhow—seemed to anthropomorphize even the rocks and clouds. "Are you saying we shouldn't intervene?"

"I'm saying the wolves are smarter than you give them credit for, and these men won't find them so easy to get rid of. Whether we should do something..." He shook his head. "If we can think of something constructive, yes."

Mercy made an impatient sound. "I can't stand this! I can't stand this feeling of not being able to prevent a catastrophe. What happens when they get rid of us and the wolves? They'll still need to deal with all those environmental concerns. People in general are becoming less and less willing to allow wilderness areas to be timbered. They won't accomplish anything useful with this...this murder!''

She felt foolish almost as soon as the words were out of her mouth. She knew better. Gray Cloud merely nodded noncommittally.

After a moment, Mercy let go of her tension and sighed. ''Somebody has to help the wolves,'' she said finally, sadly.

Gray Cloud rose to his feet in one smooth movement. Leaning forward, he passed his hand over the fire. As he did so, the flames leapt and changed color, growing blue and cold looking. ''Events have been set into motion. Powers that slumbered have been awakened. We will have opportunities to intervene. We may see some way to take action. For now... For now we wait. The forces that gather on this mountain have not yet come together fully. If we act now, we may prevent an important development.''

Slowly Mercy lowered her gaze from his stony face to the twisting blue flames. They no longer seemed to leap randomly but to weave sinuously, like dancers involved in an intricate ballet. And within those flames she thought she could see faces, almost familiar at times, nudging at her memory like a word she couldn't quite remember.

You know.

The whisper seemed to reach out of the fire toward her, telling her to remember, that she already knew. That all she had to do was recall.

Disturbed, she wanted to look away, to ignore the whisper, ignore the feelings it evoked, but as if hypnotized by the flames she continued to stare into the heart of the fire.

One face appeared to grow larger, to move closer and separate from the rest. For eyes and a mouth it had only dark holes, yet it was familiar to her. She knew that face, and if she could just fill in the eyes, she would recognize it. The memory danced maddeningly out of reach.

With a whoosh the flames leapt to man height and then subsided, turning orange once again as they did so. Beyond the cavern walls, thunder growled angrily, then shook the ground with its fury. Gray Cloud remained standing, his eyes closed as he viewed some inner vision.

Around her, Mercy heard the whispers of the elements, mocking voices that seemed to tell her to run while she still could. Beneath her, she felt the stirring power of the mountain.

Gray Cloud was right, she realized. The powers were coming together; ancient forces had been awakened. And the mountain would not care if a few innocent beings were destroyed as it sought to save its denizens. Just as the wolves would sacrifice the pups for the survival of the pack, the mountain would sacrifice some for the survival of many.

An uneasy shudder ran through her. When the mountain reacted, anything that happened to be in the way would be crushed. The mountain didn't care.

Nor, she feared, did Gray Cloud.

Sometime during the night she awoke in a state of terror. Claustrophobia hit with all the might of a falling boulder, and in an instant she was locked in a state of breathless panic.

The night was impenetrable, dark as pitch. The fire had died hours ago, not leaving even the faint glow of embers for illumination. The rushing sound of the wind filled the cavern, creating the sensation of falling endlessly through space.

Guided by deep-rooted instinct, propelled by unthinking terror, Mercy struggled out of her blankets and scrambled on hands and knees toward where she remembered the cave mouth to be.

She had to get out of here. The weight of the tons of

rock around her was crushing her, bearing down on her, slowly burying her alive. The mountain was asphyxiating her as surely as if it were strangling her by the throat.

Air! She needed air now! Her lungs dragged desperately, sucking in nothing, as she crawled frantically across the rough cave floor. There was no air. Somehow she had fallen into a vacuum and was going to die with her lungs laboring uselessly while her heart pounded frantically in her ears.

The mouth of the cave wasn't where she expected it to be. Crawling desperately, she ran up hard against a rock wall, banging her head painfully. Where had the cave entrance gone?

All of a sudden, in a moment of clarity that pierced her panic, she understood. There was no longer any cave opening. The mountain had sealed her off underground. Had buried her alive in a cavern deep within its bowels.

The cave where she had fallen asleep had become her tomb.

CHAPTER SIX

*B*uried alive.

Locked in the maw of the mountain, time became meaningless. The desperate need for air increased her panic, which increased her need for air....

But finally, at some point, she calmed down. It was not the calm of peace, but the calm of desperation, as her mind and body recognized that her only hope lay in forced composure. And as she calmed down, she discovered that she could breathe more easily, though the air was dank and heavy.

But nothing made it possible to see.

In the dark she became a young, frightened child again. The night was easy to populate with all kinds of unsavory things, and who knew what creatures might inhabit a cave like this? Insects. Spiders.

And she didn't dare move again, because it struck her that she didn't know where she was. She couldn't be sure that there wasn't a ledge here somewhere, that she wouldn't fall into a pit and plunge hundreds of feet to a painful death if she crawled in the wrong direction, down the unexplored passage.

Oh, she was cold. Huddling against the rock, she curled up and wished that she hadn't struggled out of her blankets. Now she needed them desperately, and she had no idea where they were, no way to find them. Well, she might not suffocate to death now, but hypothermia would kill her in a few hours.

How had she gotten here? The last thing she remembered

was staring into the fire while Gray Cloud spoke of forces awakening.

Gray Cloud! What if this wasn't the cave she had fallen asleep in and he had brought her here? What if he had hypnotized her in some way and then carried her off and left her stranded in this deep, dark cave? What a way to commit murder! No one would ever guess that she hadn't just gotten lost and died of exposure. Nor was there a doubt in her mind that Gray Cloud was physically strong enough to carry her however far he needed to.

But why should he do any such thing? Why? The question kept taunting her. Not for the first time, she wondered why he hadn't killed her at the outset, if killing her was his intent.

Shivering, she curled up as tightly as she could and wished bitterly that she could at least have answers to her questions before she died.

As if in response to her thoughts, she made a connection she had not made before, one that answered her questions and settled her doubts.

Gray Cloud was dedicated to protecting Thunder Mountain. He believed the mountain was a sentient being. Well, even Mercy herself had come to believe that. If the mountain wanted Mercy dead, Gray Cloud would do it, wouldn't he? What if the mountain had just decided she needed to be eliminated and had told Gray Cloud to bring her to this cavern?

He would have done it. Gray Cloud would have done it, because the mountain demanded it.

The sense of betrayal she felt was sharp and deep. She had been coming to care for the man, coming to trust him. Coming to want him. And he had become the pawn of a mountain. An insane mountain, if it didn't distinguish between threats and non-threats, but simply chose to destroy everything that was an outsider.

Oh, God! This was crazy thinking. Sheer insanity! The mountain didn't think. Gray Cloud might not have anything to do with her present situation. Anyone could have carried her to this cave and left her to die, including the gunman. All they needed was a chance to get at her, and that could have happened anytime during the night while she slept.

She didn't want to believe Gray Cloud had done this to her, and when she thought of how he had looked after her since he rescued her from the landslide, she found it even harder to believe that he might hurt her.

Unless the mountain told him to. The thought was an uncomfortable prod, a reminder that there was something Gray Cloud put above all else. A reminder that he was a fanatic. And fanatics were capable of anything in their attempts to serve their cause.

He could have left her here, whether she wanted to believe it or not.

And that hurt. Hurt terribly. Hurt with a pain that was far more than trust betrayed.

When the whispering began, she had no idea at all how much time had passed. At first she thought perhaps it was merely an illusion of the rushing-wind sound that filled the cavern. Susurrations at first sounded like almost-words, tickling the edges of her mind even in her preoccupation with her dismal circumstances. Gradually, in syllables, words began to emerge from the background noise, like a radio not quite tuned.

"Mercy...."

"...away..."

"...gone..."

Her mind, she told herself, was simply manufacturing words out of random sounds, the way in the perfect dark her eyes kept seeing brilliant flashes of light that weren't really there. The mind needed to fill the void with something recognizable, to make sense out of nonsense.

Sensory deprivation. The term floated to her out of a long-ago psychology class. If the mind was deprived of all sensory input, it would begin to manufacture hallucinations to fill the void. That was what she was doing: hallucinating.

Shivering and cold, she didn't want to lose her mind, as well. She didn't want to die insane. Squeezing her eyes shut, as if it would make a difference, she forced herself to ignore the words that seemed to be emerging from the background sounds and tried instead to focus her thoughts into a logically consistent evaluation of her present situation. Any kind of focus, she reasoned, should counteract the hallucinations.

But it didn't. Instead she found that the flashes of light in the pitch-darkness seemed to increase, becoming tiny dancing blue sparkles, not so very different from the ones that had seemed to guide Gray Cloud through the storm the night he rescued her.

And the susurrations seemed to become louder, more demanding.

"*...wolf...*"

"*...man...*"

"*...beast of...*"

It was as if the mountain was demanding her attention. The sparkles grew more numerous, the whispers became louder, until they began to sound like broken voices. The more she tried to ignore them, the more they demanded her attention.

And that was *not* the way hallucinations behaved.

In that instant she became certain that the mountain was trying to tell her something. Understanding flooded her, halting her attempt to ignore what was happening.

Listen to the mountain. The whispery voice of the wind spoke inside her head. *Listen to Thunder. Listen.*

A whirlwind snatched at her then, spinning her around, lifting her from the ground, tumbling her headlong into the pitch of night.

"Mercy? Mercy, wake up!"

A low, masculine voice yanked her out of the frightening freefall, and her eyes snapped open. She was in the cave, the dim red fireglow silhouetting Gray Cloud as he squatted beside her.

"Wake up," he said quietly. "You're having a nightmare."

Nightmare? Slowly, shaking her head, shivering internally from a cold that had seeped into her very bones, she sat up. No, it had been no nightmare, she thought. No nightmare. The cold was too real. Her hands felt like ice, and her head ached where she had bumped into the cave wall. No nightmare. Fright made her heart throb.

"Are you okay?" Gray Cloud asked. "You were thrashing around like a fish out of water."

Lightning flared brilliantly beyond the cave entrance, and thunder cracked loudly, a deafening reverberation that shook the ground. *Listen to Thunder.*

"I, uh, was dreaming that I was buried alive." The words escaped her in jerky bursts. She had no one to turn to right now except Gray Cloud, and now that she knew he hadn't kidnapped her, she was ready to trust him.

He sat up abruptly, folding his long legs and leaning toward her. With the dying fire behind him, she couldn't see much except the glitter of his eyes. "Buried alive? How?"

"In a cavern. There wasn't enough air, even though I could hear the wind rushing noisily all the time...or a waterfall, I guess. But I couldn't breathe, and it was so cold. So dark I couldn't see anything at all, except finally there were these little blue sparks dancing everywhere...." She shook her head, wincing when it throbbed where she had banged it in her dream. "I knew I was buried alive, in a cave deep in the mountain. Don't ask me how."

"Such things are known in dreams. Tell me."

"I heard voices in the wind." She could see him nod slowly. "Just a dream," she said after a moment, though her body argued otherwise.

"Dreams are real," he said. "My people never dismiss a dream. They come to tell us things. The spirits speak to us, give us guidance and warning. Dreams are real, Mercy. Never ignore them."

Listen to the mountain. Listen to Thunder. Listen.

She turned her head a little and looked past Gray Cloud to the lightning-ruptured night. Listen. Just what was she supposed to hear?

Then, as if in another dream, she felt Gray Cloud's arm slip around her shoulders, felt him draw her close to his side and hold her with an ineffable gentleness that made her throat ache. The warmth and solidity of his side against hers, the power of his embracing arm—they seemed to shelter her.

A corner of her mind rebelled briefly, feeling afraid of the comfort that was being offered, feeling afraid of long unmet needs and hungers. But after only the briefest struggle, need won, and she let herself soften and sink against Gray Cloud's strength.

It felt so good to be held!

And as she relaxed into his embrace, he seemed to relax, too. His hand began to knead her shoulder gently, a soothing stroking almost like petting. And little by little his touch filled her with a warm sense of security.

Not until that instant had she realized just how tense and afraid she had been for the last several days. Feeling safe for even a few moments was such a relief, such a release. It would have been so easy to let go of everything, just leave it all to Gray Cloud and forget the wolves, forget her mission, just...forget. Let someone else handle everything.

Such a seductive feeling, one she had never in her life given in to. But she gave in to it a little now. Just a little. Releasing a long sigh, she yielded, feeling as if she were melting into a soft, warm puddle.

Gray Cloud's arm tightened around her shoulders. When she simply softened more against him, a gentle pressure from his hand urged her to turn toward him. A touch from his fingertips brought her chin up, and the next thing she knew, he was kissing her.

It was a warm, soft kiss. A coaxing, reverent touching of lips. It conveyed gentleness, caring, hope...tentativeness. That tentativeness slipped past her last defense, softening her completely, tipping her head back in an unmistakable invitation.

Accepting it, Gray Cloud lowered her gently back onto her blankets, following her down with his mouth pressed gently to hers. "So sweet," he whispered gutturally, then took her mouth again in a deeper, harder kiss.

And she wanted more; she wanted it so badly that she opened her mouth without urging, inviting him deep inside her. His tongue traced her lips softly, then slipped within to tease gently at hers. Soft sinuous strokes led her farther and farther along a path of yearning and hunger.

Her arms lifted, closing around his broad shoulders, at last discovering how hard and powerful he felt beneath her palms. Just being free to touch him was enough to make her insides curl, but being held and kissed by him softened her and wrapped her in a warm, hazy glow.

The terror of her dream receded, as did the storm-tossed night and the hard cave floor beneath her back. Her entire being focused on the man who held her so gently yet securely, on the mouth that caressed hers so tenderly, on the powerful body that hovered over her.

A body she wanted to have pressed full-length to hers. Her hands clenched on his back, fingers digging in, trying to bring him closer. When his weight settled on her, she almost groaned with the sheer delight of it. Until this very moment she had never guessed how satisfying that feeling could be.

His hands slipped beneath her head, cradling it gently, as his tongue foraged deeper in her mouth, coaxing hers into erotic play. Her entire body arched, trying to bring him closer yet, and her insides turned liquid.

She wanted him. Oh, Lord, how she wanted him. She wanted the promise that was in every line of this man's body; she wanted the seductive promises of his oh-so-gentle mouth and strong but tender hands. She wanted the answers to mysteries older than time and hungers newer than today. She wanted the answer to her womanhood, and every instinct cried that he held the key.

Listen. To what? Listen to what? The driving drumbeat in her blood? The whirlwind of aching needs in her head? The yearning of her heart for its mate? Oh, she was listening, all right. Listening with every fiber of her being to the silent messages of her own body and soul.

Listening to the way her body yearned for other touches and twisted subtly in invitation. Touch me, her body cried, and she turned a little, begging for the caress of his hands on her breast. On her side. On her…

In a flash she lost her breath. Where before he had lain half-over her, all of a sudden he was between her legs, his hardness pressing against her softness in unmistakable demand. He wanted her. He wanted her as much as she wanted him.

But all sense hadn't been lost. The sudden intimacy of having him between her legs, even fully clothed, shattered her mood, quelling her arousal. And with stark, embarrassing clarity, she saw the dangerous game she was playing.

Her eyes flew open, and she found herself looking straight into his—dark, mysterious pools in the dim light of the dying fire. An instant later he rolled away, freeing her.

Neither of them said anything as the night crept back between them. Embarrassment welled in her, a sense of shame at the ready way she had welcomed him and encouraged him. He'd probably only meant to comfort her after her nightmare, and she'd taken it wrong....

Oh, damn!

Why, she wondered miserably, was it so hard in retrospect to remember exactly what had happened—who had been responsible for the rising passion of the embrace?

But maybe she couldn't remember because it had happened *between* them, for both of them. Maybe she hadn't been alone in her shamelessness.

What did it matter, anyway? She wasn't going to do it again or encourage it to happen again. For heaven's sake, she didn't know anything about the man except that he'd been tried for murder and he believed that mountains were alive! And what kind of recommendation was that?

Listen.

The whispered word twisted sinuously into her mind, driving back other concerns with its cold breath.

Listen.

Listen to what? She wanted to groan in frustration, to demand an answer from the source of that maddening whisper. Listen to what?

Beyond the cave mouth, lightning leapt from cloud to cloud, splitting into six or seven blue forks before vanishing. Moments later, thunder rolled through the air and the ground, causing the world to tremble.

In the moment after the thunder died, in a stillness as even the wind seemed to hold its breath, came the howl of a wolf.

Mercy's scalp prickled, and she sat up abruptly. Gray

Cloud did the same. Something was wrong. That howl was...different.

Gray Cloud rose to his feet in a single swift movement. "I'm going to check on the pups."

"I'm coming with you." The thought of that climb in the dead of the stormy night was daunting, but she couldn't just sit here and wait. Something was wrong.

The ground was slippery and treacherous from the rain. Smooth rocks became icelike, and the mud was every bit as bad. The little sparkles of blue light danced in the misty, wet air—guiding them, it seemed—and Mercy no longer questioned what her eyes were telling her. Whatever those little lights were, they were illuminating the way.

Gray Cloud never strayed from her side, keeping a hand at her elbow or back every step of the way. More than once, when she started to slip, he caught her and kept her from falling. She quickly grew accustomed to having his powerful arm snatch her about the waist and steady her.

She couldn't imagine why he wasn't having the same difficulty keeping his footing, but he appeared to be having no problem at all. Like a mountain goat.

Another howl rent the night, a sorrowful sound, and what troubled Mercy more than anything was that there was no answering howl. What had happened to the rest of the pack? Had they abandoned the bitch and her pups? Or had one of them gotten injured and been left behind?

They surely couldn't have abandoned the den—not yet, when the pups had just been born. Something was very definitely seriously wrong.

Another howl, this time more of a low groaning sound than a true howl. It made Mercy's hair stand on end, it was so unnatural, and even Gray Cloud paused a moment, tilting his head back as he listened to it.

"Damn!" he muttered.

"It's hurt, isn't it?" She knew in her heart there could

be no other explanation for that anguished, sorrowful sound.

He grunted acknowledgment as he urged her up the side of the ravine. She slipped again, but this time when he caught her, he didn't release her once she was steady. This time he kept his arm clamped around her waist.

"It's the bitch," he said.

"How can you tell?"

"I just know."

As usual. The wind had probably told him. She would have felt frustrated, except that she was far too worried about what could have made the wolf howl that way. Had a pup died? Was she sick in the aftermath of giving birth?

Where were the other wolves?

Listen.

Yeah, right. Listen. To what? That pained, painful, moaning howl? What the hell good would listening do? Something was wrong, and *listening* wasn't going to fix it!

The last bit of terrain was steep enough that Gray Cloud climbed up first, as he had earlier, then turned to reach down and give Mercy a hand up. She could have climbed it alone, but it seemed important to him to help, so she let him. Besides, arguing would only waste time, and they didn't have any to spare, to judge by the wolf's cry.

At last they came over the rise that concealed the den from them. The first thing they saw was fire.

Gray Cloud swore viciously, and Mercy cried out. Someone had built a fire at the mouth of the den, and the bitch was standing a few feet away, blocked from her pups by the flames, howling helplessly.

Gray Cloud released Mercy and loped forward toward the den. She was hard on his heels, not at all certain what she would do, but knowing they had to do what they could.

The wolf turned on them as they came running up.

Squatting in a threatening posture, she growled and bared her fangs, warning them away.

Gray Cloud ignored her, brushing past her as if she were no more than a flea. Mercy halted and held her breath, expecting the wolf to leap at the man. But the bitch didn't. Her snarl faded swiftly into an expression of perplexity, and then she tipped back her head and howled again, the same sorrowful, anguished sound. Mercy hurried past her to help Gray Cloud.

Gray Cloud waded into the burning brush and wood as if he were wearing asbestos, with total disregard for his safety. He kicked the fire apart, scattering burning brands this way and that, clearing the door of the den. No sooner had he opened a path than the wolf darted past him into the tunnel.

The burning wood sizzled in the rain, and the flames began to die as the wood scattered. The wolf reappeared a short time later with a pup in her jaws. One after another she went back for them and laid them all just beyond reach of the scattered fire.

When she had retrieved the last of them, she sat on her haunches and looked up at Gray Cloud. The man stared back down at her. "I think," he said after a moment, "that she'll let us move the pups."

"Then let's do it."

Mercy's scalp prickled again as she watched the eerie interaction between man and wolf. Their eyes met and held, hers so yellow, his so dark, and silent messages seemed to pass between them. Gray Cloud removed his jacket slowly, but the wolf appeared to be confident that he meant no harm. When he squatted and spread his jacket on the wet ground, she merely moved to one side to allow him to pick up the squirming, whining pups and put them on the jacket. She waited patiently while he tied the arms together and made a sling, nosed at them once just before he picked them up, and then stood back, tail high, to allow him to lift her litter.

"Let's go," he said.

Whoever had set the fire at the mouth of the den had intended to suffocate those pups. The fire would have drawn all the oxygen out of the den and prevented any more from getting in, and the litter would have died from suffocation. The method of execution showed a degree of intelligence that made Mercy's skin crawl even more. To not just crawl in and kill them, to not just be content to kill the bitch and let them die from starvation, but to do it this way...

It was disturbing to see the way the wolf responded to Gray Cloud, as if the two of them could read minds, as if they had spoken together in some silent language and reached an agreement about the pups.

He really was a medicine man. The thought struck Mercy as she followed him back down to the cave. It was ludicrous, but until this very moment she had refused to consider what that might mean about him. He was a medicine man. A practitioner of arcane arts who believed in powers she couldn't even imagine. Someone who caused flickering blue lights to dance in the rainy nighttime woods to illuminate their path. Someone who could evidently talk to wolves and mountains.

This was no primitive mythology that Gray Cloud practiced, but a potent understanding of very real powers. That wolf wouldn't have offered her pups to just anyone, and offer them to Gray Cloud was exactly what she had done.

Getting down was, if possible, even more difficult than getting up had been. The slipperiness of the wet ground caused problems, and Gray Cloud had his hands pretty full with the pups. From time to time he would ask Mercy to hold the sling while he climbed down ahead of her, and then he would reach up to take it from her. The wolf grew uneasy every time the exchange was made, growling softly at the back of her throat, but then calmed down as soon as the litter was back in Gray Cloud's care.

Mercy felt bruised and scraped nearly everywhere by the time they reached the cave and was glad to give up the struggle to stay upright on the treacherous ground.

The wolf seemed to have no qualms about following them into the cave. As soon as Gray Cloud settled her pups off to one side, safely away from the fire, she curled around them and nudged them to her teats before settling herself to watch her human companions.

Gray Cloud threw some more wood on the dying fire and proceeded to start a pot of coffee in Mercy's tiny tin pot. He was right, she thought; nobody was going to sleep now. Pawing around in her knapsack, she produced some trail mix and offered it to him.

"The pups would have died," she said.

He nodded.

"What *really* troubles me was the way he chose to kill them. There are so many other ways that wouldn't have required...well..."

"That wouldn't have displayed quite so much intelligence," Gray Cloud said heavily. "Only an educated person would know that the fire would suffocate the pups."

"And that required *thinking*," Mercy said. "Someone really *thought* about how to kill them. That bothers me more than if someone had crawled in there and shot them." She hesitated. "That sounds dumb, I guess."

He shook his head. "It strikes me the same way."

"Thank God we heard the howl." She looked at the wolf and shivered a little at the way the bitch's eyes seemed to glow with golden fire. These animals were far more intelligent than anyone wanted to believe, she thought. Far more intelligent. It glowed in their strange eyes in the same way it glowed in Gray Cloud's.

"This isn't good," she said suddenly. "Not for the bitch or her pups. It's not healthy for her to trust people."

Again he nodded, saying nothing as he stared into the fire and waited for the coffee to brew.

"I just don't know what we can do! We have to protect them, but we can't risk them coming to trust us. What if they trusted the people who want to kill them?"

"That's a problem," he acknowledged at last.

"So what do we do?"

"Wait. Powers are gathering. Any action now would be premature."

Frustration welled in her, and she made an impatient sound. "Damn it, you're always saying we should wait! What if we'd waited tonight? Those pups would have died."

Several heartbeats later, he lifted his gaze from the fire and looked directly at her. "Do you know how many people are out there? Who sent them? What their orders are? Without knowing these things, how can we make a plan that will be of any use?"

She drew an annoyed breath. "We *have* to do *something.*"

He nodded slowly. "*Reconnaissance* is the word, I believe. We need to learn as much as we can about our foe. Scout the enemy. Only when we know exactly what we're up against can we be sure of taking appropriate action."

It made sense. It also made her uneasy. Later, lying on her blanket as the sky began to lighten with dawn, she remembered the fire in front of the den, remembered that Gray Cloud had been out of the cave until just a short time before the wolf howled.

He could have set the fire.

She tried to brush the thought away, but it clung like porcupine quills, keeping her awake and uncomfortable. He could have set the fire. He could be involved in the trouble, which would certainly make him reluctant to take any action. He had planned to go up after the pups alone. What if she hadn't followed? Would he have come back to say the pups had died and there was nothing he could do?

She should have been trying to sleep as dawn brightened Thunder Mountain, but all she could do was stare up at the cave ceiling and wonder if she was being completely and deliberately misled.

The wolf showed no desire to move herself or her pups. The rest of the pack found her without any apparent difficulty, and came and went throughout the morning, bringing her nourishment and checking on her, as it seemed to Mercy, who noted everything she possibly could and then proceeded to name all the wolves.

The alpha female she named Stripes, because of the pattern of colors on her snout. The alpha male became Eyebrows because of the markings over his eyes. Eyebrows didn't stray very far from his mate that morning and was there every time she stirred.

Mercy was painfully conscious of two things all morning: One, that she was observing the wolves in unique circumstances and, while informative, those observations would not be as illuminating as those made of the creatures in their natural habitat. The other thing she couldn't forget was that Gray Cloud was out there somewhere, supposedly scouting, but possibly arranging another threat against the wolves.

Or against her.

Almost as if he picked up on her thoughts, Eyebrows lifted his head from his paws and looked straight at her.

"Aren't you going to leave?" Mercy asked him. "You leave every time Gray Cloud returns, and he said he'd be back by noon."

The wolf's ears pricked forward, but other than that he showed no reaction.

She was losing her mind, she thought, turning her head so she could look out at another stormy day. A nightmare of being buried alive had managed somehow to leave her feeling physically sore even this morning—she must have gotten restless enough during the dream to crack her head on something. Hearing voices on the wind that kept whispering *Listen,* as if there was anything to listen to besides the wind. Hanging around with a man who had been accused of murder, distrusting him...

If she really distrusted him, she asked herself, why didn't she just pack up her stuff and move? Leave. Climb down from this godforsaken mountain and report that she'd found wolves and leave it at that. Let someone else come up here and figure out what was going on.

If she really distrusted Gray Cloud, what had she been doing when she fell into his arms last night?

And the memory of that made her *ache.* Why couldn't she feel that way about someone who was nice and safe, like one of her colleagues? Why had it taken an accused murderer on the wild side of a mountain, a man who evidently had no home and no job other than a mystical mission to protect a mountain?

She sat there, staring out at the dark pines, staring into the deep shadows beneath them, trying to remember what had seemed so important to begin with, why she had felt it necessary to come up here and find these wolves. Gray Cloud had been right about one thing: announcing the presence of the wolves might be detrimental to them. But not as detrimental as whatever the person who had built the fire at the den had intended. That alone was enough to convince her that the wolves were a serious target for some reason. That hadn't been a random act; it had been planned.

Well, obviously, she thought, realizing that her thoughts

were running in circles. Round and round she was going, traveling the same ground in hopes that she could find some clue, some key—anything to help.

But Gray Cloud was making sense—they had to scout the situation before they could take any useful action. What *she* needed to do was keep an eye on Gray Cloud, as well, to be sure he wasn't the problem.

Because she couldn't stand the thought of anything happening to the wolves. In principle she sympathized with the desire of the Indians to keep their sacred places untouched, but from her perspective, the wolves and the environment were equally important. Perhaps more so. Merle had never understood her affinity for living things, whether plant or animal, or why she could get so upset about timbering or strip-mining. Yes, she used paper and drove a car and all the rest of it, but she was convinced there were better ways of providing these things than raping the environment for the fastest, largest profit possible.

Now the wolves were being threatened because they might stand between some company and its desire to make money from Thunder Mountain.

It was hard to believe Gray Cloud could be any part of such a conspiracy, but it *was* possible. What better cover than pretending to be here to protect the mountain?

She was never certain at what point she began to feel as if she were being watched. At first the sensation was mild, not quite as annoying as the buzzing of a lazy fly. But the feeling grew until it burst into her awareness with discomforting force.

She was being watched.

Her neck crawled with the sensation. Instinctively she looked toward the wolves, but Stripes was dozing with her pups, and Eyebrows was staring out the cave opening at the same shadows she had been staring at.

As she watched, his hackles rose and a growling began

deep in his throat. Slowly he rose to a crouch, never taking his attention from the woods.

Mercy needed no more convincing. Rolling to her side, she lay on her stomach and began to inch toward the cave mouth, hoping to get a glimpse of whoever—or whatever—was watching them.

Listen.

"Listen to what, damn it?" she muttered under her breath as she eased her way to the entrance. Listen. Listen. Useless piece of advice!

You know him.

The whisper in her head stopped her cold. She knew him? Knew who? Gray Cloud?

God, was she listening to voices in her head?

By the time she reached the cave mouth and could see a broad expanse of the forest, Eyebrows had crept up, too, and was watching the woods guardedly.

Where was Gray Cloud?

Her breath jammed in her throat as she saw movement in the shadows beneath a tree. Someone standing there and watching the cave? An animal?

A low growl emanated from the wolf, and she decided it was no small animal stirring over there. Eyebrows wouldn't be reacting this way to a raccoon. Someone was in those shadows, and she had no reason to trust anyone on this mountain after what had happened to the wolf den last night.

For the first time in her life she honestly wished she had a gun. Damn it, Thunder Mountain, she found herself thinking, you're supposed to be protecting yourself and these wolves, the trees...

A rumble, at first hardly detectable, began to shake the earth beneath her. The trees swayed as if caught in a forceful wind, while the ground bucked and heaved beneath them. And the earth sound, the horrible moaning of the tortured ground, chilled her spine.

Earthquake.

As she watched, the ground undulated like waves on the water. Even the rock beneath her seemed to ripple. Eyebrows began to howl, and when she dared to glance his way, she saw he was pacing nervously, unwilling to abandon his mate and the pups, but wanting very badly to get out into the open.

And that was what you were supposed to do in an earthquake, Mercy remembered. Get outdoors, where falling debris was less likely to kill or injure you. But the pups...

Galvanized, forcing herself to ignore her own terror, Mercy crawled back into the cave to get the pups. When she reached the litter, she found Stripes hovering nervously over the squirming mass of whining pups.

"We'll get them out of here," Mercy told Stripes. Rising to her knees, she tugged her jacket off and spread it on the floor of the cave. Just as she reached for the first of the little wolves, thunder began to roll down the mountainside, shaking the earth in a different way. The undulations of the earthquake were a counterpoint to the hammering roar of falling rocks.

Mercy hesitated. This cave might be a death trap, but rock slides were just as deadly. Perhaps it would be safer in here.

And where the devil was Gray Cloud? At this moment she would have given a great deal not to be alone in the face of a world gone mad. Without the comfort of another human presence, death looked a lot more terrifying.

She had looked death in the eye before, when rock climbing, and by itself, death did not terrify her. But the thought of dying on a lonely mountainside, without another human being nearby to know or care, *did* bother her. She didn't want to die this way. Not this way.

"Gray Cloud…"

She spoke his name with yearning, as rocks began to tumble down in front of the cave entrance. Her defenses began to crumble, too, and she whispered his name again as she scooped up the pups. They had to get out of there before the rocks sealed off the cave. They would have a better chance in the woods below.

Gray Cloud.

In a moment of yearning so intense it beggared description, she called his name deep inside her soul and felt it wing upward and outward, a silent cry of the heart. And at that very moment the hail of rocks became a torrent. With horrifying speed, the mouth of the cave was sealed shut by fallen rocks.

She was trapped.

CHAPTER SEVEN

Gray Cloud.

He heard Mercy's cry in his mind in the same instant that he realized the mountain was taking action against the intruders. In a flash he understood the danger the woman and the wolves were facing. Forgetting the deserted campsite he was investigating, he turned and began to run in the direction of the cave.

Time seemed to become mired in mud. No matter how hard he ran, stretching his muscles to the utmost, racing at a speed that caused his heart to thunder in his chest, he didn't seem to be moving at all. Not at all. It was a nightmare come true, as the air seemed to grow so thick he felt as if he were running through molasses.

Gray Cloud.

But then he burst from the obscuring forest on the slope below the cave mouth...just in time to see a river of rock slide off the side of the mountain above and seal the mouth of the cave.

"Mercy!"

His shout was drowned by the roar of the falling rock. He stood there helpless to prevent it as boulders tumbled down before the cave mouth. Some kept going, rolling into the trees below, driving animals ahead of them, but enough rocks remained that Mercy and the wolf pups were trapped.

Her nightmare had come true.

His first instinct was to race up and start burrowing a hole in that tumbled wall of rock. All that held him back was an awareness of the mountain's anger, an awareness that his interference might arouse that ire even further and cause more harm. Without the mountain's forbearance, he couldn't be absolutely certain of getting Mercy out of there.

There couldn't be much time. There was some air in the cave, but not enough. The small tunnel leading off the back only came to a dead end.

A few hours, he thought. He had only a few hours to get her out of there. And each minute of those hours would be sheer terror for her. She was buried alive.

But first he had to appease the mountain, and his medicine bundle was back at his camp. With time being of the essence, he had no choice but to scan the surrounding area for items he could use to make an altar. No buffalo skull or painted sticks were available here, but there were plenty of rocks and earth. He would call on the Stone People to help him, and hope that *Tate* and *Wakinyan*, the Wind and Thunder, would aid him.

He needed stones, large unique ones. One as smooth and round as nature could make it, representing the harmony of the world. Another cracked and uneven, to represent the power of the mountain and earth. And finally, one perfectly flat stone to represent the sky above all. Finding them, he laid the stones out carefully, in a triangle, each separated from the others by a distance equal to the length of his forearm. It humbled him to measure himself against the mountain, and that was good.

He stood before the altar, closing his eyes, and extended his arms. Usually, when he prayed, he beseeched the mountain to hear him. Today he was angry. Fury shimmered in him, a force he could not quite control, as he railed at the mountain's willingness to sacrifice the wolves and the woman to its purpose.

There were those on these slopes who were a serious threat, but the woman and the wolves were not among them. Yet Thunder Mountain had shown no compunction about harming them, had not attempted to protect them in its drive to clear the intruders from its slopes. In seeking to drive away the men below who were plotting to kill the wolves, the mountain had been willing to kill the wolves itself.

And that infuriated Gray Cloud.

Today his chant had an angry sound to it, reflecting the outrage he felt. He had served this mountain for most of the days of his life, protecting it from the encroachments of those who could not understand the mountain's power or its sacred nature. Now the mountain was seeking to protect itself without regard to the cost, and this offended Gray Cloud.

He felt betrayed.

For a while it seemed that the mountain would not respond to him, that it was going to ignore him because he was angry. They were both angry, he and the mountain, but he was just angry enough to refuse to accept being ignored.

Answer me! The demand seemed to roar out of him, though he spoke the words only in his heart. *Answer me!*

And finally the mountain replied. *The intruders have moved back down lower. Why are you angry, little man?*

Gray Cloud was used to the mountain's detachment, but today, for some reason, it bothered him, fueling his anger. "What does it matter if you drive the intruders down lower, if you also kill the wolves?"

The wolves matter little. In time other wolves will come. The mountain must be preserved so that they can come.

"And the woman? What about the woman? She only came to study the wolves, not to hurt the mountain."

She is nothing. The world crawls with her kind.

Nothing. The world crawls with her kind. The intense heat of rage Gray Cloud felt at that dismissal blinded him to the danger inherent in confronting the mountain, made him forget the vision that had called him to protect this mountain, made him forget the sacred nature of the being with whom he dealt.

"Mountain!" he argued. "Her kind may be one of many, but *she* is unique, and she does not deserve to be killed simply because she was in the way!"

The earth trembled and shook beneath his feet, and the stones he had found moved a little, breaking the symmetry of the triangle. Gray Cloud stood his ground, prepared to face the mountain's ire.

"I am here," he continued as the ground bucked again, and another hail of rocks fell from above. "I am here, and I will free the wolves and the woman. If they are of no consequence, then they may as well live."

The mountain shrugged. Another torrent of rock spilled down the slopes, but when the clatter died away, no more was forthcoming. Gray Cloud gathered up the stones into a pile, then turned toward the rocks that blocked the cave. He didn't know if he would be able to dig the woman and the wolves out in time.

He could only try.

No light filtered into the cave. Mercy huddled near the wolf and her pups, listening to the pups whine, and shivered from the cold. Another shudder of the earth shook debris down from the cave roof.

Buried alive. It was even more terrifying than her dream last night had been, perhaps because she knew that this time she couldn't wake up. This was *real*.

The pups wouldn't stop whining, and they squirmed back and forth between their mother and Mercy. They were blind and deaf so soon after birth, and had no way of knowing the world had turned dark and threatening. But they could feel the rumble of the ground and could probably smell the fear on Mercy and Stripes.

Eyebrows had vanished. Mercy hoped he hadn't been hurt or killed in the rock slide.

Stripes moaned low in her throat, an unhappy sound. Without even thinking about it, Mercy reached out and touched the wolf, digging her fingers into the thick fur and tugging gently. Stripes shivered and then moaned again, accepting the touch.

There was a flashlight in her pack, if she could find it. She crawled around in the dark on the floor of the cave for a while, realizing with a vague sense of shock that the cave was bigger than she had realized. Either that or she was crossing and recrossing her own path again and again.

Ah! Her pack. Memory told her the flashlight was tucked into a back pouch. Feeling carefully, she found the long aluminum cylinder and pulled it out. With an eager push of her thumb, she threw the switch and then watched in dismay as a thin, yellow beam gleamed, flickered and died. The batteries were gone.

Despair welled in her, nearly choking her, and she had to battle it for long moments, but finally she was able to shove down the impending tears and start thinking again.

The tunnel at the back of the cave crossed her mind, but she quailed at the thought of climbing into its narrow confines when the earth was shaking. If it collapsed...

It didn't bear thinking about.

Her heart was still hammering in her chest, and she was still gasping like a sprinter near the finish line, but adrenaline had cleared the panic-induced fog from her brain, and she was thinking again.

Without light she didn't dare try to dig herself out. Even with light, she might precipitate another rock slide, right into the cavern. *Think, Mercy! Think!*

Licking her finger, she held it up and waited, but could detect no movement in the air. That meant the tunnel at the back didn't lead to the outside, so there was no point in exploring it. That left the sealed cave mouth as her only hope of escape.

And it was no hope at all.

Closing her eyes, she turned inward, seeking some glimmer of an idea, seeking what clarity and strength she could summon to help her deal with her impending death.

Because she believed she was going to die. The mountain had won.

The mountain seethed, but so did Gray Cloud. He had dedicated his life to protecting this mountain, and in theory he understood that sometimes individuals must be sacrificed to preserve the greater good. He even agreed with the idea—in principle.

Reality was a different matter.

Despite the damp chilliness of the day, he grew hot and sweaty as he strove to clear a tunnel into the cave. Anger goaded him, as did an inexplicable sense of betrayal. Troubled, his mind ran over events again and again, trying to find the reason in what had occurred. He knew that in the larger scheme of things, a single life was insignificant. That an individual being was less than the single blink of an eye in the span of a lifetime. He knew this.

He also knew that all life was sacred, and while killing was sometimes necessary, life deserved more respect than to be dismissed as utterly insignificant.

But what really disturbed him was the uneasy sense that the mountain and the developer were both using the same reasoning. After all, didn't the developer tell himself that a few Indians were insignificant, that for the greater good the mountain must be timbered and mined and developed?

Did the end truly justify the means? That question had haunted him ever since he had taken a man's life. The taking of life was sometimes justified, yes. He believed that, and would kill again if necessary. But it was not jus-

tified to take an innocent life simply because it was incon-
sequential and was in the way.

When he cut willow branches to make a sweat lodge, a
man should ask the forgiveness of the willow. When he cut
a tree to make a lodge pole, he begged the forgiveness of
the tree.

Life must be treated with respect and never ended with
wanton indifference. The mountain evidently felt differ-
ently, and the mountain was an ancient and powerful being
with much wisdom. Gray Cloud, who had promised to
serve the mountain, wrestled with himself as he tried to
come around to the mountain's way of thinking, as he tried
to accept that perhaps the mountain was right.

As he faced the possibility that his role of protector
might require him to harm the innocents who got in the
way.

As he wondered yet again if Mercy was as innocent as
she appeared.

The timing of her arrival was suspicious, coming as it
did at the same time as the arrival of the men who had
killed the deer and tried to kill the wolves. The men working for the developer who wanted to rape the slopes of
Thunder Mountain.

Perhaps she was one of them, despite her concern for the
wolves. Perhaps she was helping them. Perhaps the mountain had known what it was doing when it sealed the cave
and drove the men below farther down.

If she was one of them, she would have to die.

The ground seemed never to be quite still. It quieted from
time to time, but then the mountain would stir again, shaking loose more debris. Stripes howled each time the earth
shook.

The air was growing stale. Mercy forced herself to remain as calm and motionless as possible to conserve air.

She had to believe that someone would try to rescue her, that Gray Cloud was even now trying to dig his way into the cave.

And beneath her she felt the heartbeat of the mountain. In the dark, with the earth moaning and rumbling all around her, she felt the power surrounding her, felt the touch, however faint, of an alien mind.

The mountain lived.

At times Gray Cloud believed the mountain was not going to let him rescue the pups and the woman. Each time he thought he must at last be making headway, Thunder Mountain would rumble and tremble again, and rocks would cave in on the tunnel he was so laboriously digging. When he looked back, he could see how far he had come. When he looked forward, he could see only how much of his work had been undone.

The mountain was annoyed with him. The Stone People whispered sibilant warnings, the Wind murmured of dangers, and Thunder tolled an alarm overhead. What did the woman and the pups matter in the larger scheme of a world billions of years old?

But while the Stone People and Thunder seemed to chastise him, the Wind sided with him. *Tomorrow Woman listens,* the Wind murmured. *She hears.*

Hears what? wondered Gray Cloud as he lifted yet another boulder with aching, exhausted arms and felt his back twinge a sharp protest. What did the woman hear?

Another rumble of the ground started to shake rocks loose, and the rein on Gray Cloud's temper snapped. Rearing up, he bellowed, "Enough!"

For the space of a heartbeat the universe seemed to hold its breath. Even Thunder grew silent, and the Wind stilled in the treetops.

And then Thunder Mountain began to rumble. From deep

within came the creaking, snapping groan of rocks on the move. As the heap of fallen rocks beneath his feet began to tremble violently, Gray Cloud turned and scrambled down from them, acutely aware that the temblor could shake all those loose boulders into another landslide.

Rocks started following him down as he hurried toward safety. The mountain was going to teach him a lesson. He hoped against hope that his lesson wouldn't cost the pups and the woman their lives, if they hadn't already died. But if it did, he would have no one to blame but himself.

Small rocks had been the first to shake free, but soon there were larger boulders bouncing downward. He reached the bottom of the rock heap just in time to dart to the side and miss being struck by a tumbling boulder the size of a man's head. Others rolled down behind it, parts of the mountain on the move.

This tremor would probably fill in the entire passageway he had labored so hard to clear. Frustration filled him, causing him to grind his teeth and clench his fists in an attempt to avoid challenging the mountain again.

Another violent shudder shook the mountain, causing the earth to buckle and heave, and turning dirt into a liquid that swallowed some of the smaller rocks. Bigger and bigger boulders tumbled down from the heap as a new landslide was unleashed.

Despair filled him as he watched rocks from farther up begin to tumble downward, too. The woman and the wolves were going to be freshly buried, and there wasn't a thing he could do to prevent it.

The temblor started deep within the heart of the mountain. Mercy felt it coming, as did Stripes, who nudged her pups even closer to Mercy, as if the two of them shared the task of protecting the newborns.

It was going to be a bad one, Mercy thought. A very bad

one. Some part of her seemed to feel the mountain's intent, and that was almost as unnerving as the tremor itself.

Listen.

Listen to what? She wanted to shout the question in frustration, but she was afraid any sudden loud noise in the cavern would bring more of the roof down on them. It was only a distraction, anyway, the frustration. Something to feel besides the fear that had plagued her for hours now.

At least, she *thought* it had been hours since the rock slide sealed off the cave. And now, from the sound of it, she was going to get buried even deeper. Not that she had long left to worry about it. The air was getting thicker—so stale it was difficult to breathe. Her heart was beating rapidly now, and her respiration rate had increased significantly as her body struggled for the oxygen that was getting rarer and rarer with each breath she took.

The trembling grew, shaking more rock chips loose from the ceiling. This time Stripes didn't howl. Instead she gave a small, brief moan and wrapped herself more tightly around her pups.

At that moment Mercy didn't know whether she would rather have the roof collapse and end it all swiftly or wait until suffocation put her to sleep. Either way, she would be dead, free of this awful fear. She wouldn't have to sit here any longer while the ground heaved like an angry beast and rocks pelted her head with stinging force.

Hope hadn't died, but the renewed earthquake came close to killing it. She couldn't imagine that the rock surrounding her and creating this cave wouldn't crack and rupture under the strain of being twisted this way. And when it cracked…

Another rumble, sounding like a subway train approaching the station, worked its way up from deep within the mountain and shook the cavern again. More rock rained down on her, and Stripes yelped sharply as something struck her, but she didn't abandon her pups.

The dark was endless, fathomless. Not a ray of light reached them. From time to time one of her eyes would signal a brilliant flash of light to her brain, but it was illusory. Beautiful, though, as brilliant colors momentarily decorated the endless night.

Despite the flashes, the darkness was as suffocating as the air. Her mind cried out for light in the same way her body cried out for fresh air. The darkness was confining, crushing. An almost palpable weight bearing down on her.

And behind it all was the sense of an alien presence, of a mind so very different from her own that its merest touch was chilling. To that mind, she and the wolves had as much substance and importance as ants did to a human. She was negligible. Too small and ephemeral to be considered.

For the human mind, it was almost impossible to comprehend the perspective of a being that lived for aeons, a being as massive as this mountain. What she could understand, though, was that the fate of the wolves, and the fate of Mercy Kendrick, didn't matter a whit. And it was terrifying indeed to think of all that power unleashed, not caring what it crushed.

The ground shook again, more violently this time, and Mercy found herself clinging to Stripes. The wolf didn't try to shake her off but seemed to burrow even closer. More rocks shook free of the ceiling and pelted them, and a terrible clatter came from the rock slide that had sealed the cave mouth, as if the rocks there were falling, too. More rocks were probably falling onto them, sealing the cave ever deeper.

Mercy felt tears running slowly down her cheeks as she faced the most terrible helplessness of all. She couldn't save herself or the wolves; there wasn't anything she could do. And if Gray Cloud had been trying to help them, this newest quake would have defeated him, as more tons of rock fell across the cave entrance.

This was the end, she thought. Buried alive in a dank cavern, her entire life an unfinished story. In these final moments, the most important things had become the things she hadn't done. The true love she had never given, and the children she had never had, suddenly seemed of far greater importance than anything she had achieved in her career to date.

She was going to die on the side of a mountain in remote Conard County, Wyoming, and her only legacy would be a few dry and dusty scientific papers that only a handful of people would ever read. What a waste!

Thunder Mountain rumbled again, a violent upheaval that felt as if it were going to shake everything off its shoulders—every man, beast and tree. The hail of stones from the ceiling grew thicker, and Mercy curled up, folding her arms over her head instinctively.

Stripes unleashed a mournful howl and curled around her pups.

This was it, Mercy thought. The whole cave was going to collapse on them.

Thunder Mountain bucked violently, and Gray Cloud fell to his knees, unable to maintain his balance on the wildly heaving earth.

Angry. The mountain was angry, striking out at those who had annoyed it, uncaring what others it might harm. Just like the timber people, Gray Cloud thought. Uncaring, blind to all but a single-minded purpose.

His purpose and the mountain's were the same. Gray Cloud had known that all his life, but for the very first time a part of him grew doubtful about the wisdom of that. This mountain must be protected for all the generations to come, for it was a sacred place. And as the sacred places diminished, it became harder and harder for a man to find his vision, his purpose, the meaning of his life. And without meaning, a man had nothing.

No, he could not doubt the rightness of the mountain's actions. He must not. The mountain knew more, saw more, viewed the centuries rather than the years. The good of the many far outweighed the good of a few.

But he thought of the wolves and the woman and was saddened, for surely they were no threat. Or were they? Had the mountain perhaps seen what he had not?

It was possible. It was always possible. There could be some tie between the woman and these men sent by Stockton-Wells. At least, he *thought* the lumber giant had sent them, because that name was stamped on some of the things he had found at the campsite earlier. He knew of Stockton-Wells, of course. They were famous throughout this part of the West, employing thousands in their timbering and mining operations. They were a formidable foe, too big for a single man to take on, but not too big for Thunder Mountain to deal with.

But what about the woman? Could she be involved somehow? Was she an innocent pawn...or a scheming player? No, she had been too upset about the wolves to be one of the people who would hurt them. He doubted she could be that good an actress.

But perhaps Stockton-Wells was using her in some way? Perhaps there was some connection between her and the timber company that had aroused the mountain's ire? For it seemed to Gray Cloud right now that the mountain was angry at him, and at Mercy Kendrick. If she still lived within that buried cave, she must be terrified beyond belief as she experienced the full force of the mountain's anger.

If there were any answers to his questions, they lay in the cave with the woman. As the ground heaved beneath him, as the earth shrieked and rocks tumbled from above,

Gray Cloud looked down at his hands, which were bloodied and bruised from trying to dig a tunnel into the cave.

He had to get her out of there. He had to. He had to know.

Just then, with a thundering roar of rupturing rock, the mountain bucked violently one last time, and a cascade of boulders poured down from the heap of fallen rock, racing downward like stampeding bulls.

When the last echo of falling rocks had faded, the day turned stunningly quiet and peaceful. The ground no longer trembled, and even the ever-present thunder was silent.

It was over. Gray Cloud felt it in that part of him that was attached to the mountain. It was over. Without a moment's hesitation, he measured the rockfall that covered the cave entrance, sighted the best location and clambered up the treacherous slope to begin digging again. There wasn't a moment to spare.

Suddenly he halted, going perfectly still, even holding his breath, not certain he had heard...

Yes! Long and low, muffled but recognizable, came the howl of a wolf from within the buried cave. If the wolf still lived, then perhaps the woman and the pups did, too. And if he could hear them, then perhaps this wall of rock wasn't all that thick everywhere.

The howl sounded again, faintly, and Gray Cloud cocked his head, trying to determine where it seemed to come from, so that he would know where to begin digging. Moments later he had chosen his location, near the top and to the side.

There was no time to waste. Ignoring the pain in his hands, the ache of his back and his battered legs, he began once again to tunnel into the cave.

The wolf's howl was getting on Mercy's nerves. Even the quieting of the earth, which had come as such a relief initially, no longer seemed as soothing. But there was no way to silence the wolf, no way at all.

The air was getting still thicker, almost impossible to breathe. If only she could see where to dig, had some idea of how to start. She needed to do something—anything—to feel as if she were helping herself, but even the poor air hadn't addled her brains enough to make her forget that if she pulled the wrong rock or boulder off that heap she could cause hundreds of pounds of rocks to tumble right down on her. And she couldn't see.

But that no longer seemed terribly relevant. She was dying in here, slowly asphyxiating. Pulling a ton of rock down on her head would only be a little quicker, but at least she would be doing something to help herself.

Listen.

The whisper in her head caught her attention, dragging her back from the edge of her ragged, exhausted thoughts.

Listen.

Okay, she thought, almost belligerently. Okay. Damn it, I'm listening. What the hell am I supposed to hear?

Scrunching her eyes closed, she strained to hear whatever it was. And into her senses poured an awareness of the mountain's vitality. Beneath her, she could feel the deep, slow heartbeat of the granite, the pulsation of alien life, so real and so different.

Was that what she was supposed to feel? Was this sensation the power that made this mountain so sacred to Gray Cloud? How could this possibly help her?

Listen.

The wolf howled again, a long, low cry for her mate, for her pack. Listen?

And then she heard it, the sound of rocks moving, the sound of...someone digging. Gray Cloud! She was sure it must be Gray Cloud, trying to get her out of here. Opening her eyes, she listened intently, trying to locate the source of the sound.

Then she crawled toward it, as swiftly as she could, trying not to drown the hopeful sound of the digging with sobs and scrambling noises, because she needed the sound as if it were the breath of life itself. Someone was trying to save her!

Wisdom fled before imminent rescue. She clambered up the dangerous slope of fallen rock toward the sound of boulders being moved, and when she thought she was exactly opposite the sounds, she began to dig, too. Rocks bruised and scraped her hands and made her fingers ache, but hope was within sight and nothing could stop her. Nothing.

Stripes gave forth another howl, this one longer and more excited, as if she, too, sensed the possibility of rescue now.

And through her tears, Mercy saw a faint glimmer of light. They were saved.

With hands that were bleeding and sore, Gray Cloud reached into the opening and pulled Mercy out into the watery light of an overcast late afternoon. She was sobbing, tears making white trails in the grime on her cheeks.

Relief slammed him hard, with unexpected force. For a moment he couldn't even breathe. She was alive.

His first thought was to get her to safety, to get her as far from the path of the rock slides as he could, so the mountain couldn't harm her again.

He folded his arms around her, holding her snugly to his chest. Then, ignoring the shrieking ache in his back and legs from his labors, he rose stiffly and carried her cautiously down the unstable rocks toward the trees, where she would be safe for at least a few minutes.

"The mountain," she whispered hoarsely, through a throat so parched it felt cracked.

"What about the mountain?"

"It's alive...."

He glanced down at her, but her eyes were closed. She knew the mountain was alive. It was incredible to him that she realized that. She wasn't like some of the *wasicu* who came here and pretended to be Indians while they made up a mishmash of ceremonies culled from books. She showed none of that interest or disrespect for the beliefs of his people. Yet she had realized the mountain lived.

And he wondered, with an uneasy tingle at the base of his spine, just what she had been through during her hours in the darkness to bring the mountain to life for her.

He set her down among the trees, well out of the path of the landslides. If the mountain shrugged again, she should be safe. Then he turned, intending to go back and help the wolf bitch save her pups. He didn't really want to crawl back into that cave, though, because he no longer trusted Thunder Mountain not to crush him as carelessly as it had tried to crush Mercy.

If he got in the way, he would die.

But even as he hesitated, in that briefest of seconds as he faced his own growing doubts about the vision that had sustained him all his life, the wolf pack materialized from the trees as if summoned. All of them.

As Gray Cloud watched, they climbed in silence to the tunnel opening he had managed to carve out and disappeared inside. A short time later they emerged, one at a time, each carrying a pup in its jaws.

"I don't believe that."

Mercy's soft whisper caught his attention long enough that he glanced her way and saw her watching with awe as the wolves rescued the litter.

He grunted an affirmative and turned back to the wolves, who were now carrying the litter toward the man and woman.

Take her to the Sun Tree....

Gray Cloud closed his eyes, forgetting the wolves as he realized the mountain was speaking with him.

Take her to the Sun Tree....

The Sun Tree? Gray Cloud looked down at Mercy and wondered why the mountain should want her there, one of the most sacred places. The Sun Tree was the tallest of the lodgepole pines on Thunder Mountain, thus called because a tall lodgepole was used in the traditional Sun Dance, and this tree was the tallest of them all.

Why should she go there? She didn't belong there at all, in such a holy place of great power.

Take her...

The woman was exhausted; she didn't look as if she could walk that distance. Yet to defy the mountain could be dangerous. There had to be a reason why it was so insistent.

Take her...

"We have to go," he told Mercy. "To get away from here. The mountain is warning me."

She looked up at him for the first time without any skepticism at all. "Then something else is going to happen." Without waiting for an answer, she pushed herself wearily to her feet. "I just needed the air," she told him. "I just needed to breathe. I can't tell you how good this fresh mountain air smells after being trapped in that cave." Pine-scented, clean and fresh with rain. Chilly, but good.

Then she remembered. "My pack. I have to get my pack."

Gray Cloud hesitated, weighing the dangers. "There's something important in there?"

"My wallet, my notes, all my money and credit cards." She bit her lip. "Nothing worth dying for, I guess."

"I'll get it." The decision was made in an instant, en-

couraged by a sense that the mountain wouldn't tremble
again immediately.

Mercy's hand shot out and grabbed his forearm. "No!
It's not worth it. Truly, it's not worth it!"

He ignored her, shaking off her hand and heading for the
tunnel. This was important to him, a way of testing the
mountain's mood. If the mountain let him rescue the pack,
he would know where he stood after his rebellion this afternoon.

He couldn't ignore the opportunity.

Mercy instinctively started to follow him, still protesting,
but he waved her impatiently back. "You don't understand.
Just wait."

Climbing up the unstable pile of rocks and boulders, he
felt uneasiness run along his spine like icy little fingers.
Crawling into the tunnel he had wrested from the rockfall,
he was acutely conscious of how easily even a small tremor
from Thunder Mountain could crush him. Each time he
eased forward, the skin on the back of his neck crawled.

And then he reached the dark pit of the cavern. As he
slipped forward on his belly, from the tunnel into the cave,
his mind was filled with the awareness of how easily the
mountain could entomb him.

But nothing stirred. The air was still stale, rife with the
smells of the wolves and Mercy's fear, but breathable. Beneath his feet, even through the thick soles of his hiking
boots, he could feel the faint pulsation of the mountain.
Alive.

Just enough thin, gray light poured through the tunnel
opening to make it possible for him to locate Mercy's pack.
He almost stumbled on her flashlight, and scooped it up,
even though it didn't work. The blankets he saved, too,
because nights could get very cold on Thunder Mountain.

Moments later, aware that he had been granted a very
special reprieve, he climbed slowly and carefully back out

the tunnel, pushing the backpack and blankets ahead of him.

The mountain wasn't angry at him.

A minute later he was leading Mercy toward the Sun Tree, the most sacred of places on the sacred mountain.

CHAPTER EIGHT

"The Sun Tree," Gray Cloud told Mercy, "is believed by some to be the tree that was seen in the vision when the Sun Dance was first given to us."

"Is there something special about it?"

"It's a very tall, very straight tree that has branches only at the very top, and the way they droop down reminds some of the leather thongs that are tied between the top of the tree and the Sun Dancer's chest below."

"I've seen drawings of that dance," she said. "I think."

"Then you should see the resemblance."

The climb was steep, not something Mercy really felt like doing, but if the mountain wanted it, she wasn't going to refuse, not after what she had experienced today.

The transition from believing mountains had moods and personalities to believing that *this* mountain, at least, was a sentient being, was not as difficult as she would have expected. After lying for hours trapped in the maw of the mountain, sensing the power and strength all around her, she couldn't doubt that Thunder Mountain lived.

And if the mountain lived, then surely it would do as Gray Cloud said and act to protect itself and its denizens. She had to hope it considered her worth protecting, along with the wolves and Gray Cloud.

The wolves followed them. Not closely, but near enough that Mercy glimpsed them briefly. Each of them carried a pup, and she hoped that all this traveling wouldn't be bad for the litter, all of whom were far too young to be bounced around like this.

"There." Gray Cloud halted and pointed to a clearing just ahead.

Mercy, who had been watching the wolves disappear and reappear at either side of the trail as they wove among the trees, lifted her head and looked.

She drew a long, appreciative breath as she forgot for a moment her fatigue and soreness and her earlier fright. The clearing was large, an almost perfect circle around the base of a towering lodgepole pine, a tree so tall it reached well above the rest of the forest. And from its very crown drooped branches that, just as Gray Cloud had said, were reminiscent of the leather thongs used to tie the Sun Dancers to the tree.

Gray Cloud started to step into the clearing, but as he did so, one of the wolves darted in front of him, causing him to stumble and halt. Mercy, following, just kept walking, her attention fixed on the beautiful tree, and she tripped, falling to her hands and knees when a wolf darted in front of her. She swore softly and pushed herself back to her feet.

"Wait." Gray Cloud's voice was low and intense, and he reached out a hand and stayed Mercy as she started to move forward again. She turned and looked up questioningly. "The wolves are trying to tell us something."

That was when her fascination with the beautiful tree gave way to a recognition that the wolves had indeed acted oddly. Slowly she looked around and saw the pack gathered about them, each wolf carrying a pup, and all moving nervously. "Something's wrong."

Gray Cloud nodded. "Stay where you are." When she nodded, he took another step toward the center of the clearing. Immediately a wolf set down the pup it carried and darted forward, leaping up a little to snatch at Gray Cloud's sleeve with its jaws. When Gray Cloud halted, the wolf sat back on its haunches and waited. When the man started to take yet another step forward, the animal leapt up and snatched again at his sleeve.

Gray Cloud turned around and began walking back to the edge of the clearing. At once the wolf snatched up the pup and headed back into the woods with its fellows.

"We'd better get out of here," Gray Cloud told Mercy.

She never hesitated. It couldn't have been any plainer to her that the wolf had been trying to tell Gray Cloud exactly that. After this day, she wasn't inclined to question such things. If the wolf didn't want to go into the clearing, neither did she. Later she would have the rest of her life for trying to rationalize all these events.

For now, there was only an urge to heed the warning of the wolves.

She had barely gone two steps when a flash of light blinded her. In the same instant, it felt as if a giant hand shoved the back of her jacket and threw her facedown on the ground.

Gray Cloud turned onto his back and looked up at the flaming, split trunk of the Sun Tree. There wasn't a doubt in his mind that the mountain had intended to kill Mercy. And possibly him. He had been leading the woman like a sheep to slaughter. The thought sickened him.

Twisting, he levered himself to his feet and reached down to help Mercy up. "Let's go," he said roughly. "We've got to get out of here."

She gave him no argument as he guided her stumbling feet into the woods. "Was that— Was that lightning?"

"Yes." The Sun Tree had been destroyed. Anger simmered in the pit of Gray Cloud's belly like a pot over a blazing fire. A thing of remarkable beauty, something unique in the world, had been carelessly destroyed in an attempt to destroy something else. That infuriated him.

But at the same time, he was uneasily aware that the

mountain knew what it was doing. Something was wrong in his perception of Mercy Kendrick, something was there that he, Gray Cloud, failed to see, but which the mountain knew. There could be no other explanation for the mountain's determination.

But he would have to find out on his own. It was not his place to question the wisdom of Thunder Mountain, nor would the mountain tell him. Certainly not now that he had defied it.

A chance, he said inwardly to the mountain, hoping it would heed him. *Give me a chance to understand and banish the threat.* He couldn't bear the thought of another loss such as that of the Sun Tree. Couldn't bear the thought that this sacred place might be carved up, either by *wasicu* businessmen or by the mountain itself. His vision was to preserve Thunder Mountain for his people, and he would do whatever was necessary, even if he must face the mountain itself.

Even if he must kill the woman. For it was clear to him now, so very clear, that she must somehow be involved with the problem. With Stockton-Wells.

Because this had been a deliberate attempt to kill her.

The wolves seemed to be leading the way, Mercy realized, and Gray Cloud was following them without any hesitation, as if he trusted their instincts.

Well, she supposed she did, too, after the incident at the Sun Tree. The wolves must have felt the building charge of that lightning bolt at a level well below human perception...although that certainly didn't explain why they had chosen to aid the humans, or why they had acted in such an incredibly intelligent fashion to make their point.

Gray wolves slinking through the dim forest depths, while another of the endless storms of Thunder Mountain built up over their heads. Slipping, sliding, gliding on soundless paws as they carried the pups in gentle jaws. From time to time, one would turn to look back at them, its eyes glowing eerily, like golden flame, in the shadows.

Where were they going?

Not that any answer anyone gave her to that question would have made much sense. They were going somewhere with the wolves, and right now she was willing to trust herself to the wolves' instinct for safety, since their instinct for danger had been so much better than her own.

"We're going to the cirque," Gray Cloud said abruptly.

"The cirque?"

"It's a hollow in the side of the mountain, left long ago by a glacier."

"I know what a cirque is. It's just that the way you said it, it sounds especially important."

"It is."

She glanced over at him. "How so?" He moved as soundlessly and as fluidly as the wolves, she thought, blending with the shadows as well as they did.

A couple of minutes passed before he answered, and he did so grudgingly. "It's the place of strongest power on the mountain. My people go there to pray, or cry for a vision. The wolves think we'll be safer there."

Great, she thought. Now he was talking to the wolves as well as the wind. "What'll we do there?"

"Figure out how to deal with Stockton-Wells."

"Stockton-Wells? *Stockton-Wells?*"

The way she spoke brought Gray Cloud to an abrupt halt, and when he stopped, so did the wolves, wraithlike among the trees. Like an escort, Mercy thought vaguely. The wolves looked like some eerie kind of escort.

"You know Stockton-Wells?" he asked her.

Dragging her attention from Stripes, who was watching with tawny eyes from the shadows, Mercy looked up at Gray Cloud. "Yeah, sure. Everybody knows Stockton-

Wells. Unfortunately, I also used to date the heir to Stockton-Wells. What a...a turkey!''

Gray Cloud's eyes narrowed, becoming dark, mysterious slits. ''Why was he a turkey?''

''Because he just was! Oh, he made me so mad!'' Suddenly realizing how childish she must sound, she shook her head and calmed herself. ''We met in graduate school. He was studying forestry, and I was in wildlife biology, and we had a few classes together. We both liked rock climbing, so we took some day trips together and finally some big ones to do faces like El Capitan at Yosemite. We kind of got emotionally involved. At least, *I* thought we did, only it turned out he was engaged already, something he didn't bother to tell me. I didn't like his politics, anyway.''

''What were his politics?''

''Oh, he pretended to be conservation-minded and concerned about endangered species and all those issues, but I don't think he was. Not really. Couldn't have been. I hear he's his dad's right-hand man these days.''

She glanced up, wondering what Gray Cloud's reaction to all of this was. His face revealed nothing, but she still had the feeling she had said a whole lot of wrong things.

And that upset her, she realized as they resumed their trek across the mountain's rugged shoulder. That upset her, because she wanted the things she was beginning to feel for Gray Cloud to be reciprocated. She wanted him to want her as much as she wanted him. Wanted him to feel those warm, soft, gooey feelings that kept sneaking up on her whenever she forgot to hold them at bay.

Wanted him to wonder if her hair felt as silky as it looked, the way she wondered about his. Needed him to wonder if...

Oh, Lord, this had to stop now! The way the man had just looked at her, he would as likely kill her as make love to her. And she had to remember that she still didn't know diddly about him. Being acquitted of murder could mean so many things, from being freed on a technicality to being absolutely innocent. Could she afford to believe what she wanted to believe?

Besides, she didn't want to get carelessly involved with anyone. If she ever gave herself to a man again, it would be with love in her heart and a future ahead of her. Gray Cloud didn't look like the type to want to settle down to home, hearth and kids. Nope. Any woman foolish enough to love him would have to give up all those dreams.

The afternoon was growing darker, and the day's exertions and scares had taken a toll on Mercy. She began to stumble occasionally in small ways, and her mind wandered to thoughts of a warm fire and a hot meal, both of which were probably out of the question unless she and Gray Cloud could find some kind of shelter in which to build a fire. The rain was beginning to fall again, just a light sprinkle, but that wouldn't last. Soon it would be a drizzle, then a downpour, and they would get the usual violent display of lightning and thunder, which wouldn't be very fun out in the open on the side of this mountain.

Suddenly Stripes halted right in front of them and set one squirming, whining pup down on the ground. Slowly, like four-legged ghosts, the other wolves appeared from the shadowy forest depths and placed the rest of the pups with their mother. She twisted herself around them, nudging them close until they found her teats, then settled down to nurse them. So lovely, Mercy thought, her throat tightening inexplicably. So absolutely lovely.

"Here," Gray Cloud said. "Here is where we stay tonight." He jerked his chin to the right, and for the first time Mercy noticed what appeared to be a hollow in a huge boulder a little way back in the trees. Not a cave, not by any means, but it might keep the rain off enough to make a fire.

It did better than that. There was enough dry ground for them to spread their blankets to sleep on, as well as build a fire. Gray Cloud fetched water from a nearby brook, and Mercy invited him to join her in some reconstituted, freeze-dried stew.

Night gathered around them, rumbling irritably with the secrets of Thunder. The wind moaned in the trees, a cold and lonely sound, and in the distance the rush of the brook could be heard. The sounds were so incredibly clear on the night air, Mercy thought, staring past the fire into the darkness.

A huge pair of tawny eyes blinked back at her, and she almost smiled. Well, her purpose in studying the wolves had been blown all to hell, she thought. These animals weren't exactly wild, though they were far from domesticated, and she wasn't doing a darn thing to help keep them wild. Nope. Instead she was cooperating in the process of turning them into some kind of...of pet? No, that wasn't right, but then, neither was this. These animals should be avoiding humans, not hanging around the campfire like this. However, these animals shouldn't be showing quite this much intelligence, either.

Oh, wolves *were* intelligent—incredibly intelligent, by all reports. But the notion of them recognizing the danger at the Sun Tree and saving two humans from being fried by lightning was, well, a little difficult to put into words, even though she'd seen it happen. It would certainly be impossible to include in her study. Anecdotal evidence was not scientific.

The tawny eyes blinked again and continued to stare straight at her. Eyebrows, probably. He seemed to like to watch her, for some reason.

Anthropomorphizing again, she chided herself. And that was the real reason her study had been blown out of the water, she admitted at last. These wolves had become individuals to her. They had become *people* to her. No scientific objectivity in that. No way could she settle back in a blind and watch these animals and coldly record their behavior.

So she was going back empty-handed, she guessed, except for the news that there was indeed a viable wolf pack on Thunder Mountain. Some other researcher would come up here and study them, and she would get a brief acknowledgment for having located them.

Unless she could find some way to see these wolves as quadrupedal animals again.

Sighing, she rested her chin on her knees and stared back at Eyebrows, wishing in the vain way of the tired and worn-out that life didn't have to be so damn complicated all the time. Why did she have to worry about the future when all she wanted to do was make love with Gray Cloud? Why did she have to feel like a failure because these wolves were so spectacularly unique in some ways? Why should she feel like a fool because she had named them?

Why couldn't she just turn her head and press her cheek to Gray Cloud's shoulder and say to hell with it all, just once in her life? Why did she have to be so damn responsible and aware?

Another sigh escaped her, and she forced the yearning away. All that could possibly come of it would be grief, she told herself. Grief. She had enough of that without asking for more.

Gray Cloud spoke. "Do you know anyone at Stockton-Wells right now?"

For some reason an icy trickle seemed to run down her spine. She lifted her head and turned it slowly to look at him. His eyes, always dark, seemed darker now somehow, and the flames of the fire reflected in them, dancing hellishly. Why did she trust this man? she wondered wildly. Why?

"No," she said finally. "No one. I never knew anyone there except Merle."

He nodded ever so slightly but never took his gaze from her. "So you don't have any idea what they might be planning on this mountain?"

Her chin snapped up as she realized the direction of his questioning. "No! Absolutely not! How could you even think—" She bit the question off and looked away, suddenly so mad she couldn't even see straight. "No! Just because I knew Merle Stockton doesn't mean I'm privy to the secrets of the company! Damn it, Gray Cloud!" Suddenly she turned and glared at him. "Guilt by association, huh? Maybe I should wonder if you really killed that man!"

His expression never flickered by so much as a muscle. Horror filled Mercy like rising river waters, portending a flood but climbing slowly. Oh, God, how could she have? She wanted to snatch the words back, but they hung on the air as if branded there in fiery letters. Her throat locked, so she couldn't even apologize.

But even as she scrambled for some way to defuse the moment, he spoke, his words dropping heavily into the night, like stones into a pool.

"Yes," he said. "I killed a man."

Just that, and not another word.

The night crowded steadily in on them, thick with threat. Mercy lay on her back beside the fire, a rolled-up shirt making a pillow, and stared up at the patterns the flames made on the overhang above.

No explanations. No excuses. Just "I killed a man." Didn't he feel even the slightest normal compulsion to explain? To excuse himself or his action? Didn't he feel any urge to claim self-defense or something?

With that attitude, it was a wonder he *hadn't* been convicted. And with that attitude, it was hardly any wonder that everyone hereabouts remembered he had been accused of murder and referred to him as the Renegade of Thunder Mountain. Lord, that kind of answer was about as belligerent as they came.

The wind made a lonely sound in the treetops, like the rushing of water, as the night air grew colder. Voices seemed to murmur at the edge of consciousness, and Mercy found herself drifting into fractured half dreams of distorted faces that whispered warnings she couldn't quite hear.

Stockton-Wells. Merle Stockton's face floated before her, too well remembered even after all this time. He was a handsome devil, but what had attracted her had been his insouciant attraction to danger. Her attraction to him, however, had worn thin when she had discovered that was essentially all there was to him. Merle Stockton didn't have a feeling, caring bone in his body...except toward himself. His devotion to environmental concerns had been superficial, she had discovered, merely politically correct camouflage he'd worn while in graduate school.

In reality, Merle's one great passion had been Stockton-Wells, Inc., the company he would inherit from his father. His one burning goal had been to make some grand coup that would bring huge profits to the company and establish Merle as a power in his own right.

Maybe Merle thought Thunder Mountain could be his long-sought coup.

Oh, she could see it, all right. He would be scheming and conniving for ways to get around the Park Service and environmental groups, determined to somehow get away with doing more than was really permissible, because that would be the victory, figuring out how to do an end run around the law.

Turning her head a little, she looked across the crackling fire at Gray Cloud, who was sitting upright and staring out into the night. "Why do you think Stockton-Wells is involved?"

"I found some things at a campsite. That name was on them."

"It wouldn't be surprising."

"No." He turned his head and looked at her steadily.

He was waiting, she realized. Waiting to see if she would volunteer anything. But after her reaction earlier, he wasn't going to question her. Nor did he trust her now. The fact that she knew Merle Stockton had driven a wedge of distrust between them that was as wide as the fire burning in the pit. He was no longer willing to believe that she was nothing but a wildlife biologist who meant no harm to either the mountain or the wolves.

And that made him dangerous, she realized with a shiver down her spine. All this time he had been giving her the benefit of the doubt, allowing that she might be exactly what she said.

But now he considered her connected to Stockton-Wells and her margin of doubt was gone.

She shivered again and pulled the blanket up until it covered her to her chin. "I know Merle can be ruthless," she said finally. "I've seen it. If he wants something, it's dangerous to get in his way."

Gray Cloud nodded, absorbing this. "How ruthless?"

"He'd kill if he thought he wouldn't get caught." Another river of ice trickled down her spine as she thought what an unnerving thing that was to say to a man who *had* killed. A man she had believed herself to be in love with. "In fact, I don't think there's anything he *wouldn't* do if he thought he stood to gain enough. Thunder Mountain probably looks like an incredible opportunity to him. All this timber...."

She shivered again and dragged her gaze from Gray Cloud, who was regarding her with a steely intensity that was growing steadily more and more unnerving. "Merle wouldn't stop at much," she said finally. "But then, I guess neither will the mountain."

Gray Cloud felt the night close around him after the woman finally drifted into troubled sleep. Ordinarily he welcomed the night, but tonight it wasn't peaceful. Tonight there were hard things, uneasy things, in the darkness. And murder was in the air.

She had said Merle Stockton wouldn't stop at much and then had likened the mountain to him. That troubled Gray Cloud at a very deep level. The mountain could hardly be compared to a man who would probably sell his grandmother if the price was right, but…perhaps there were similarities, anyway, and those possible similarities hovered in the pit of his stomach like a sickness that wouldn't quite go away.

The mountain had tried to kill Mercy this afternoon at the Sun Tree. Gray Cloud thought of that and felt his innards twist with horrified rage. He had been used to take the woman to a place where the mountain intended to execute her.

Perhaps she deserved to be executed. She was connected, by her own admission, with Stockton-Wells. Perhaps she was more connected than she had told him, and Thunder Mountain had discovered that. But to use Gray Cloud in that way…

The man released a harsh breath and tilted his head back, listening to the restless night sounds and hoping the wind would bring secrets to soothe him.

He needed more, he realized. He needed more than the mountain's perception to guide him now. For the first time in all the years he had served his vision, he truly needed to separate himself from the vision long enough to make his own decision. He needed to find out what was happening, who was really involved, and what they intended. He could not be blindly obedient this time. Not this time.

Glancing over at Mercy, he saw that she still slept. He had killed before, and if it was necessary, he would do so again, but he didn't want it to be this woman. He needed far more than the mountain's perception of matters to allow any harm to come to her.

The feeling made him uneasy, and he looked away, not wanting to admit his own yearning for the warmth of a woman's body and, more importantly, for the warmth of a woman's smile. He'd been alone far too long, but that was the way of the road he had been given. Few women these days had any desire to live on the side of a mountain with a medicine man.

He was alone and would remain alone, but being alone hadn't stolen from him an awareness that he owed something to his fellow man, at least as much as he owed this mountain and his vision. That debt required him to learn what was really happening here. To figure out whether Mercy Kendrick deserved the death the mountain seemed determined to inflict on her.

He could not stand idly by and just let it happen. Not without understanding why it was necessary.

So he had to learn his foes, and discover what it was they were after, what they intended to do. He had to discover the depth of Mercy's involvement. And then, for the sake of every living thing on this mountainside, he had to try to find a way to prevent Stockton-Wells from triumphing, so the mountain would not have to act again.

Because when the mountain acted, the innocent died. Gray Cloud didn't want to see one more thing die, not even the smallest raccoon. Everything sheltering on this mountain was to be protected, according to his vision, and right now the best way to do that was to handle the problem himself.

Out in the dark, he saw the strange golden glow of wolf eyes. The big male had come to look upon them again. Strange behavior for a wolf. Protective.

Why did the wolves of Thunder Mountain seem so protective of Mercy Kendrick? What did they know that the mountain didn't? Or did they know something about the mountain that Gray Cloud didn't?

The fire had died to a few glowing embers; the wind sighed through the tops of the trees like the voices of lost souls. The night was dark, unrelieved by even the faint glimmer of starshine. The tops of the tall trees were merely darker shadows swaying against shadows.

Something moved out there.

How Mercy knew that, she couldn't have said. She came wide-awake in an instant, filled with an absolute certainty that something out there was moving in some sinister fashion. Not a wolf or any other creature of the night.

Something else.

For long moments she lay paralyzed, straining to hear some sound that would identify whatever was out there, doubting finally that she had heard anything at all, but unable to convince herself that she hadn't.

Listen.

The whisper in her head seemed almost friendly now, and she heeded it, no longer trying to convince herself there was nothing out there. Listen. Straining to hear, she held her breath and tensed....

And caught the merest whisper of sound. So faint it was almost beneath the threshold of audibility. But it was there. Her scalp recognized it, prickling as her hair stood on end. Something was moving. Either some small creature too tiny to make any appreciable noise, or something that was attempting a surreptitious approach.

Something that didn't want to be heard.

Her heart pounded in her chest, and she weighed her limited options. Sitting up abruptly would startle whoever or whatever was out there. That might either send them into flight or precipitate an attack. But what else could she do? Any movement or sound might alert whatever was out there.

Turning her head, she tried to see Gray Cloud on the other side of the very faintly glowing coals of the fire. The little bit of red light that was visible was just barely enough for her to make out the contours of his face.

"Gray Cloud..." She whispered it so softly that she couldn't hear the sound herself. Too softly, she thought, and opened her mouth to try again...when his black eyes snapped open and reflected the faint red glow.

"Don't move." His whisper was slightly louder than hers, just enough to reach her ears.

He had heard it, too, she thought. Now what? An eternity seemed to pass as they both lay there, eyes locked, ears straining.

The sound came again, still almost too faint for her to be sure it was there, still unidentifiable. But Gray Cloud had heard it, too. Of that Mercy was sure, for he tensed and shifted slightly beneath his blanket. Getting ready for whatever was coming, she guessed.

It had to be a person, she thought. One of the Stockton-Wells people must be closing in on them for some reason. No bear would approach this way, wary of detection. Someone intended to kill them both.

Again the faint sound. A twig bending? Something being crushed under a stealthy boot? Her heart scrambled right up into her throat as she realized the sound was growing more distinct, which meant it was coming closer.

Listen.

The wind sighed through the trees, then moaned softly.

One of the wolves howled in the far distance. Where were the pups tonight?

And suddenly, as if stirred by some unseen hand, the coals in the fire pit suddenly brightened to a brilliant red glow, illuminating their shelter. Gray Cloud rose to his feet in one swift motion and darted into the darkness.

Mercy instinctively sat up, needing to know what was happening, but unable to see into the night beyond their shelter.

She heard a thud, followed by a sharp grunt...and then the sound of one pair of running feet as someone ran away into the dark woods. Moments later the world was silent, except for the normal sounds of night.

Gray Cloud must have been hurt. The thought chilled Mercy, but she could think of no other reason for the sounds she had heard, for the fact that someone had run off into the night and that Gray Cloud hadn't either pursued or come back to the fire. He must have been hurt.

Oh, God, could he have been killed?

What would she do if he were seriously injured?

Oh, God!

Scrambling to get out from under the blankets, she struggled at the same time to see into the impenetrable darkness and get some idea of where Gray Cloud was.

He could be bleeding to death out there. Concussed. Oh, Lord...

She got her feet beneath her and into her boots, then haphazardly tied the laces around the ankles so she wouldn't trip. Then she eased from beneath the deceptive protection of the overhang and into the restless night.

Lightning flickered in the distance, soundless, backlighting the anvil of a thunderhead. The wind slipped through the trees, whispering of losses and woes in the dead of the night. Beneath her feet she felt the heartbeat of the mountain, a steady, almost imperceptible throb. Beyond that, the night was empty.

Just ahead. To the right...

The wind whispered to her, guiding her straight to Gray Cloud, who lay facedown on a carpet of pine needles. She could barely see him—he appeared to be a shapeless lump until she knelt beside him and bent close.

She could smell the metallic odor of blood, and then she saw the black stain on the side of his face. Reaching out with a tentative finger, she felt sticky wetness. Someone had bashed him in the head.

For an instant she froze, uncertain what to do. Every instinct cried out to her to help Gray Cloud, but she didn't have any way of evaluating the threat. If she went back to the fire and built it up so she could see, she might be exposing them even more to watching eyes. But she couldn't leave Gray Cloud there, and she couldn't do anything for him in darkness so thick she couldn't even evaluate the extent of his wounds.

With a queasy lurch of her stomach, she suddenly realized just how alone she was in the night, on the isolated side of this mountain. Alone. Completely.

CHAPTER NINE

Alone.

The whispered word mocked her from the forest's depths.

Alone.

Exposed. The night was alive with threat, a sussurating, taunting threat. The trees loomed over her, pressing in, crowding her, as they murmured of dire things. Thunder laughed hollowly in the distance.

Alone.

It was too dark to tell what lurked beneath the trees in the shadows. Too dark to gauge the threat or measure her safety. There was no one within shouting distance who she could turn to for help. No one at all except the person who had attacked Gray Cloud.

An urge straight out of childhood nearly overwhelmed her. She wanted to curl up in a tight little ball, hide her head in her arms and just be invisible until dawn. Her heart thundered like the hooves of a racehorse in sight of the finish line. Her lungs desperately dragged in air and couldn't seem to get enough of it. She was terrified.

But she had to do something. Almost anything at all would be better than sitting there waiting for doom to overtake her and Gray Cloud. She couldn't leave him unconscious in the open air like this. It might start raining at any moment, and hypothermia could kill him, even if his head wound didn't. She had to get him under the overhang.

But what if someone was out there? Watching. Waiting.

The icy river of fear trickled down her spine again, raising goose bumps all over. Her back felt mercilessly exposed, and even as the urge to look behind her grew until she could hardly stand it, she was terrified to turn her head for fear of what she might see.

Like a child, she hoped that if she didn't see it, it wouldn't see her.

Dumb. Really dumb. Get it together, Mercy, she scolded herself.

But her skin crawled and her scalp prickled with an awareness that couldn't be denied. She was exposed. Completely and utterly exposed, and her only defense was perfect stillness, perfect quiet. To become invisible to the predator by being motionless.

Only the predator was human, and motionlessness wouldn't fool him.

She was just beginning to shake her paralysis when a soft sound froze her again. Something had moved. The sighing wind snatched the sound and carried it away before she could identify it or locate the source, but she knew she had heard it. Her hair was standing on end.

Trying to hear anything over the cascading rush of the wind in the treetops was a hopeless proposition, but she tried, anyway, because instinct wouldn't let her do otherwise. How could she move unless she was sure she wasn't moving closer to the threat?

Listen...

She listened with all her might, straining to hear anything that might give her a clue.

Alone...

Yes, she was alone. Completely, utterly, terrifyingly alone. This aloneness was unlike anything she had experienced before. The vastness of the Wyoming night stretched around her, empty and comfortless...populated only by the person who had hurt Gray Cloud.

Tomorrow Woman...

Her head jerked around at the unmistakable whisper of

the name Gray Cloud had said the wind had given her.
Tomorrow Woman. Who else would know to call her that
except Gray Cloud…and the wind?

She shivered violently. Not the wind. It couldn't be. But
who else…?

Move…

Another sigh, but this one sounded like a command. And
somehow, released from her paralysis, she bent toward
Gray Cloud, thinking that if she turned him over she might
be able to take him under his arms and drag him toward
the overhang where they were camped. Once she had him
safely away from the inevitable rain, she could think about
what she needed to do.

Thunder crackled with sudden violence, a goad to action.
A storm might break at any moment.

And if someone was watching her from the shadows, he
could kill them as easily while she sat frozen here as he
could if she moved.

Another sound, barely audible over the wind. Oh, how
she wished that damn wind would stop for just a minute so
she could really listen and figure out if she was truly hearing something.

A groan. This time unmistakable. Gray Cloud! Bending,
she brought her face to within inches of his and called his
name. She didn't dare say it loudly, afraid that she might
attract unwanted attention. This night was full of the potential for such things.

Oh, how she wished she had listened to Sara Ironheart
at the Conard County sheriff's office. Sara had urged her
to bring a radio with her. She might have been able to reach
the Park Service or a patrolling ranger for help. Instead she
had shrugged off the suggestion because she was familiar
with camping in the wild. Because she was confident she
wouldn't get into trouble. Because she was always careful.

Because she was foolishly arrogant.

And now her isolation was absolute.

Move...

When she tugged gently on his shoulder, Gray Cloud stirred and moaned again. She whispered his name again, and he lifted his head.

"Can you hear me?" she asked. "Do you think you can get up?"

A few moments passed, then he answered, "Yeah. Yeah. I'm okay."

She seriously doubted that, considering he'd been knocked unconscious and was bleeding from a head wound, but at least he was conscious and coherent. "Let's try it, then."

She steadied him as they took it in stages, getting first to their knees and then to their feet. He was definitely woozy, reeling just a little when he first stood, but then his head seemed to clear up.

Thunder growled a warning as lightning stabbed the clouds, leaping from thunderhead to thunderhead. A large, cold drop of rain splattered hard on Mercy's cheek, stinging, and the wind gusted restlessly. The air smelled scorched.

"Let's get to cover." Gray Cloud spoke rustily, but it was clear he was alert and thinking again. Relief nearly swamped Mercy, but another drop of rain slapped her cheek, prodding her toward their camp.

She felt chilled to the bone by the time they reached their bedrolls. Grabbing up blankets, she threw one around Gray Cloud's shoulders and another around herself, then sat beside him on the hard ground.

"We need to do something about your head," she told him. "You're bleeding. You might be concussed. You need to see a doctor."

"No. I'll take care of it."

She opened her mouth to ask how, but swallowed the

question when he lifted his hand to his wound and began
to chant softly. He was healing himself. Mercy's Western-
educated mind rebelled, until she thought of the things she
had sensed and felt during her time on Thunder Mountain.
If a mountain could think, then Gray Cloud could heal himself.

In the dark, it was easy to see the faint blue shimmering
that appeared around his hand where it touched his head.
Easy to see it pulse and sparkle, dim as it was. The life
force, he had said.

Several minutes later, the glow faded and he dropped his
hand. Then, without so much as a by-your-leave, he
reached out with both hands, gathered Mercy to him and
wrapped them snugly together in the blankets.

She should have rebelled. She should have snapped at
him for his presumption and demanded he let her go. She
should have been afraid.

Instead all she felt was a wonderfully weakening sense
of security. The heat of his body was as welcome as the
blast from a furnace on a frigid night. When he tucked her
head into his shoulder, she gave up any thought of struggling. She hadn't felt this secure since early childhood, and
right now she didn't want to consider that she was in the
arms of a man who had killed, a man who might well
decide to kill her. Right now she just wanted to be in the
arms she had been longing to feel around her for what
seemed like half a lifetime. To forget for just a little while
the terror that stalked them.

More childishness, but she gave in to it, promising herself it would be for only a few minutes. Just these few
minutes.

"We've got to do something about this mess," Gray
Cloud said. His voice was a rumble deep in his chest beneath her ear. "If that man had reached us while we were
sleeping..."

He didn't finish. He didn't need to.

"What *can* we do?" Mercy asked. Funny, she thought, how only yesterday she had been trying to convince Gray Cloud that they had to do something, and now that he was saying the same thing, she couldn't imagine what it might be.

"Get down from this mountain and alert the Forest Service and the Conard County sheriff. We've got something the sheriff can go on now. I was attacked."

"The wolves..."

"I don't want to leave them unprotected, either, but there's nothing we can do by ourselves. Nothing legal, anyway."

She almost tipped her head up to look at him, then remembered that it was too dark to see him, anyway. The sheriff, he'd said. Funny. She wouldn't have thought Gray Cloud a man to turn to the authorities, or to worry about whether his actions were legal.

But what *could* they do, short of killing someone? And if they hung around here, they were apt to get killed themselves. Gray Cloud was right: the authorities needed to know what was happening here. That alone would probably put a severe crimp in whatever illegal doings Stockton-Wells had in the works. It would do more to protect the wolves than she could. And Gray Cloud was right about another thing: they had more than the claim that something illegal was going on now. Now, with that gash in his head, they had proof of wrongdoing. Proof that someone had intended harm to them.

And certainly the authorities could do an awful lot more than she and Gray Cloud could to protect the wolves and the mountain.

"We have to act quickly," Gray Cloud said. "If we start to head down the mountain, perhaps they'll think they've scared us off and they'll relax. That'll give us some time."

"And maybe they'll realize we're running for the authorities."

His arm tightened around her shoulder. "That's a possibility. The mountain will keep trying to drive them away, but..." He hesitated.

"But other animals may get hurt," Mercy said for him. "Like the wolves that were trapped with me yesterday. Like me."

He didn't have to reply. Mercy shivered and turned her head to stare out into the restless, wind-tossed night. Stockton-Wells evidently wouldn't balk at killing them. The mountain apparently wouldn't hesitate, either.

"Talk about a rock and a hard place," she muttered.

A soft, unexpected chuckle escaped Gray Cloud. "The mountain and Stockton-Wells come close, don't they?" Then he sobered. "We'll leave at first light."

"The wolves—"

"Will take care of themselves."

Yes, she thought, they probably would. Heck, just yesterday the wolves had taken care of her and Gray Cloud. But how much could those poor little pups take?

The storm still hadn't broken at dawn. Gray light silhouetted the swaying treetops, and thunder growled almost ceaselessly, the way it always seemed to here on the mountain.

As they set out, Mercy again felt that brush of a strange mind, that touch of something not human. Thunder Mountain. It was watching them, she realized. She wished there was some way to tell if it objected or approved of what they were doing. She sure didn't want to end her life beneath a ton of rock.

Or any other way, for that matter.

Eyebrows showed up briefly, pacing them as they trekked in the general direction of the Park Service headquarters. Mercy hoped the wolves were paying this much attention to the activities of the Stockton-Wells people. And briefly she wondered if Merle was here with his men or operating at a sanitary distance from the violence. Somehow she thought Merle might actually be part of this.

She wondered if he had learned about the wolves from old contacts at the university. If he had learned about her research proposal and perhaps followed her....

She couldn't bear the thought that she might have led him to the wolves.

Sheet lightning flickered, giving a surreal quality to the forest. Mercy tried to keep her attention on the path, to keep her thoughts from the fact that they might even now be followed by more than a wolf.

From time to time Gray Cloud paused and closed his eyes, listening. Mercy doubted he could actually hear anything over the restless rustling of the wind in the trees, but she didn't think he was listening with his ears. No, he was probably listening to the wind, and after what she'd been hearing, she didn't doubt the wind had plenty to say.

And then there was his head. The wound had scabbed over and looked as if it had happened several days earlier, not just a few hours ago. Another one of the inexplicable happenings of the past few days. The usual rules of reality evidently didn't hold here...or perhaps her view of such things had always been too narrow.

She shivered again, looking around at the shadowy forest, uneasily aware of just how many hiding places there were among the trees, boulders and ravines. An army could be hidden out there and never be spotted, let alone a few men bent on murder.

They traveled until midday without incident, though. When they halted for a lunch break, Gray Cloud left her in a relatively concealed place among some boulders and then circled out and away, looking for any sign that they were being followed. He moved as soundlessly as a cat, she thought as she watched him slip away. Even in boots.

The loamy ground was soft here, like a firm pillow, and she stretched out, deciding to catch up a little on her sleep if she could. Too many disturbed nights. Too much excitement. She was getting to the point where she honestly wouldn't have cared if Merle showed up right now, just so she could get this over with and get some sleep.

Damn, maybe she still had his picture in her wallet. If she did, she could give it to Gray Cloud in case he ever saw any of the men and could find out if Merle was among them.

At least it was something she could *do*. Pawing around in her backpack, she came up with a granola bar and her wallet. One of her failings was that she never cleaned out her wallet or her purse. Here was a grocery store receipt from…good grief, a year ago? And a credit card slip from last December…. A photo of her first college sweetheart.

And Merle. Sure enough, his handsome face was tucked in behind her insurance card. The problem with villains, she found herself thinking, was that they looked like ordinary people. The kind of people you met every day. Merle was no exception. You would never guess from looking at that rugged face that he had the instincts of a shark.

But after her initial infatuation with him had begun to ease, she'd noticed things that left her feeling vaguely uneasy. And later, when he'd become confident of her, he'd begun to poke fun at her. At the time she'd been hurt and confused, and too ready to forgive. In retrospect, she could all too clearly see the cruelty behind the barbs. She still wasn't sure that he'd intended to wound her with his remarks, but even if he hadn't, they said plenty about his lack of compassion.

And in retrospect, his attitude toward the mountains they had climbed together probably said a lot, too. Mercy had climbed because she enjoyed the challenge, enjoyed the mountains, enjoyed the backbreaking effort and the contest with nature. Merle had climbed to prove himself.

And proving himself was something he was undoubtedly trying to do here on Thunder Mountain. It had to be hard to be the son of an extremely successful father. Merle might never be able to meet or exceed his father's achievements, but there wasn't a doubt in Mercy's mind that he would do anything he considered necessary in an attempt to prove he could.

And the more she thought about the probability of Merle's involvement, the more she began to feel that perhaps she had been used, probably to find the wolves that were rumored to be on the mountain. It absolutely horrified her to think that she might have led the person who built the fire right to the den. That Gray Cloud had trusted her enough to show her the wolves, and that his trust might have been inadvertently abused.

Shaking her head, she tucked the picture back into her wallet, this time where she could find it easily. She wouldn't show it to Gray Cloud, she decided. He would never believe that she wasn't involved with Stockton-Wells if she showed him Merle's picture after claiming to have broken off with him so long ago. No, Gray Cloud wouldn't believe she simply never cleaned her wallet. Heck, she would hardly believe it herself if someone else gave her a story like that.

Things were tense enough with Gray Cloud, and there was no point in making them any worse. Hugging her knees, she tilted her head back and watched the low clouds scud overhead. Such a gray and gloomy place, Thunder Mountain. And what if the mountain believed she was still involved with Stockton? How would the mountain come to such a conclusion, anyway? Because Merle had followed her...if he had?

If the mountain figured she was part of the attack on the wolves, or responsible in some way for it, that might explain why she'd come so close to being buried alive. Or did the mountain even think in those terms? Had it just struck out, catching her and the wolves in the slide simply because they happened to be there? Or had it struck at her deliberately?

Would she ever know?

Thinking like this was enough to make her head reel. There couldn't possibly be any answers to questions like those. Heck, she couldn't believe she was even asking.

But she could feel the mountain around her, feel something more in the atmosphere than the raw chilliness of impending rain or the scent of the pine needles. Given a million years and a million words, she doubted she would be able to describe exactly what she sensed that convinced her the mountain was alive and aware. It just *was*. Like a crackle of static in the air, or an aroma so faint you couldn't quite identify it.

Life, she found herself thinking, had a sensation to it. Gray Cloud held blue sparkles in the palm of his hand and called them the life force. She felt something emanate from the mountain that told her at some primitive level that the mountain lived. Life force.

All of a sudden Gray Cloud appeared among the tumbled boulders, carrying some pine boughs. "Lie down," he ordered quietly. "We're being followed. They'll be here in a few minutes, and I want them to get past us without knowing we've stopped here."

He crawled into the crevice with her and pulled the pine boughs over them. Then he lay beside her on his back, cocking his head from time to time as he listened.

Mercy felt strangely secure there in the crowded crevice with the pine boughs over them like a tent. It was as if the mountain were cradling her protectively in its arms like a baby. As soon as the thought crossed her mind, she stiffened, wondering how she could so quickly forget that just yesterday this same mountain had tried to kill her.

Cautiously, she turned her head and looked at Gray Cloud. He was staring up into the pine boughs and listening for the sounds of their pursuers. What were they going to do now? she wondered. Followed already. It wouldn't be long before the Stockton-Wells people discovered Mercy and Gray Cloud were no longer ahead of them and backtracked. How could they be sure of getting a big enough lead to escape?

She wished she could just turn and curl into Gray Cloud's arms the same way she was curled into the mountain's embrace. Stupid way to feel about a man who might decide she was a problem that needed eliminating.

Gray Cloud tensed beside her, and Mercy instinctively held her breath, listening intently. They weren't being very quiet, probably because they weren't worried about being heard. They were far enough behind where they believed Gray Cloud and Mercy to be that noise wasn't a significant problem. They were even talking in low voices, and Mercy strained to make out a word or two, without success.

Gradually the sounds of the men faded into the normal background sounds of the forest, the wind and the thunder. They were once again alone in the clearing. As they waited, Mercy's thundering heart slowed down to nearly normal.

"There were four of them," Gray Cloud said quietly.

"How could you tell?"

"Four different voices."

They waited a few more minutes; then Gray Cloud pushed the boughs away and rose cautiously. "Okay," he said finally, and reached down to help her up.

"It won't be long before they discover they've lost us," Mercy said as she picked up her backpack. "What are we going to do?"

Gray Cloud hesitated only a moment. "Head higher up the mountain, to my home."

It shocked her to realize that she had never wondered where Gray Cloud lived. It was as if she had assumed he lived in the open, like the wolves, without a roof or any of the other comforts. Yet he was dressed decently, and was clean; if he had been living as she assumed, he would not have been.

Heading higher up the mountain would surely confuse their pursuers, she thought. The only problem with that was whether she and Gray Cloud would be able to get the help they needed. Could he possibly have a phone? No, not on the side of this mountain. No way.

"Do you have a radio?" she asked.

"No. No radio, no telephone."

"Then maybe going to your place is a mistake. We could get trapped there."

"I'm going to send a smoke signal."

For a heartbeat she couldn't even absorb what he was saying. "A—what?" The words came out on a nervous laugh.

"A smoke signal. I'm going to burn some trash in my wood stove and make enough smoke that the rangers will investigate."

It sounded like a good idea. "But that will alert the Stockton-Wells people, won't it?"

He shrugged. "Maybe. It's our best chance."

Mercy nodded reluctantly, admitting he was right. It seemed like an awfully slender thread of hope, but there wasn't another one in sight. "I just can't imagine why they should want to kill us. Not really. I mean, it seems like such an extreme act. Maybe they just want us to get out of the way."

Gray Cloud shook his head. "Human life is cheap compared to the millions and millions of dollars of timber on this mountain, compared to the potential for development. You think human life is precious, beyond price, but I assure you, that's not how others see it. Killing one or two people is simply a minor inconvenience, no more significant than moving a rock out of the way of the roads they'll have to build.''

''In short, we're simply obstacles.'' Somehow she found it easy to believe that Merle thought that way. An obstacle. She was an obstacle to Merle's plans for this mountain. And that thought, striking her for the first time, sent chills running down her back. She knew how Merle viewed obstacles.

The climb was rugged, and Mercy suspected Gray Cloud had chosen a difficult path to slow their pursuers and make them harder to track. Rain started falling, a cold drizzle that slowly soaked them. Her hair hung limp and dripping around her face, and for the first time she genuinely wished she had worn a hat.

Too late now, she thought, shivering as the cold began to penetrate her jacket and jeans. She was just trying not to think about how they were headed up the side of the mountain, away from help. Trying not to think about how they might actually be trapping themselves.

She wondered what his home was like. A tepee wouldn't be much protection, but given Gray Cloud's attitudes and his role as medicine man and protector of Thunder Mountain, she wouldn't have been surprised at all if he had chosen to live in a traditional dwelling.

What she hoped for was a log cabin, something with walls thick enough to stop bullets. Of course, that could be burned down around their ears. Well, then, how about a stone fortress?

She almost giggled, and that was when she realized she was getting hypothermic. Woolly-headedness and loss of coordination were both warnings, and she was stumbling over her own feet now. Gray Cloud frequently had to shoot out a hand to steady her.

And his touch affected her like electricity. Sparks zinged from his fingers on her arm, even through all the layers of clothing she wore, and shot straight to her womb, filling her with an impatient tingling, a restless need to be touched and caressed.

She wondered if he felt anything at all for her. Anything at all.

Long ago, someone had built a large log cabin on the side of Thunder Mountain. Four rooms and a shed, all tightly chinked with mud. Gray Cloud had taken over the cabin when he had come to the mountain to live, had fixed it up a little, cleaned it up a lot, and turned it into a comfortable place where he could work and sleep.

The furnishings were all rough-hewn, handmade. Minimal. But the walls... Mercy turned in slow circles, drawing one awed breath after another as she drank in the surprising beauty of Indian blankets and rugs, of beadwork and leatherwork crafted by patient, talented hands.

And the shields. Beautiful leather shields decorated with feathers and beadwork were lined up along one wall—more than a dozen of them. She looked at Gray Cloud questioningly.

"I make the shields," he said almost grudgingly. "My friends made the other things."

Such talent! Mercy squatted before one of the round leather shields and touched it. "You do it all?"

"Start to finish, from rawhide to beadwork."

"You're very talented."

He shrugged dismissively. "It keeps clothes on my back."

Sensing he was uncomfortable with her admiration, she

rose and forced herself to turn to other things. There would be time later, she promised herself, to learn more about this enigmatic man. "You live here alone?"

He nodded.

"What about family? Do you have any?"

"A sister." He scowled faintly. "Why?"

"Just curious about you. Aren't you curious about me?" Her heart hammered a little with nervousness. If he said he wasn't, she would be crushed.

But he didn't answer. Instead he turned away and began to close heavy wooden shutters over the windows, barring them in place. Next to a stone fortress, she thought, this cabin would certainly do.

Window by window he locked out the fading afternoon. A gust of wind moaned around the corner of the cabin, muffled by the thick walls, and rattled noisily in the stovepipe. When Gray Cloud squatted before his wood stove and opened the door to the firebox, there was a hollow sucking sound as wind skimming the chimney top created a vacuum.

He arranged kindling and split logs, then, with the flick of a match, ignited the fire. The draw was good, and in no time at all a bright blaze was burning. The stove door had a glass window in it, and Mercy found herself hypnotized by the dancing flames. She was tired. So very, very...tired. Moments later, she nodded off.

It was dark when she woke, the only light coming from the fire in the wood stove, a bright orangy glow. Gray Cloud sat before it, his back to her.

"Hungry?" He asked the question without turning to look at her. She wondered how he had known she was awake and decided there must have been a change in her breathing.

"Yes, I am." Hungry. Tired. Lonely. Achy. Too many things she didn't want to think about.

"I'll make some sandwiches." He stood, still without glancing at her, and headed toward the kitchen.

"Can I help?" Mercy called after him.

"No, thanks."

Somehow she had gotten to the couch, and a pillow had been tucked under her head. She must have sat down here just before she dozed off, but she sure didn't remember it. The last thing she remembered was standing in the middle of the room while Gray Cloud lit the fire.

"Do you think anyone saw your smoke?" she called.

"I hope so. Fire danger isn't exactly high right now, but the rangers usually keep an eye out, anyway. It should have been spotted from one of the fire watchtowers."

"And they'll come to investigate? Wouldn't they just fly over to make sure there isn't a forest fire?"

"They'll come because I sent the smoke up in puffs. Anybody would recognize that someone was signaling."

A smoke signal indeed, she realized. A smile touched the corners of her mouth, the first smile she had really felt in what seemed like a lifetime, though it couldn't have been more than a couple of days.

Gray Cloud returned with sandwiches for both of them— thick turkey, lettuce and tomato.

"How do you keep food up here?" she asked him. "You don't have electricity, do you?"

"Ice. The old-fashioned way. That shed outside is an ice house."

"Oh!" Lord, she couldn't imagine that, even though her own mother had told tales of the icebox when she was a little girl. This man was self-sufficient, and there was no reason to be surprised because he had an icehouse and knew how to use it. He probably hunted a lot, too. "Do you get into town often?"

"Often enough." He was sitting on the floor, watching the fire while he ate, but now he turned around and looked at her. "I go in every couple of weeks. I sell my stuff and buy whatever I need."

"Where does your sister live?"

"She's in Rapid City now."

"Did she used to live here, too?"

He averted his face for a moment. "She used to be married to Cal Witherspoon, who owned a ranch just east of here."

"I know the place. Wasn't he murder—" Too late she realized and bit her tongue, wishing she could snatch the words back, miserably aware that she couldn't. For a long time the only sound in the room was the dull pop from the fire, muffled by the fire door on the stove.

"I killed him," Gray Cloud said presently.

He had killed his sister's husband. Mercy sat transfixed, sandwich forgotten. The fire popped and flames leapt, and outside thunder rumbled until the cabin shook. Finally she found her voice. "There was... There was a reason, wasn't there?" And she suddenly thought she knew what it was.

"There's never a good reason for killing."

He spoke with flat condemnation, offering no apology or explanation. But Mercy stared at the back of his head, thought of what she knew of him, and would have bet right then that he had killed Cal Witherspoon because Witherspoon was abusive. "He beat her, didn't he?"

Gray Cloud's head jerked minutely. Seconds ticked by in utter silence before he turned his head and looked straight at her. "I knew he'd been beating her, but she wouldn't admit it."

"That's common enough." Hard to believe, but true. "An awful lot of abused wives keep it secret. Was it...? Was it really bad?"

His eyes looked almost hollow, dark pits in his face in

the uncertain light. "I caught him beating her with a crow-bar."

"My God!"

"I pulled him off her, and he came at me, and I...killed him."

And now she knew why he'd been acquitted. Self-defense was a strong justification, one she could readily accept. And she couldn't imagine that any person worth his or her salt could have stood by while that kind of abuse was going on. No way.

"How—how's your sister now?"

"Recovering. She still has some paralysis of her left side, but other than that, her worst problems are the scars on her mind and spirit."

"I'm so sorry, Gray Cloud. So sorry."

Thunder boomed again, rattling the walls despite their thickness.

"I don't think our pursuers will get here tonight," he said. Changing the subject, Mercy realized. He'd given her a view of his guts, and he wasn't comfortable about it. "It's going to be a bad storm."

Mercy offered a quiet sound of agreement and let the subject of his sister go. She knew now the kind of man he was, and she wasn't sure it gave her any comfort at all. He was capable of killing in the right circumstances. Perhaps he was capable of killing to protect Thunder Mountain. What if he decided she was a threat?

But it was hard to hang on to such concerns when the fire was warm, the night was deep and the wind howled beyond the door. It felt cozy in here, safe. She could feel herself softening and melting, sinking into a state of comfort she hadn't felt in a long, long time.

And all she wanted was to share it with the man who sat cross-legged on what was probably an extremely expensive Navaho rug. She wanted to melt into his arms and feel his strength surround her. She wanted to know how his body would fit with hers and how it would fill hers. She wanted to know him.

And he knew it. He turned his head, and it was as if he could read her mind. His eyes seemed to flare like brilliant flames of jet, and then he rose to his knees, facing her.

"Come here," he said.

strength surround her. She wanted to know how his body would fit with hers and how it would fill hers. She wanted to know how.

And he knew it. He could tell, and it was as if he couldn't breathe. His eyes seemed to hate like brilliant licks of jet, and then he knew he was naked, facing her,

CHAPTER TEN

The orange glow of the fire gilded the room. Outside, a storm raged, but inside the world had grown still, caught between breaths of anticipation. Slowly, feeling as if she were moving through molasses, Mercy rose from the couch and took the two steps that carried her to Gray Cloud. When he reached up for her hand, she dropped to her knees facing him.

He lifted both hands and cradled her face gently in his palms. Black eyes looked down at her, as dark and deep as the night sky. Eyes she could fall into and drown in gladly.

"I want you," he whispered. "I want you."

She couldn't find air to answer. It took the greatest effort to nod her head. Her muscles felt syrupy, her head heavy; nothing wanted to move. She simply wanted to melt until she became one with Gray Cloud.

As if he understood, he slipped his hands to her shoulders and then to the bottom of her forest green turtleneck. Slowly, so very slowly, he raised the hem.

She wore no bra. Her breasts were small and firm, and a bra was an unnecessary encumbrance when camping and hiking. For an instant she was almost embarrassed, realizing he would find out that she was naked under her shirt, and then she thought how silly that was....

His appreciative look told her he was glad he hadn't found a bra. He liked what he saw and lifted his head so he could smile at her. "Pretty," he said in a husky whisper.

He couldn't have chosen a better word. It was the only one she could almost believe. Did his hands tremble just a little as they tossed away her shirt and then gently cupped her breasts?

She stopped wondering as the electric shock of his touch ripped through her. So good. So warm and dry and welcoming. She ought to be embarrassed or nervous or something, she thought hazily, but she wasn't. Not at all. Her entire being had yearned for this moment, and now that it was here, it felt so right. So very, very right.

A wispy sigh escaped her, and she leaned into his touch, savoring the gentle kneading of his fingers on her tender flesh. Little rivers of warm sensation seemed to flow through her to her core, heating her, making her weak and restless all at once.

Gray Cloud leaned forward and lightly brushed his lips against the side of her neck. A delightful shiver ran through her, and a soft moan was drawn from her. Again and again he brushed his warm lips against her soft skin, sending wave after wave of pleasure through her.

Everything inside her was growing soft in the most delightful way, as surrender filled her.

"So sweet," he whispered. "So sweet..." His lips trailed up the side of her neck to her ear, and then he electrified her by plunging his tongue inside. Another low moan escaped her, and her hips began a helpless undulation.

Carefully, so very carefully, never taking his tongue from her ear, he lowered her gently to her back on the rug. Coarse woven wool met the bare skin of her back, another stimulus, strangely delightful in its prickliness. When he reached for the snap of her jeans, she lifted her hips, silently beseeching him to hurry.

Her eyelids fluttered open in time to see his sleepy smile of satisfaction as he pulled her zipper down and then tugged her jeans over her hips. There was no doubting that he wanted her, and while some corner of her mind warned her not to place too much importance on that, her heart leapt, anyway.

At last she lay utterly naked before him. Kneeling between her legs, he let his eyes wander over her. Slowly his gaze returned to hers, and he gave her a warm smile. "Lovely," he said huskily. "Just lovely."

Joy bubbled up in her, filling her with a sudden happiness. She lifted her arms, reaching for him, and he lowered himself over her, covering her. He still wore his shirt and jeans, and she found the sensation incredibly erotic as denim rubbed against the soft skin of her inner thighs and the flannel of his shirt caressed her breasts and belly.

And then there was the absolutely exquisite sensation of his weight on her, holding her down, promising her so much more. A long sigh of happiness escaped her as he caught her head between his hands and held her steady for his kiss, this time a deep, plunging one that claimed her.

The world whirled away, fears and worries all forgotten in the warm blissfulness that filled her. It was as if his weight sheltered her from everything, as if his tongue had stroked her into purring contentment. Nothing else mattered.

As he kissed her, he began to rock his hips against her, a gentle, suggestive pressure that fueled the ache in her center. Her arms wrapped around his broad back, fingers digging in with delight. Closer. Every cell of her needed him closer, closer....

This is madness.... Some corner of her mind reminded her that she didn't fully trust this man, that she believed him capable of killing her if she threatened his precious mountain. Mercy brushed away the warnings with a soft sigh of surrender. She had lived long enough to know how rare were the feelings this man evoked in her, and she was old enough to accept that she would probably be hurt.

But the magic he cast about her was too fine and beautiful to deny. She wanted these moments and this man at any price.

There were no words of love, just whispered words of praise as he encouraged her in her surrender. He wasn't shy about letting her know that he approved of her, or reluctant to let her know what he liked. His honesty was an aphrodisiac beyond compare and elicited her own in return.

"Oh…yes…"

"Like that…"

"…please…oh, please…"

He slipped lower and took her breast into his mouth, the entire small mound vanishing into the warm, moist heat of him. A soft cry escaped her, and she arched into his touch, feeling consumed in the most delightful way. When his tongue swirled around her nipple, ribbons of sensation seemed to draw her tight on a rack of sheer pleasure.

Her hands tightened on his shirt, grabbing it and pulling it up, needing the feel of his skin against her palms. Needing to be skin to skin with him in the most intimate embrace of all.

His teeth nipped her gently, shooting exquisitely sharp pain-pleasure sensations racing to her core. Then he reared up and pulled his shirt over his head without unfastening the buttons. She reached at once for the button on his jeans, but his fingers were there ahead of her, working the zipper, helping her yank the denim down over his hips.…

Everything stilled inside her, catching the moment in amber. Eyes wide open, she looked up at him, drinking him in with all her senses. He was magnificent in the ruddy glow from the fire, muscled and smooth and powerful. Her palms itched to run over him, to feel that sleek smoothness everywhere. Her body yearned to feel his weight bearing her down again. She needed him on her and in her with a ferocity that might have shocked her if she hadn't been caught so fully in its grip.

But he wanted to tease her, and tease her he did, with light touches of his fingers, first across her breasts, then down over her belly to her dewy core. Light touches, like the merest brush of butterfly wings, maddening touches that soon had her twisting and reaching, straining for harder and deeper touches.

Deep inside her, the heavy ache grew until it seemed to consume her. She felt so open, so aware, so exquisitely filled with sensations...and she needed more. So much more.

Reaching out, she caught his forearms and tugged. A smile creased his face in response, and slowly, slowly, he lowered himself onto her.

"Ahh..." The long, soft moan escaped her. Skin on skin, no sensation in the world more exquisite or more intimate. And then... And then the thrill of his penetration—that incredible, indescribable frisson of pleasure.

And when he was buried deep within her, he lifted his head and looked straight down into her eyes. She would never wonder if he knew who he was with, she realized with an inward melting. It was Mercy Kendrick he was looking at, and Mercy Kendrick he was loving as he moved slowly within her, lifting her higher and higher on an updraft of incredible sensation.

Her body took over completely, causing her to arch up toward him so she could take him deeper, feel him better. This was what she had been meant for. This moment, this place, this man's arms.

And almost before she was aware it was going to happen, she shattered in an explosive climax.

Firelight flickered faintly on the ceiling, and the red glow filled the room. Gray Cloud's fingers brushed lightly against her feminine curls, a soft, teasing, subtly exciting touch. Her head was cradled on his arm, and one of his legs was thrown across hers. He made her feel as if he didn't want to let her go just yet, nor did she want him to let go. The afterglow was sweeter than she ever could have dreamed, and she didn't want it to end.

From time to time he kissed her cheek or shoulder, and when she turned her head toward him, he took her mouth in soft, sweet kisses. Surprising tenderness, she thought dreamily. The kind of tenderness she'd often wished for but had never found. Unexpected in this rough, wild man. So perfect she could have lain there forever and soaked it up like a contented cat.

But gradually passion began to build again. Contented movements began to grow restless, and she finally turned toward Gray Cloud, giving her hands the freedom his had taken. Smooth, sleek, warm... She reveled in the way he felt and loved the way he responded to her touch.

Hard and smooth across his chest, small pointed nipples that responded instantly to her lightest touch...that dragged groans from him when she lipped and nipped them gently. A smooth, flat belly that rippled and quivered beneath her fingers. Long, powerful thighs that flexed beneath her palms.

When she at last cupped his sex, the groan that escaped him sounded as if it had risen from his very toes. Exultation rose in her, strong and joyous, as he reached out and lifted her to straddle him.

"Take me," he whispered hoarsely. "Take me."

She did, deep and hard, with an instinct as old as the mountain below them.

Dawn crept around the edges of the shutters, a pale, rosy glow, surprising after days of grayness. Gray Cloud was up to see pink fingers stretch across the eastern sky as they reached for the western horizon. Beyond the open door where he stood, the shadows beneath the trees were still dark, pregnant with threat. They were safe for the moment, he thought. The mountain offered no warnings about intruders nearby, nor did the wind whisper alarms. All was peaceful for these few minutes.

Turning, he looked at the woman who slept naked beneath a quilt on the floor before the fire. She was a gentle, tender lover, eager to please, and generous. After the initial shyness had worn off, she had become a tigress of sorts. When he moved he could faintly feel the superficial scratches she had left on his back, and the awareness made him smile inwardly.

She was a woman fit for a warrior, he thought. *Tomorrow Woman.*

While it was safe to do so, he took a bucket out to the stream and filled it with fresh water. It would need boiling, of course. The *wasicu* had managed to spread parasites everywhere throughout the West, and the beavers, picking it up from human waste left too close to streams, carried it everywhere else. Water that had been safe to drink even twenty years ago was now rife with unhealthy organisms.

A disgrace, he thought as he carried the water back to the cabin. A disgrace. Nothing tasted sweeter than fresh, icy water from a mountain stream, flavored with minerals and moss.

He set the bucket on the porch and turned to look at the rising sun. There was a cliff a hundred feet from the porch, and the sudden drop opened a view to the east of Conard County and beyond. The sun was rising beneath the high overcast, bathing the world in a rosy glow. For once Thunder Mountain was free of the clouds that usually shrouded its peak, giving unlimited visibility.

That wouldn't last, he thought. Dipping his hand into the bucket, he sprinkled water with his fingers, scattering it in each of the four directions. Then, keeping his voice low so it wouldn't carry, he chanted a prayer to Tunkasila, the grandfather of the world.

"Mitakuye oyasin." He ended the prayer with the ritual words *All my relations,* a reminder that all the world was one.

"That was beautiful."

At the soft whisper, he turned swiftly and found Mercy standing behind him in the open doorway. He hadn't heard her open the door, so involved had he been in his prayer.

There was a look to her this morning, he thought, a look of tenderness that could shred a man's soul, if he let it touch him. The rosy dawn light bathed her face, emphasizing her feminine softness, heightening the drowsy, just-awakened look that was both vulnerable and erotic. In a single instant he wanted to both make love to her and protect her.

Instead he looked away, toward the rising sun, and cleared his throat. "I was praying."

"I thought so. It was beautiful, somehow." She stepped out onto the porch and drew a deep breath of appreciation when she saw the view over the cliff. "Oh, it's wonderful! How can you ever bear to leave here?"

He didn't answer her, simply watched her drink in the morning's splendor. Then, reminding himself that he couldn't be sure that this woman wasn't assisting Stockton-Wells, he picked up the bucket and went inside.

As he walked past one of the chairs by the wood stove, the bucket knocked Mercy's backpack over, spilling some of its contents. He set the bucket aside, then knelt and began to gather up granola bars. And her wallet.

The wallet lay open, and Gray Cloud froze when he recognized a familiar face staring up at him from a color photograph. It was a face that belonged to one of the men he had seen at the Stockton-Wells campsite yesterday morning, just before they had moved out.

He stared at the photo, letting its significance resound

through him. Then, swiftly, because he couldn't bear to look at the proof of her betrayal, he snatched up the wallet and jammed it into the backpack. By the time Mercy followed him inside, he was setting the steel bucket on the wood stove to start the water boiling.

You can't trust her.

The view from Gray Cloud's porch was breathtaking. The world seemed to be spread out below like a giant relief map. The air was so clear this morning that the valley looked close enough to touch. Mercy had seen views similar when she went rock climbing, but none had ever been quite this beautiful. She wondered if Gray Cloud saw this often, or if the habitual storm clouds usually concealed it from him.

The sun rose higher, and the rosy glow vanished as fresh storm clouds began to build around the peak. Even as she stood there and watched, swiftly racing patches of fog moved in, dripping strands of cloud as they coalesced and formed rapidly into storm clouds. The valley vanished, and Thunder Mountain was once again cloaked in a storm.

Sighing with reluctance, she went inside to ask Gray Cloud what they should do next.

She knew instantly that something was wrong. He didn't quite look at her when she spoke to him, and he seemed stiffer somehow. Surely she was imagining it?

But as he prepared fry bread for breakfast on the wood stove, she grew increasingly certain that something was the matter. Even when she had first met him, he hadn't seemed quite this distant. Nor had he seemed then to be avoiding her, and right now she got the definite feeling that he was avoiding her.

"Did something happen?" she asked him finally; when he passed her a tin plate loaded with bread, his eyes never lifting to hers.

"No."

Something had. The very fact that he didn't ask why she wondered was a giveaway. Something had happened, and he couldn't quite look at her. Last night, of course. He must be having second thoughts about it. Fears that she might expect a long-term relationship, which of course she didn't.

Did she?

The sinking sensation in the pit of her stomach told her that she was lying to herself. She wanted more, much more, from Gray Cloud than a one-night stand. It was folly, of course. Their lives would never mesh. She had to return to the university, and he wouldn't abandon his precious mountain. There was no future of any kind in that. None at all. He certainly realized that as clearly as she did, and that was why he couldn't look at her.

Wasn't it?

Uneasiness stalked her, making her stomach hurt and killing her appetite. She hardly touched the fry bread, even though it was delicious. He should have asked what the problem was. He didn't. Which meant that something was very definitely wrong.

He never lifted his eyes from his own plate as he spoke. "How long did you date Stockton?"

"Almost two years." Her stomach clenched hard, and knifelike pains radiated through it. Back to Merle, she thought. Gray Cloud might have made love to her last night, but he didn't trust her. And she didn't know how she could get him to.

Or even if she should try. He might decide she was a threat that needed eliminating. Maybe he already had. Maybe she ought to be running as hard and as fast as she could. He would do whatever he thought necessary to protect his damn mountain, and if he thought she was tied up somehow with Stockton-Wells...

Mercy jumped up and hurried toward the door, needing

fresh air, needing to escape the miasma of suspicion that filled the cabin. She didn't trust him. He didn't trust her. The gulf between them had never been wider.

And maybe she ought to concentrate on that gulf. Damn it, Mercy, this man might decide to kill you! He might already have decided it! How could you have slept with him last night? How can you be so stupid now? He'd killed once; he could kill again! He was not the kind of a man she ought to be falling in love with.

He caught her at the door, his fingers biting into her upper arm, not quite hard enough to bruise, but hard enough that she felt his grip. It infuriated her, and she tried to yank free.

"Stop it!" he commanded in a low voice. "You can't go out there. Those people are bound to be on their way up here."

"Let me go!"

He gave an impatient shake of his head. "Not until you promise to stay here."

"Why should I? You think I'm involved with Stockton-Wells, don't you? You think I'd actually hurt those wolves, or help turn this mountain over for timber exploitation. Why should I stay with you when you believe that? So you can kill me?"

The gauntlet was thrown, the challenge thick in the air, as thick as the suspicion. He didn't answer her, and his silence confirmed her suspicions. He *did* think she might be involved with Stockton-Wells. Nor did he deny that he might kill her. Funny sort of honor, she found herself thinking, as everything inside her seemed to freeze into ice. He couldn't lie, but he could kill.

And then she realized what was really happening. He had no intention of ever letting her go. She was his prisoner.

Listen.

The day dragged endlessly. Gray Cloud sent up another

smoke signal, burning pitch-soaked rags that must have produced huge clouds of black smoke. A forest ranger would surely have to investigate, Mercy thought. Soon. That smoke would be so anomalous that they couldn't overlook it.

But it would probably also alert the Stockton-Wells people.

The thought of a ranger showing up was comforting, for it meant that Gray Cloud must intend to let her leave the mountain. He wouldn't be trying to get the rangers up here if he intended to kill her, would he?

But it would be so easy to kill her up here. Drop a rock on her head. Push her over that cliff out front. If he really intended to kill her, he would have done it already, wouldn't he? He wouldn't have rescued her after the rock slide trapped her in the cave, would he?

Would he?

But something had changed this morning. Something had definitely happened. This was not the man who had made love to her last night; this was a stranger with a hard face and cold eyes who didn't even want to look at her.

The time dragged. Noon crept up on them so slowly that Mercy felt as if days had passed. Thunder began to rumble again, promising more lightning and rain. The early afternoon darkened, and even though only one shutter was open, the change in light was enough to make it feel as if the day had passed into night.

Gray Cloud went to the window often, listening and watching intently, but no one appeared, and the forest seemed to remain undisturbed.

"They could have lost us," Mercy said finally, her voice cracking after hours of silence. "Maybe they lost us and never picked up on our new direction when they doubled back."

Gray Cloud shook his head. "They track too well. Anyone who could follow us as far as they did knows enough to find where we changed our direction."

"Merle always did talk about tracking like it was some mystical art. Maybe he finally learned how to really do it."

As soon as she spoke, she regretted it. Gray Cloud turned to look at her with eyes as cold as the depths of space. "Stockton."

"Yes, Stockton!" Her chin lifted, and she glared back at him, even as a corner of her mind warned her frantically that provoking this man could be a big mistake. "I told you I used to date him. Is that a crime?"

"You still know him."

"No, I don't! I haven't spoken a word to him in two years! He's a sleaze, and I never wanted anything to do with him again after we broke up!"

"But you carry his picture."

That explained it, she realized with a dull sense of loss. That explained the change in him. He had looked in her wallet. Damn it, she should have given him the photo last night instead of deciding against it, because any way you sliced it now, she looked guilty as hell.

And then anger ripped through her, as hot and fierce as a summer brush fire. "How dare you," she said in a low, angry voice. "How dare you snoop in my personal belongings! You are beneath contempt!"

For a couple of heartbeats it seemed as if he wouldn't answer. When he finally spoke, his voice was as cold and distant as his gaze. "I didn't snoop. Your wallet fell out of your pack, and I found it on the floor. Open."

"Right! While you're at it, try to sell me a bridge, why don't you! You snooped and pried and then leapt to conclusions, and you weren't even going to tell me! Just how the hell would it have been for you in your murder trial if the court had treated you the way you're treating me?"

Before she could say another word, before he could respond in any way, thunder cracked and rumbled deafeningly, shaking the cabin and rattling the window glass in its frames. On and on it rolled, as if it would never cease, and Mercy's hands knotted into fists as she wondered if it was going to shake the cabin down around their ears.

Listen.

She wanted to scream, to shout, to tell the whisper to leave her alone, to get out of her head...or at least tell her what the devil she was supposed to be listening to. Her entire life seemed to be coming to an ignominious conclusion at the hands of a mountain and a fanatical medicine man, and she didn't want to riddle with the wind. Listen to *what?*

Thunder roared again, trumpeting angrily, shaking the world. The mountain replied with a rumble of its own, a deep shaking from within the earth and a groan of tortured rock.

Something was happening. Scared, aware of the power of the storm and the greater power of the mountain, Mercy forgot her anger and looked at Gray Cloud. "Wh—what's happening?"

He shook his head. "I don't know. Something's... wrong."

She could feel that herself. There was no escaping the sense that the storm and the mountain were crying out in outrage. Gray Cloud turned to look out the window again, and Mercy, forgetting her fear of him in the face of a stronger fear, hurried over to stand beside him.

The day was dark, almost bottle green, and fingers of deep gray cloud hung down so low they skimmed the treetops. It looked every bit as threatening as it sounded. Forks of lightning leapt from cloud to cloud, and some speared downward, as if seeking a target.

The ground shook again, and this time Mercy couldn't

tell if it was the rumble of the thunder or the mountain moving.

As she watched, a doe suddenly leapt out of the woods to the right and dashed across the clearing as if it was being pursued.

"Something's definitely wrong," Gray Cloud muttered. "Damn it, what are those Stockton-Wells people up to now?" He turned abruptly, glaring down at her. "What are they doing?"

"I don't know!" Her anger at him seemed unimportant in the face of a world going mad. "I honestly don't know! Gray Cloud, I swear I haven't talked to him in years!"

"One hell of a coincidence that he shows up on this mountain at the same time you do!"

Mercy wanted to deny it—she even felt her jaw open on the words...but she couldn't make herself say them, not when the same suspicion had crossed her own mind. "He must have heard about my research grant. It's not a secret that I was coming to Thunder Mountain to look for the wolves."

"You told him."

"I did not!"

"You expect me to believe he just stumbled on it? How many research grants are made every year? Every *month?*"

"He has ties at the university. Lots of them! He took a graduate degree in forestry there. That's how I met him. Any number of people could have mentioned my grant. He has lots of friends there, damn it!"

He regarded her with steady coldness a moment before returning his attention to the forest beyond the window. He didn't say anything.

"Damn it, Gray Cloud!" Mercy felt as if she were fighting for her life, needing to convince him that she hadn't been lying to him. "It's just a coincidence that the wolves turned up on a mountain he wants to timber. If I'd found them on another mountain, he never would have turned up. If any other biologist had come out here, the same things would be happening. It doesn't have anything to do with the fact that I *used* to know him. Nothing at all! Believe me, I wouldn't get involved in anything like that. I wouldn't. I *couldn't!*''

He kept his face averted, his attention on the woods outside. There was no way she could convince him, she realized. No way at all. He would believe what he wanted to believe, and if that meant he would believe she was involved with Merle, she didn't stand a chance in hell of changing his mind.

The pain she felt at that realization was crushing. In that instant she realized just how much this man had come to mean to her. Past reason, past common sense, she had fallen in love with him. Oh, God, how could she have been foolish enough to fall in love with someone who might actually intend her harm? Someone who wouldn't hesitate to kill her if he felt it necessary.

She was crazy, she thought numbly. Crazy. Totally and completely out of her mind. What she needed to do was just give it all up, give up any hope of studying the wolves or protecting them. Just get off this mountain while she was still in one piece and breathing.

The ground shook again, a violent trembling that was accompanied by the anguished groan of rock. Thunder cracked like a gunshot, deafening, and then growled angrily. Lightning stabbed at the ground, seeming to march toward them.

''Smoke.'' Gray Cloud spoke the word like a curse.

''Where?''

He jerked his chin to the right, and after a moment Mercy was able to see a haze of dark smoke against the dark sky. ''Forest fire?'' Wet as it had been, she couldn't imagine that the fire danger was any too high, but that didn't mean trees full of pine pitch couldn't burn.

"I don't know," he said. "Stockton wouldn't be stupid enough to burn down the forest he wants to cut, but it's a big forest."

"Controlled burns are part of forest management, aren't they? Maybe he's started a controlled burn. But it could be the lightning, too. Lightning starts fires all the time."

Gray Cloud shook his head slowly. "The mountain is angry. It wouldn't be angry if lightning had started the fire. That's a natural thing, part of the order of life and nature."

She kind of thought that herself. Which left only one conclusion. "Can we get out of here?"

At last he turned and looked at her. "Only by going farther up the mountain."

Which would trap them more, she thought. How far could they go up without limiting their options? She had a good idea how a tiger felt when the hunters began beating the bush to drive him out into the open. "There's no other way?"

He indicated the smoke with a jerk of his chin. "The only way to this cabin is along a ridge between two very deep gorges. It looks like they're burning the trees along the ridge."

There was no doubt in her mind that Merle could read a topographical map and see the terrain as clearly as if he were walking over it. She'd seen him do it. He would have recognized that ridge and its significance as soon as he looked at a map of the area. He knew he would be driving them upward, and he undoubtedly had some plan for trapping them.

"He's driving us into a trap," she told Gray Cloud. "I'm sure of it." She saw the distrust flicker across his face. He didn't want to accept her word without a fight, but there was no argument he could offer in the face of her greater knowledge of Merle Stockton. For now he had no choice but to accept that she knew what she was talking about.

But he didn't have to like it. He scowled at her and finally managed a reluctant nod. "It wouldn't be too difficult." He looked out the window again, toward the thickening smoke cloud and the threatening sky. "It's a good day to die."

Mercy found that the most chilling thing he had said yet.

Fire. A fire meant to kill, set by the men who wanted to rape the mountain. Anger grew until it was a seething fire in the mountain's belly. They must be stopped—at any cost. And Gray Cloud...he who was chosen by Thunder protected the woman, and the woman was linked to the man who wished to rape the mountain. Even Gray Cloud...

There was sorrow, but there was even more rage.

No human could be trusted. Not one.

Gray Cloud filled Mercy's pack with dried foodstuffs and tied a fresh bedroll to it. Then he filled a pack of his own with more food and another blanket. He evidently thought they might be stuck in the wilderness for some time.

If they lived. Mercy was learning to ignore that qualifier, learning to ignore the chilly sense of unease that never quite let go of her spine, or the tension in the pit of her stomach that never quite let her relax. She hadn't really relaxed since the moment she had felt she was being watched as she climbed the mountain. With each passing hour it had only gotten worse.

Now they were setting out again, with Merle and his henchmen on their heels—or so she would be willing to bet—being driven into a trap of some kind. And as if that wasn't enough, they were going to climb the side of an angry mountain that at any moment might decide to smash them with a rock slide or zap them with lightning. She wished she had never wanted to leave the safety of her desk for the wild side of this mountain.

They left the cabin by a back entrance, slipping out into the forest's depths quietly. Just as long as no one was watching from nearby, they had escaped unseen.

Not that it would make any difference, Mercy thought. Merle wasn't stupid. He would have planned this carefully and probably knew exactly which way they would have to head. It would be a miracle if there wasn't already someone up above waiting to ambush them.

As soon as the thought crossed her mind, she voiced it to Gray Cloud. He merely gave her a short nod. "Wouldn't the mountain know if someone's up there?" she asked him. The absolute absurdity of the question struck her, but she was past caring whether she was crazy to believe the mountain was alive. The way things were going, she wasn't going to be around long enough to worry about such things.

"Yes."

"Well, wouldn't it warn you?"

Gray Cloud spared her a distant glance. "Perhaps not."

Perhaps not. Once again a chill seeped into her as she realized that Gray Cloud no longer trusted the mountain he served.

CHAPTER ELEVEN

It ought to be raining. It just ought to be raining. The air was so pregnant with the impending storm that it was thick, almost too thick to breathe. Perspiration from exertion soaked her and wouldn't dry, and finally she had to rip the bottom of her shirt to make a sweatband so she could keep her vision clear. Gray Cloud pulled a shoelace out of a shirt pocket and tied his hair back.

Thunder continued to growl and grumble like an irritable beast. The light turned so green it felt like they were walking underwater. Long fingers of cloud dipped down, looking as if they wanted to touch the ground. The lightning, though, stopped spearing from cloud to cloud, and from cloud to ground. It subsided to a flicker deep within the stormy sky, barely discernible despite the darkness of the afternoon.

And Thunder Mountain growled angrily. The ground never stopped vibrating, not quite strongly enough to make walking difficult, but enough that it was impossible to forget the mountain was angry and might at any moment lash out.

Before long, Mercy noted that Gray Cloud tended to avoid places where a rock slide might be a distinct danger—places where the slope was really steep, or the trees were really thin. Several times he skirted such places with evident caution, telling Mercy as clearly as any words that he was concerned about what the mountain might do.

And Mercy began to get angry. Very angry. It wouldn't do any good, so she bottled it up inside and chewed on her tongue to prevent the words from escaping. But what she wanted to do was stomp her foot and give the damn mountain a piece of her mind.

And the wolves. Where were the wolves? She and Gray Cloud had lost contact with them sometime yesterday. She assumed they'd gone to dig themselves a den somewhere for the pups and hoped they'd gotten well out of harm's way. But she was worried about them and wished she could at least catch a brief sight of Eyebrows.

But the afternoon waxed, then waned, and there was no sight of wildlife of any kind...which was really strange.

It was as if the forest was dead.

At some point she realized that they hadn't seen any living thing in hours, not a squirrel or a bird. Not a hint or sound of life. It was as if every living animal, bird and insect had vanished.

The silence echoed, and uneasiness stalked her. If the animals had fled...

She wasn't aware she had voiced the thought until Gray Cloud turned to her and nodded. ''Very wrong,'' he said. ''Something's very, very wrong.''

Behind them, black smoke rose to meet the gray clouds, testament to Merle's willingness to destroy anything to get what he wanted. A doe had leapt out of the woods this morning, fleeing the fire. The ground trembled, but the animals of Thunder Mountain had in the past seemed used to that and unthreatened by it. This afternoon...perhaps they were scared by the fire, distant as it was, and had taken flight.

Or maybe they sensed that something else was about to happen. An earthquake? A really bad one?

They didn't pause long but continued the rough climb. Frequently Gray Cloud reached out to help her, and she wondered if he remembered last night at all, or if he had killed the memory ruthlessly. This morning he certainly seemed to believe her capable of consorting with Merle to destroy the mountain and using him callously in the process.

Suddenly Gray Cloud shot out an arm and motioned her to stop.

"What is it?" she asked in a whisper that was almost lost in the sudden gusting of wind through the treetops.

He shook his head, silencing her. With great effort she bit back her questions and waited, watching him as he tipped back his head and closed his eyes. It looked, she thought, as if he were opening his senses to the wind, seeking a sound or a smell that would tell him something.

Thunder rumbled again, a distant, angry growl. A large raindrop splattered Mercy's cheek, cold and stinging like an icy slap. The temperature was dropping, and it seemed likely that they might see snow, which wouldn't be unusual for this elevation even at this time of year...but would be absolutely miserable to hike through. She shivered and wished Gray Cloud would reach some kind of conclusion about the threat they were facing.

Where had all the animals gone?

Why had all the animals gone?

The wind whipped through the treetops with a sudden, ferocious moan. *Listen...*

A prickle at the back of her neck warned her. Forgetting Gray Cloud's injunction to silence, she whirled around and gasped as she saw a huge hawk perched on a low bough and staring straight at her with eyes that seemed to burn right through her. At her gasp, Gray Cloud spun around and saw the hawk, too.

It was watching them. It was watching them and following them. Mercy shuddered as frigid awareness seeped through her. There was no escape. Everywhere they went, they were being watched.

Gray Cloud muttered something she didn't understand. It didn't matter; she knew what she was seeing, and it didn't need a name. Those small, black eyes pinned her like twin knives, holding her motionless...almost helpless.

"Let's go." Gray Cloud clasped her elbow, dragging her out of the paralyzed state she had fallen into. For once she didn't mind a gentle tug that pulled her away, back into the real world.

If this world could be called real, she thought as she followed Gray Cloud farther up into the mountain. The hawk's eyes seemed to bore holes in her back even after the trees must have screened her from its view.

"It was watching us," she said. The altitude and exertion were making her breathless, and the words came out on small puffs of hard-won air.

"Yes."

"For who?"

"The mountain. The hawk is the eyes of the mountain."

She scrambled up a steep incline, scraping her knuckles a little as she grabbed handholds. The injuries didn't bother her; if such small hurts had mattered, she never would have become a rock climber. The back of her neck still seemed to burn from the hawk's gaze, and when she dared an upward glance at the stormy sky, she saw the bird above them, circling slowly.

The altitude must have been affecting her mind, because it was a while before she got to wondering why the mountain should be watching them. Gray Cloud, after all, was trusted by the mountain...wasn't he?

The possibility that the mountain had some reason not to trust him was awful to contemplate. She had seen some of what the mountain was capable of, and she suspected it was capable of far more than that. If for some reason it had come to distrust Gray Cloud...

The thought was chilling.

Just when her legs were turning to putty and she was beginning to stumble over her own feet, Gray Cloud called another halt. Sitting side by side on a low, flat boulder, they stared back down the way they had come. Beneath them the mountain continued to tremble, but so slightly it was almost possible to believe she was imagining it. For some reason her mind hopscotched to the seismograph the Forest Service kept on Mount Rainier. She'd seen it years ago, while taking a summer trip through the Northwest, and had been fascinated by the way the apparently quiet, lifeless mountain never really stopped trembling. Mount Rainier was a dormant volcano, and the seismograph was a reminder that the mountain could awake at any instant, that it merely slumbered.

Thunder Mountain was slumbering no longer. The entire Rocky Mountain area was seismically active, so it was hardly surprising that this mountain was rumbling and groaning as if waking from a centuries-old sleep.

But that wasn't all that was happening. Thunder Mountain was more than an accident of plate tectonics. A sleeping giant had been awakened by the threat of Stockton-Wells, and the more Mercy thought about it, the more likely she considered it that none of them would survive. Despite all the power and force contained within this mountain, she seriously doubted a surgical strike was within its capabilities. Everything that got in the way would probably be destroyed. The only hope she and Gray Cloud had of escaping would be to stay well away from Merle and his henchmen.

She turned to Gray Cloud. "Why is the mountain watching us? I thought you were its friend."

He turned slowly and looked straight at her. "I saved your life."

Her breath jammed in her throat as his meaning drove home. He was no longer the mountain's friend because he had dug her out of the cave. That must mean the mountain believed she was a threat, and if the mountain believed that...

"No!" She spat the word like an oath. "No, damn it, I'm not going to be hanged without a trial! Are you and this mountain both deaf and stupid? I came up here to study wolves, not to hurt one damn thing. I haven't talked to Merle Stockton in over two years, and his picture was in my wallet because I never clean my wallet, not because he's still a friend of mine! Don't you hear me?"

"I hear you." But the words conveyed no belief in what she was saying. None at all.

Right then, Mercy came as close as she ever had to committing an act of violence. The urge to swing at Gray Cloud, just to get his full attention, was nearly overwhelming. This man had made love to her just last night with a tenderness the mere memory of which made her breath catch, and yet now he was treating her as if she were a total stranger. He had convicted her on the basis of one lousy photograph.

And he wouldn't even listen to her explanation.

Tears pricked at her eyes, and she looked quickly away, trying to repress the sense of betrayal. She had trusted this man with everything that she was, had trusted him enough to open her body to him, making herself completely vulnerable. And instead of treating that gift with the respect it deserved, he had turned his back on her, choosing to disbelieve everything she had told him because of one stupid photo.

"You're worse than Stockton," she heard herself say. "You're even worse! What if I hadn't believed what you told me about killing your sister's husband? What if I believed you had made up a story that would make you look sympathetic and explain away your reputation! How would you feel?"

"That you were being wise and cautious."

Stunned, Mercy watched him rise and turn away.

"Let's go," he said roughly. "It's time. Something is

brewing, and I want us to get up higher before it happens. There's a place where we'll at least have a chance if the mountain goes wild.''

She wanted to scream and shout, to stamp her feet and insist that they weren't going anywhere until he listened to her, but even as she had the impulse, she was climbing to her feet and following him up the ravine. Screaming and shouting wouldn't change his mind. Nothing could do that except himself. If his mind was made up, no protest would alter it.

And that saddened her beyond words. She had given him her heart, and he didn't care. Not even a little bit. He had used her last night, that was all. Used her.

Listen...

The wind sighed the word through the treetops as evening darkened the sky even more. Gray Cloud settled them on a wide expanse of granite, a firm bit of ground that appeared as if it would resist buckling if Thunder Mountain shook harder.

For the mountain had never stopped shaking. The vibration was small, but it could be felt, and to Mercy it seemed as if something were building beneath them, like a pressure cooker. Some kind of explosion was imminent.

Dinner was a silent affair, a quick meal without even a passing word to lighten the atmosphere. The lightning began to play among the clouds, bright and colorful, beautiful but subtly threatening. Mercy curled up in her blankets and tried not to feel mercilessly exposed on the rock slab. More drops of rain spattered them, but not enough to make them wet. Just enough to remind them that they *could* get wet.

Gray Cloud defied the storm, standing tall and straight as he prayed, holding his arms up toward the clouds in supplication. Thunder had chosen him, she remembered.

The Thunder Spirits had given him the vision that guided his life. He probably didn't fear the storm at all.

Lying on her back, she watched the wind toss his hair and whip it around him. With his hands turned palm upward, he seemed to be inviting the storm to come to him. Little blue sparks of light appeared in his cupped hands as they had once before, but this time, instead of remaining small little flickers, they grew until they filled his hands. And then blue light seemed to run along his arms, down his sides to his feet, until he was limned in glowing blue light bright enough to emphasize every detail of his face and body. She could see him as clearly as if he were standing in a bath of daylight.

And then, from his fingertips, the light reached outward, two strands of blue stretching up toward the clouds. Mercy held her breath, hardly daring to believe what she was seeing. She blinked repeatedly, but nothing made the image go away. Gray Cloud was bathed in lightning.

She cried out when a fork of blue lightning suddenly leapt down from the clouds and met the blue streamers flowing from his hands. She was sure he was a dead man then, that the lightning would kill him in an instant or burn him so badly that he would never get off this mountain....

But he remained standing, his arms upraised as he continued to chant his prayer. He was talking to the lightning, she realized, communing with the power of the storm. Speaking with the Thunder Spirits.

Her world had been turning topsy-turvy since she began her climb up Thunder Mountain, but now the last vestiges of her old reality slipped away as she crossed the threshold completely into the world of Thunder Mountain.

Into Gray Cloud's world. A world where thunder spoke and lightning touched on the power of life. A world where a medicine man could call upon the powers of nature to aid him.

For there was not a doubt in her mind that that was what he was doing. If the storm could aid them, he would ask it to. If the mountain hadn't condemned him, he would probably call on that, as well. And there was a sense that the light that bathed him was protective, that it would shelter him from harm. From evil.

Primitive instincts were awakening within her, and without realizing it, she rose to her knees. It could be harmful, she thought...or it could be helpful. And Gray Cloud was pleading for help.

He glowed with blue fire now, almost as if he were aflame, a brightness in the night that drove the shadows back. Slowly he turned toward her and reached out a flaming hand.

Her first instinct was to back up, run, get away. She could only be hurt by that blue fire.

Listen...

The wind dipped down from the treetops and wrapped around her, the caress of the breeze catching at her short hair and lightly touching her cheeks.

Listen...

In spite of herself, her hand lifted and reached out for Gray Cloud's until their fingertips met. And as she watched, the blue light began to flow to her, to cover her fingers, then her hand, and slowly, slowly creep up her arm. She felt nothing at all except a very faint warmth. It was going to consume her just as it had consumed him.

Listen...

The wind curled around her as the fire slipped over her, and something inside her grew still with expectancy.

Listen...

Then wind and thunder claimed her.

The evil men were waiting above for Gray Cloud and the woman. They had laid a trap, and the mountain saw it all through the eyes of the hawk. Once they all came to-gether, the mountain could free itself of the blight forever.

It was good.

The mountain settled down to wait, a mere blink of time until the sun rose again and the puny little humans on its slopes began once again to move.

It saw Gray Cloud speaking to Thunder, and saw Thunder take the woman in its embrace, and knew that Thunder would see through her to her heart and discover the evil there. Thunder would not protect her once it knew her.

Mercy didn't remember falling asleep, and when she woke to the first pearly light of dawn, she was astonished to find herself tucked up against Gray Cloud. When she moved, his arms tightened around her and tugged her even closer, so that her head was cradled on his shoulder. He couldn't be awake, she told herself. No way.

The last thing she remembered was watching the blue light crawl up her arm. She didn't even remember it reaching her shoulder. It probably had, though, because this morning she felt a subtle tingling everywhere, not so very different from what she had felt as the light crept up her arm.

She wished she understood what had happened last night. Wished she understood what all this meant. The rules of reality that she had been living by for so long were evidently meaningless on Thunder Mountain. Lightning had reached down from the sky and touched both her and Gray Cloud without harming them. Thunder had spoken to them, and she remembered it somewhere deep inside, though she couldn't remember what, if anything, she had learned.

What was different this morning, she realized suddenly, was that she no longer felt that she was running from something. Instead she felt that she was heading *toward* something. That she had a purpose.

Had Thunder given her a vision of some kind?

No. Her mind recoiled from the thought, not because she considered such a vision impossible, but because she wasn't the kind of person who had visions. Or a person who should receive such visions. Who was she that Thunder should talk to her? Nope. If anyone had had a vision last night, it would have been Gray Cloud.

But the lingering sense of rightness persisted, generated, she told herself, by Gray Cloud's arms around her. From the start she had felt a sense of belonging with him, even when he was being his most critical of her. The rightness and peacefulness were illusory, she told herself, but that didn't keep her from soaking them up while she could.

But the sense of purpose that filled her now...that was harder to dismiss.

Listen...

Listen to the feeling? Why not? What difference could it possibly make, except to ease the next hours? If she continued this climb with a sense of purpose, that would make it easier to face whatever lay ahead. Why not believe that she had come to this point in time for a reason, that there was some cosmic scheme behind the horrible things that had been happening and would still happen? Would it really make any difference at all if she believed she had been guided here rather than that she had wound up here by accident?

Easier to believe that something had guided her. Easier to think about it when she remembered Jason Nighthorse from the anthropology department dropping in last autumn to mention the wolves he had heard about on Thunder Mountain...when Jason didn't have any interest in wolves. Then there was the way the grant opportunity had just fallen into her lap without a hitch almost before she had really started to think about seeking one. The way everything had come together to get her on this mountain at the same time as Merle.

A chill crept along her skin as she considered the size of that coincidence. Oh, it was easy to say Merle had heard about her research and followed her, but when she really thought about it...well, there were some awfully unlikely coincidences in the string of events that had put them both here.

If Merle was even really here. But she would have bet that he was. Merle was like that—he might hire a bunch of people to do the dirty work for him, but he would keep control for himself, and for Merle that meant being right there to superintend everything. Oh, she was familiar with that trait of his, all right. She'd even teased him about how awful it would be to work for him.

But that was neither here nor there. Some part of her knew he was on this mountain, and that for some reason or other they were going to have a final confrontation. She knew that as surely as she knew the sun was rising higher on the far side of the low clouds.

Listen...

She was listening. She wasn't sure what she was hearing, but she was listening. Inwardly, she knew this was all meant to be. That what was going to happen on the side of this mountain would affect the course of the future. That she would never again be the same.

Well, of course not. She had discovered that a mountain was capable of thinking and acting. That the rocks beneath her feet were sentient, and that the wind could whisper tales. She had discovered that the world was alive in ways she had never before imagined.

She had stepped out of the objective, impersonal Western world in which she had been raised and had entered a realm where the life force animated every molecule. She had stepped from her own world into Gray Cloud's.

No, she would never again be the same.

She tried to sit up but as soon as she stirred, Gray Cloud's arms tightened again and tugged her closer still. Instinctively she tipped her head back to see if he was awake and met the obsidian of his gaze. Not a single line of his face betrayed his thoughts. He looked as hard and forbidding as the mountain that surrounded them.

Then, without even the flicker of a muscle to betray his intent, his mouth swooped down and captured hers.

Joy erupted inside her like holiday fireworks. He wanted her. He still wanted her. And if he wanted her, perhaps he didn't entirely distrust her.

But did she trust *him?*

The question caused winter frost to creep through her. No, she didn't trust him.

As if he felt the chill strike her, Gray Cloud pulled away suddenly and in one swift movement rose to his feet.

Mercy watched him stride away into the woods and told herself that he had kissed her only because he'd been half-asleep and aware of nothing but the fact that there was a warm woman in his arms. That was all it had been. Any woman who had been pressed to him that way would have been kissed.

Sitting up, she ignored her stiff body and aching muscles and tried to find the calm that had been with her upon awakening. Matters were coming to a head.

Today everything would be decided.

Thunder was strangely silent that morning as they climbed up over increasingly difficult terrain. Gray Cloud paused often, giving her a chance to catch her breath in the thinner air, and checked things out. Or at least she assumed that was what he was doing when he tilted his head back and closed his eyes, appearing to listen.

Merle was waiting for them up ahead. Mercy wasn't sure

exactly how she knew that, except that it wouldn't have been like Merle to start that fire until he was already in position to spring his trap when he drove his quarry upward.

"It has to be soon," Gray Cloud said finally. "Soon. If we get up much farther on this ridge, we'll be able to cut across and come back down the mountain. Our options will open up again."

"We could stay right here and wait for him. Pick our own ground." She was surprised when he gave her suggestion consideration and didn't say that she was simply encouraging him to do what Merle wanted him to do.

"Usually," he said, "picking your own ground is an advantage, but there's no good ground between here and the place where he's probably waiting for us. We'd be at a disadvantage everywhere, on the downhill side."

"Okay. It was just an idea. But if he really is already up there waiting for us, we're going to be at one hell of a disadvantage."

"He's up there," Gray Cloud said with conviction. "He's waiting."

"Shouldn't we make some kind of plan? Do something to try to save ourselves?"

He looked at her for a moment, then squatted and began to draw absent patterns in the dirt with his forefinger. "Thunder Mountain is a manifestation of Makan, the earth spirit, but it is not all-powerful. Thunder is more powerful. The wind is more powerful. These spirits are greater than the mountain." He glanced up questioningly, and she nodded that she understood what he was saying.

"I've asked *Wakinyan* and *Tate,* Thunder and Wind, to help us. We must trust that they will, and be ready to take advantage of whatever aid they give us. As for the mountain..." He shook his head. "I don't know what the mountain intends, but we have more to fear from it than we do from Stockton and his friends."

Mercy didn't like the sound of that at all. Not at all.

"I'm going to take you a little farther up," he continued. "There's a place there where you should be safe while I scout around and see if I can discover a way to take care of Stockton."

"I'll come with you."

He shook his head. "I can track more silently alone."

The thought of being left in isolation on the mountainside didn't appeal to her at all, but she couldn't come up with a good reason why he should take her with him. She didn't know how to track, and she certainly didn't know how to fight. She was a biologist, damn it, not a commando.

Feeling uneasy and grim, she had no choice but to follow Gray Cloud. Thunder rumbled uneasily from higher up, and the mountain trembled faintly. Forces were gathering, creating a tension in the air that was inescapable, a tension as palpable as that on a drawn rubber band, and to Mercy it felt as if something might snap at any moment.

The place Gray Cloud took her to was a table of granite surrounded by volcanic dikes that looked as if they reached to the very bedrock. "You'll be safe here," he told her. "Safe enough. The dikes will stop a rock slide."

So he thought there was a chance the mountain might try to kill her again. Mercy wanted to argue with him, tell him that he had to take her with him, but the words didn't come. Instead she sat on the table, surrounded by the bony fingers of upthrust rock, and watched him disappear into the dark, silent depths of the forest.

Alone, she listened...and heard nothing.

CHAPTER TWELVE

The woman sat on the table of rock, thinking herself safe. Gray Cloud had underestimated the power of the mountain. With one shrug of its shoulders, it could send that entire table tumbling down to the valley below.

But not yet. The man who wanted to cut the trees and kill the wolves was closing in on the table. He would find the woman, and then the mountain could take care of the entire problem at once. Easily.

As for Gray Cloud... The mountain ruminated.

The day was growing colder as noon approached. Mercy watched the occasional snowflake fly and tucked her hands up beneath her arms to keep her fingers warm. What was taking Gray Cloud so long?

He was checking out a wide area, she told herself. The side of this mountain was pretty big, and rough terrain besides. Of course it was taking him a long time.

Standing, she hopped from one foot to the other, trying to build up some body heat inside her clothing. The pack was beginning to feel as if it weighed a ton, too, but it served to keep the wind off her back.

And the wind was beginning to develop a real bite, teeth of ice that nipped right through her clothing and were making her earlobes hurt. Roughly she chafed her ears with her hands and then covered them with her palms. What she needed to do was find something to tie around her head, she thought. Maybe one of the shirts tucked deep into her backpack.

Before she could slip the pack off, movement in the corner of her eye caught her attention. She turned swiftly but could see nothing in the woods beyond the table where she stood.

Something had been there. Something had moved. And it had been bright enough to snare her attention, which meant it probably wasn't an animal, which would have blended into the background.

Someone was out there.

For a few moments she allowed herself to think it must have been Gray Cloud, but when he didn't reappear, didn't emerge from among the trees and approach her, she knew it had to be someone or something who didn't want her to see them. One of Merle's people, perhaps. Or Merle himself. The unpleasant sense of being watched returned.

The hawk. Remembering the hawk that had followed and watched them yesterday, she looked around her, trying to find a large bird. *Hoping* to find a large bird, because that would explain the movement and the sense of being watched. But if the hawk was out there somewhere, she couldn't see it.

Where was Gray Cloud?

Thunder rumbled deeply from clouds that seemed to be closing in on her, curling downward around the trees, bringing the sky down to them. Lightning flickered, as yet not forking down to strike the mountain.

Feeling too exposed and too vulnerable, Mercy squatted down and hugged her knees, making herself as small a target as she could. If it hadn't been the hawk, then it was a person, and if it was a person, it was unquestionably Merle or one of his friends...and that was not good. Not good at all.

Scanning her immediate vicinity, she tried to see some way she could defend herself or escape if someone attacked. Running in the opposite direction was a simple option, but what if they came at her from *all* directions? And what if the mountain got involved? If the mountain struck out at the Stockton-Wells people, she would probably get caught in the cataclysm...which was why Gray Cloud had left her here, wasn't it? To keep her safe from another rock slide. These jutting dikes of basalt would unquestionably provide a shield against falling rocks from almost any direction.

But was a rock slide all the mountain could accomplish? Oh, God, she didn't even want to think about it. It was too much to contemplate. Her mind had absorbed so much strangeness in the past few days that it was getting balky. No more.

But not thinking about it wasn't going to change the reality, which was that Merle was stalking her and Gray Cloud, probably to arrange an accidental death for both of them so that no one would hear about the wolves, and any serious objections to his plans would be silenced.

Well, was she just going to sit here and take it? But what could she do? Keeping her eyes open, scanning the forest's edge continuously, she tried to think of some way to protect herself and stymie any attempt by Merle to hurt her.

And she tried not to feel as if she were the Judas goat set out to attract the tiger.

Because the longer she sat here, facing the threat alone, the more a small voice in her head kept saying that Gray Cloud had left her here purposely as a lure. That he had wanted to draw Merle out here for some reason, instead of meeting him some other place. That she was bait in the trap.

And bait was expendable.

Lord, it was getting so cold! Shivering inside her jacket, she considered what, if anything, she could do to draw the men out...and if she managed to draw them out into the open, what would she do then? Maybe the thing would be just to get up and try to walk away from here. If she moved before they were ready to act, she might have a chance, but the longer she stayed here, the more opportunity she was giving them to get ready to take her out. To make it look as if it was an accident.

There had to be *something* she could do, besides sit here and feel that she had been thrown to the predators by the man she loved.

Not that he loved *her.* Damn, he could hardly even bring himself to look at her today. Pain pierced her heart, an ache beyond description, as she considered what would never be. *Could* never be. How had she been so foolish as to give her heart to a man who didn't want it, a man who had set her out as bait in a trap and probably didn't care if she lived or died as a result? Well, the Judas goat usually died, didn't it, devoured by the tiger it had lured into the trap?

She shivered again and told herself it didn't matter. Nothing mattered. She had had a broken heart before; it wouldn't kill her. Nor was this the time to be moaning about that, not when her life might actually be hanging in the balance.

There was no more sign of movement from the woods, and it occurred to her that Merle could settle in just as well as she could, waiting for Gray Cloud to return so he could handle things all at once. There was no reason why he should act immediately. After all, his assumption would be that Gray Cloud would return to her, and it would certainly be less messy, and less likely to cause problems, if he killed them both in a single "accident."

But what kind? Shivering violently, she tipped her head back and looked around at the mysterious trees, the mountain slope rising away to her right, falling away to her left. A rock slide wouldn't be able to reach her very easily because of the upthrust basalt. Gray Cloud had been right about that.

So what other accident could happen here?

Beneath her, the ground trembled with suppressed power. The mountain was stirring again. The wind reached down and tugged at her hair.

Listen...

Giving herself up to the wind, Mercy forced her thoughts to quiet down and tilted her head back so the frigid air could nip at her unimpeded. *Listen.* All right, she would listen. To the wind. To the thunder and the lightning. And even to the mountain that might want to kill her.

Listen...Tomorrow Woman...listen...

She heard the earth groan and realized it was about to move again. This movement would be more than the small tremors that had been coming almost nonstop. This movement would be violent. An attack.

Deep within the mountain, stressed rock groaned and fractured, transferring its confined energy upward toward the surface.

Listen...

She heard the stressors, heard the anguish of the tortured rock and felt the earthquake push up toward her. The fingers of basalt that guarded her began to hum and vibrate as the shock wave deep within the mountain struck their buried bases.

Listen...

She heard the wind carry its warning along the mountain slopes to the small animals, herding them away from the epicenter.

Heard the wind whisper her name again. *Tomorrow Woman...run...run...*

The epicenter was beneath her. Directly below her. She saw it in a fractured moment out of time, as if the ground beneath her had become transparent, and she saw that the shock wave was racing straight up toward her feet.

Listen...

Thunder boomed hollowly, and the wind snatched at her hair, tugging.

Run...

Lightning forked down, dazzling her, terrifying her. She felt so exposed.

Run...

Lightning was trying to push her, she realized. Thunder was trying to warn her.

Run...

She rose from her crouch, ready to flee but not sure where to flee to. Barely had she reached her feet when the table of granite beneath her began to shudder violently. She teetered from side to side, finding it almost impossible to maintain her balance.

The upthrusting dikes of basalt trembled, too, shaking as if they were working their way out of the ground. The ground shrieked its agony now, crying out as it rent itself, severing ancient veins, tearing itself apart.

Run!

A crack opened at the edge of the rock table, and Mercy stared in horror as it widened, separating the table from the surrounding ground. Then slowly, so terribly slowly, the table began to tip.

Dread held her frozen, disbelief making it almost impossible for her to comprehend what was happening. The rock table was separating from the ground around it. The mountain was breaking it free, tipping it, trying to shake her off....

A sudden lurch tipped the table precariously. Galvanized by the same fear that only moments ago had paralyzed her, Mercy tried to scramble upward but slid backward as the rock tipped further. Looking behind her, she almost cried out. The ground back there had vanished, leaving a gaping hole. A cliff edge.

A nightmare place to fall into.

She had never forgotten the tale she had heard of the Alaska earthquake, had never forgotten the man who had seen a crevice open beneath his wife, had seen her fall in, had heard her cries as the crevice closed around her.

No, damn it, she wasn't going to die that way, swallowed alive by the mountain. No way!

Falling flat on the tipping table of rock, she used every one of her rock-climbing skills to edge her way higher. Handholds were almost nonexistent, but the surface of the rock wasn't perfectly smooth, either, and she was able to wedge her feet against small bumps, to claw a slippery grip on barely discernible ridges with her hands. In no time at all her fingertips were sore and bleeding, but she hardly noticed. It was reach the top or tumble into the pit behind her.

The attempt to survive demanded all her attention, but somewhere deep inside was the sorrowful, angry realization that Gray Cloud had left her here to die. He had indeed handed her to the mountain, like some sacrificial lamb.

An angry tear escaped, but she ignored it as she struggled upward on the violently shaking slab of rock. As soon as she felt her feet were braced securely enough that she wouldn't slide backward, she stretched her arms up and felt for handholds. More than once she slipped back a little, but more often she managed to inch upward.

Another strong tremor shook the rock, nearly shaking her off it. Just as she was sure she couldn't hang on another second, that she was going to slide backward into the pit the mountain had made, into the grave it had dug for her, the tremor let up and her grip held. Not even wasting a moment to allow herself to feel relief, she pushed upward again with her toes and then reached with her hands.

And felt the edge of the slab. For an instant she froze. What if all she found when she looked over the edge was another crevice…a deep pit that could swallow her as easily as the one behind her? What if there was no escape up there?

What alternative did she have? She should have run the instant the wind advised her to. The very instant.

Tomorrow Woman...listen.

To what? Oh, God, listen to what? Her breath was coming in sobs now, her fingers ached so badly from clinging to the bucking rock that they were cramping, and her thigh muscles were beginning to quiver.

Pull up!

The wind nipped at her ears, slapped her cheeks and forced her attention back to what she needed to do. This was no time for self-pity, no time to stop and moan. So what if her fingers cramped and her thighs ached? So what?

With her arms fully extended, she gripped the edge of the table and pulled with all her might. As if the rock realized she was close to achieving her goal, it shuddered wildly, like a horse trying to shake off a fly. That was what she felt like—like a fly plastered to the side of the rock— and about as significant.

Move!

She struggled, hauling herself up against all the resistance of gravity, against the friction of her clothing and body against the rock itself, inching higher and higher as her arms began to quiver and protest.

And finally she looked over the edge.

Into a crevice as black as night. Into the very maw of the mountain.

Jump!

Across a gaping hole five feet wide. How could she find a position from which to get stable enough to jump with any surety? What if she tumbled into that hole?

What alternative did she have?

Turning her head, she looked back down the slab of rock and saw the pit that waited there. It was far wider, far more of a threat, a sinkhole in the side of the mountain. At least she had a chance of jumping over the crevice.

Pulling herself up the last little bit, she clung for dear life as the rock bucked and shuddered beneath her. There had to be a place where she could stand just long enough to jump.

"Mercy, here!"

A voice from out of the past, a voice she had never wanted to hear again. Raising her eyes, she saw Merle Stockton standing on the other side of the crevice with a coiled rope in his hand. A vision from the past in woodland camouflage.

"I'll throw you a rope!"

She would have loved to tell him where to stick his rope. Although she was exhausted and scared, although it was likely she would die if someone didn't help her, she wanted to hurl his offer right back in his face.

But as soon as the resentment rose in her, it faded away, replaced by common sense. If he threw her that rope and she fell into the crevice when she jumped, there would at least be a chance he might pull her out. If he didn't pull her out...well, she wouldn't be any worse off, would she? And why would he throw her a rope if he wanted her to die? No, he must need her for some reason.

And that meant he would help her now.

She nodded her understanding to him, unable to speak as the rock shuddered yet again and tipped more.

"Catch it, Mercy!"

The earth shrieked again and trembled fiercely. Merle stepped back a little farther from the edge of the crevice and flung the coiled rope toward her. She shot out her hand but missed. Quickly Merle coiled the rope again, and again flung it out toward her. This time she managed to catch it and hang on.

"Tie it around your chest," he called to her. "Then stand

up and try to jump. I'll stabilize you as much as I can when you get up.''

She loosened her pack cautiously, watching Merle tie his end of the rope around himself, under one arm and over the other shoulder so he wouldn't asphyxiate if it yanked tight. She slipped a little as she shook her pack off her shoulders and watched it tumble down into the waiting pit. Then, wedging her feet as best she could, she wound the rope around herself, arranging it just as Merle had tied his end. She hesitated a moment, aware of the risk she was taking, aware that Merle could tumble her right into that crevice now if he chose.

But what choice did she have?

She tied the rope. When it was secure, she inched her painful way back up the shaking slab, feeling it tip even more, as if it wanted to turn over on her and bury her. When she reached the top again, Merle was still waiting.

"Ready," she called to him.

"Okay. Find a place to stand, and then jump. I'll brace you as best I can."

Which really wasn't bracing at all, since the rock slab had become as active as a bucking bronco. Time was running out, she realized. The mountain was going to turn that rock over with her on it.

Wedging one foot against the edge of the slab, she eased herself into a position where she would be able to rise and jump in one smooth, quick movement. The rock shook hard, and then steadied…just enough.

She shoved herself up and jumped.

The minute her feet left the ground she knew she wasn't going to quite make it. The chasm was just too wide, and it yawned beneath her like a hungry mouth. No, not quite, but she hit the far side with a thud that nearly knocked the wind out of her. At once her hands clawed for purchase on the edge of the crevice, seeking a hold to keep her from slipping down into the abyss below.

Damn it, why wasn't Merle pulling on the rope? Dirt crumbled beneath her hands, and she felt herself slip a little. The earth shuddered again, trying to shake her down into the crevice. She slipped a little more.

And then the rope around her torso tightened, and with a strong tug she felt herself being pulled upward. The earth groaned deeply, a sound of angry protest.

"Help me," Merle shouted at her from above. "The crevice is closing!"

Spurred on by the terror of being crushed to death in the maw of the mountain, Mercy managed to dig her fingers into the hard, dry dirt and pull herself upward a little.

"That's it," Merle called. "Keep it up, honey!"

She was past wondering why he should be helping her, or why he'd call her "honey." The ground was shaking hard, and it was all she could do to keep from slipping downward. The rope around her was a reassurance, but she wasn't getting up the side of the crevasse fast enough. It could close at any moment, and she was willing to bet that was exactly what the mountain wanted to do.

"Come on," Merle called encouragingly, and all of a sudden, with a shove of her feet, a tug of her hands and the upward jerk of the rope, she got her torso up and over the edge. A few more seconds and she was out of the crevice and able to roll safely away from the edge.

Lying facedown, she gasped for air and hugged the shaking earth, grateful for its apparent solidity...a solidity that was frighteningly deceptive, as she'd just seen. Creeping coldly along her spine was the realization that the mountain could open another crack right beneath her, that if she held still long enough it could gather its energy and focus it in one place, and cause the earth to try to swallow her again. And it never stopped rumbling beneath her. Never.

Merle swore almost disbelievingly, and Mercy lifted her head in time to see the crevice close like snapping jaws. If she'd been in there...

She shuddered and watched the earth open again, this time as the rock table on which she'd been sitting heaved up a little more and finally tumbled over backward, falling into the sinkhole.

"My God," Merle said. "Let's get out of here. Now! It looks like this whole place is gonna fall apart."

He reached down to grab her hand, pulling her to her feet. Together they ran uphill toward the trees, away from the bucking, buckling ground behind them.

In the thick pine woods, the ground trembled but didn't buckle and shake as hard. Perhaps the roots of the trees interfered with the shock waves, or perhaps the mountain didn't want to harm the trees. Whatever, it felt almost safe there, and Mercy had no qualms about falling to the ground to catch her breath. Merle didn't seem especially inclined to go any farther just yet, either. He fell to the ground beside her and drew breath raggedly. The air was thin up here near the tree line. Very thin.

"In all my days," Merle said finally, "I've never seen an earthquake like that. I've never seen *anything* like that."

That was because he'd never seen anything like Thunder Mountain, Mercy thought. But she knew better than to speak of such things to Merle. He'd made such fun of her for thinking mountains had moods, a purely artistic reaction to their shapes and colors. Or had it been? Maybe...maybe she'd sensed the life force in the rock even then. Even before Gray Cloud.

And what had happened to Gray Cloud? Not that it mattered, she told herself angrily. He'd left her there, and considering his relationship with this damn mountain, it was entirely possible that he'd conspired with the mountain to kill her.

"God!" Merle said. "That was incredible!"

Mercy suddenly remembered that she needed to appear ignorant about Merle's presence on the mountain. If she let him know that she'd been aware of his presence and purpose, he might perceive her as an even bigger threat. Certainly pretending ignorance was the only possible protection she had now. Sitting up, she reached for the knot of the rope wrapped around her and tried to look casual.

"Wherever did you come from?" she asked him. "I couldn't believe it when I heard your voice!"

"I came looking for you."

That answer astonished her enough that she forgot the knot she was untying and looked at him. She'd expected him to make their meeting sound accidental, not baldly say he'd been looking for her. Her heart began to beat uncomfortably as she realized that the only excuse he could have for being so blunt was that he was going to kill her, anyway, so it didn't matter what she knew.

"Looking for me?" Her voice quavered ever so slightly. "Why?"

Merle looked away. "You won't believe me."

"Try me." Damn, she thought, he was as handsome as ever. But now, when she looked at him, she could only think how pretty he was. Gray Cloud was much more...attractive. But Gray Cloud had tried to kill her. All because he'd seen Merle's picture in her wallet he'd been willing to convict her and sentence her to death.

Merle hesitated. "I haven't been able to forget you."

Mercy's jaw dropped. For a moment everything else was forgotten as she considered this man's unbelievable gall. "Oh, come on!"

He shook his head. "No. No, really. I told you that you wouldn't believe me. But the honest truth is, I haven't been able to forget you. Joanne and I are getting a divorce, and all I've been able to think about is you, and the times we used to spend together rock climbing and white-water kayaking…. Mercy, there isn't one woman in a hundred like you.''

He was good, she found herself thinking, as she met his brilliant blue eyes. Oh, he was very good. Those eyes couldn't possibly be lying…except that she knew Merle better than that. ''I'd have preferred to be one in a million.''

He looked a little startled, and then a chuckle escaped him. ''Well, I'm beginning to think you might be. I was a fool not to recognize it then. Mercy, you're exactly the woman I need, the woman I want to spend my life with.''

A couple of years ago, she might have believed it. A week ago, under other circumstances, she might even have considered it. But too much had happened in the last few days. Too much. This man had been responsible—or so she believed—for the attempt to kill the wolf pups in their den. He would mow down the trees on Thunder Mountain, leaving this beautiful land denuded of all except a few seed trees. Perhaps he would be required to replant, but Thunder Mountain wouldn't look the same again for a century or two. All this beautiful old-growth forest would be gone. And with the loss of the trees would come the loss of so many animals and birds.

It wasn't that she objected to the timber industry. But she did object to clear-cutting, and she certainly felt that some areas ought to be left alone in their natural state as a legacy to the future. Let timber companies replant and harvest the same areas again and again. If that drove up the price of paper, so be it. Maybe there would be more recycling. But certainly this beautiful mountain ought to be left untouched for all the generations to come.

All Merle could see though, was all this pristine lumber. Not trees, but lumber. That was what he saw. And dollar signs. He wouldn't care about the wolves except as an obstacle, or about the owls and birds and mice and all the rest of the little creatures. He would come up here and cut away every last tree that wasn't jealously guarded, and would call it progress and profit. He would never count the losses.

So it didn't really matter whether he was telling the truth about wanting her. But she didn't believe he was. He was trying to manipulate her, to get her into his camp. He knew how much trouble he could save himself with a wildlife biologist on his side. Did he really think he could maneuver her so easily? Had she been such a wimp when they'd dated?

Probably.

And it would probably be best now to seem to believe him. If he thought he could control her, maybe he wouldn't be so eager to eliminate her. And the longer she survived, the more chance she would have to escape somehow.

So she managed to keep any trace of sarcasm out of her voice, and even managed to inject a trace of hopeful breathlessness, as she replied, "Really?"

Because she didn't believe him, it was easy to see the satisfaction in his answering smile. "Really," he said. "I know you'll need time to think about it, but honestly, honey, I've never been able to forget you. I think you're the primary reason I never made Joanne happy...because I was always wishing I was with *you.*"

She wanted to gag and looked quickly away, hoping the urge wasn't visible on her face. Hating every word, she forced herself to say, "I don't know, Merle. I mean...I hurt an awful lot over you. I cried for a long time."

"It'll be different now, I swear. Honestly, honey, I was a fool. I didn't know how lucky I was to have you, and I'd already made a promise to Joanne. I don't break promises, honey."

No, but you lie easily enough, Mercy thought angrily. What now? Trapped on the side of a murderous mountain in the company of a lying man who wouldn't hesitate to kill her if he thought it would make him a profit, abandoned by a man who had made love to her and then left her to be killed—a man who couldn't possibly love her, because he didn't believe in her basic honesty. No, he had used her. *Used her.* But anger at Gray Cloud wasn't going to help her deal with Merle.

She forced herself to bite her lower lip, a habit she had when she was undecided about something, a habit Merle had teased her about more than once. He would know what it meant, and it wouldn't occur to him that she was doing it deliberately to hide the anger and disgust she was feeling. And the fear. With everyone on this mountain determined to kill her and the wolves, how could she spare any emotion for anything else? But she did. She felt plenty of hot rage right now.

A flicker of motion caught her eye, and she turned her head a little, just barely managing to swallow a happy exclamation when she saw Eyebrows regarding her from deep within the forest shadows. He stared straight at her, then turned suddenly and slipped away. She had the strongest feeling that he'd been trying to tell her she wasn't alone.

"Mercy?" Merle was demanding her attention, the faintest trace of impatience in his voice.

"I don't know." She tried to sound truly doubtful but not skeptical. She hoped it sounded as if she really wanted to believe him. Oh, God, this was an impossible game to play! She was no actress. "I mean...if you'd really loved me..."

"Oh, honey, I did! I do! Just say you'll give me the chance to prove it to you. Just the chance."

She summoned a smile. "I think... I think I'd like that."

There was absolutely no mistaking the satisfaction in his smile now. He felt he had her, which was a comment on how easy she'd been for him the first time. There wasn't a doubt in his mind that he could exercise a little charm and that she would tumble like an overripe apple into his waiting arms. It might almost be interesting to actually do it, just so she could find out what he hoped to accomplish. Did he think she would be willing to claim the wolf pack didn't exist?

No, even Merle couldn't possibly be so mistaken about her. What he probably intended to do was kill the wolves and then have her testify to the fact that they were gone and that it wasn't likely any wolf pack would come to the area again in the foreseeable future. Yes, that would be within the realm of possibility. That was something she would be able to do without lying and compromising her conscience. With the weight of her reputation and university behind whatever he wanted her to say, it would be believed and not questioned too closely. No one, for example, would believe that she had colluded in the murder of the wolves, so whatever had happened to the pack would be assumed to be natural or accidental. No one would look too closely.

God, he was despicable! She shivered, feeling the ground shake with renewed vigor. "I've got to get off this mountain." That much was absolute truth.

"We will, honey. I promise we will. But first...well, I understand you came up here to study some wolves?"

Ahh. This was it. She managed a nod, but couldn't bring herself to look at him. Instead she seized on what had happened on the rock table. "Did you see the way that rock tipped up? Oh, Merle, I thought I was going to slide down into that pit!"

"I know, but you're safe now, honey." He slid over closer and started to put his arm around her, but just then Thunder Mountain gave a huge tremor, one strong enough that Mercy and Merle both lay back to ride it out rather than try to balance against it.

Mercy held her breath, hoping against hope that another

crevice wouldn't open right under her. It was possible; she had seen what this mountain could do, and if it wanted to kill her and Merle both...

"Let's keep moving." The words were out of her mouth before she consciously formed them.

"You must be kidding! We won't even be able to stay on our feet!"

But the ground continued to shudder, and beneath her Mercy felt it buckle as if it were about to give way. Panic filled her, and she scrambled to her feet, swaying like a drunk as she tried to maintain her balance. "We've got to move!"

"Mercy, don't be stupid!"

The ground heaved upward now, doming beneath her feet, beneath Merle. That evidently connected in Merle's mind with Mount Saint Helens, because he scrambled to his feet, too, and stopped protesting. "Where?" he asked, as if she had all the answers.

"Anywhere. Anywhere away from here." Because it took the mountain time to act, and as long as they could keep moving, they might stay one step ahead of it.

They might survive.

CHAPTER THIRTEEN

They scrambled upward toward the mountain peak. As the trees grew thinner, the terrain grew steeper, and climbing became more difficult. Some corner of Mercy's mind wondered why she was heading upward instead of downward, why climbing seemed so imperative.

Listen...

Well, she was listening to something, she thought half-hysterically. Something was driving her higher up this mountain, and Merle was following without protest, probably because she seemed to know what she was doing.

Did she?

A different kind of thunder resounded from somewhere to the left; it sounded like a massive rock slide had been unleashed by the mountain's restlessness. Sobbing for oxygen in the thin high-altitude air, Mercy tilted her head and looked upward, afraid she would see some overhang or talus just waiting for the proper shake to set it loose. Much to her relief, there didn't appear to be anything that could easily be turned into a landslide.

But then she remembered the table, an apparently immovable, stable platform that had tried to tip her into a pit. Thunder Mountain had the power to do whatever it chose. No matter how stable and safe any portion of it looked, the mountain could turn it into a threat.

But she kept climbing. Running downward wouldn't make them any safer, and some instinct was demanding that she climb, that she get beyond the trees, if possible.

"Some friends of mine are up here a ways," Merle said breathlessly.

A corner of Mercy's mind registered his choice of words as odd. "Friends? You didn't come alone?"

"No. A bunch of us are, umm, camping out."

A small bubble of anger burst in Mercy. *Camping out* was a strange way to describe what these men had apparently been attempting to do. It infuriated her beyond speech to remember that fire set at the mouth of the wolf den. "I thought you came to find *me*."

"I did," he said as swiftly as his breathlessness would allow. "I did. But when I mentioned I was coming up here, a group of my pals decided to come along."

Right, thought Mercy. Right. Even for Merle, it was pretty damn thin. "How many of your pals?" That information might at least prove useful...if she lived long enough. Damn it, what had happened to Gray Cloud? She had a vision of him hiking happily down the side of the mountain while the mountain took care of all the problems, namely her, Merle and his friends. Another bubble of anger rose and burst within her.

"There are... There are four other guys with me," Merle said. "Good buddies."

Good murdering buddies, she thought bitterly. "Well, maybe if we all work together, we can get off this damn mountain." Hah.

"Yeah."

Just then, up ahead, she saw Eyebrows again. He stared straight at her and wagged his tail ever so slightly, as if he were greeting a member of his pack. Then he slipped away again into the shadows.

Climb...higher....

The trees were getting much thinner, and the barren slope above the tree line had just come into view when Merle reached out and stopped her. "Let's head south a little. That'll take us to my campsite."

Mercy hesitated, looking up the slope beyond the trees

with something that felt very much like longing. Why should she want to get up there? There were fewer places to hide up there where nothing grew.

Listen...

At twelve thousand feet, the lack of oxygen was distinctly uncomfortable. Had they been flying this high in a small airplane, they would have been required to wear oxygen masks. She was sure the altitude was fogging her brain a little, and she hesitated for too long, looking from Merle to the slope above, unable to decide.

"Come on, Mercy, it's not far. Six of us together will stand a better chance, because we can help each other."

She wasn't sure about that, but there didn't seem to be an alternative. She couldn't argue without a reason, and her only reason was a sharp longing to get higher.

And somehow, without being aware of making any decision, she found herself traversing the slope behind Merle, heading toward his campsite. What was he going to do with her when he got her there? Keep up the pretense that he loved her? Make a prisoner of her? Or kill her?

The mountain shook, and thunder rumbled hollowly, bouncing off the mountain and echoing through the canyons below, so that it sounded as if it came from everywhere all at once. With startling suddenness, lightning forked downward and hit a tree only fifty feet away. Blinded, Mercy stumbled to a halt as the thunderclap deadened her hearing.

The brilliance of the light seemed to have burned a hole in her retina. Everywhere she looked there was a black spot dead center in her vision, and she was afraid to move.

Merle swore savagely and reached out to hang on to a tree trunk as if he were afraid of falling. Long moments passed, and he just kept right on swearing.

When Mercy could finally see again, it was as if the world had been transformed. Black, roiling clouds had covered the sky, nearly turning day into night. Lightning flickered within the dark depths of the clouds, looking like the spluttering and spitting from a downed power line. Thunder Mountain's tremors had subsided a little, but the vibration of the ground beneath her feet was steady, a reminder.

They were greeted before they reached the campsite by one of Merle's "friends." Mercy took in the gun the man carried slung over his shoulder and recognized that it was no simple hunting rifle. These men weren't armed for deer, and it wouldn't matter, anyway, because it wasn't hunting season. The man looked from her to Merle in a way that made Mercy's skin crawl.

"My fiancée," Merle said, looking at Mercy with a smile. "At least, I hope she will be soon. Mercy, this is my buddy Vince."

She managed a smile. "Hi, Vince. Nice to meet you."

Vince didn't even bother with the smile. He nodded shortly and turned back to Merle. "Need a word with you."

The two men stepped away and spoke so softly that Mercy didn't have a hope of hearing. She pretended disinterest, turning away to look up through the trees at the barren slope above.

Listen...

She was listening. She was listening with every fiber of her being, trying to determine what she needed to do now. If she went to the camp with Merle, she might well be walking into her own grave. If she didn't...

Walk away....

The wind whispered the words to her, and she found herself walking slowly upslope, toward the tree line, away from Merle and Vince. Slowly, steadily, apparently unnoticed, she just kept going.

There was Eyebrows. He appeared again before her, staring straight at her with his strange golden eyes, and then turned, leading the way as if to encourage her.

Something was compelling her to get above the tree line. She wasn't sure what it was, or whether it was even the right thing to do, but she couldn't seem to stop herself. When finally she heard Merle shout after her, she was almost there, and she just kept going.

Listen...

Eyebrows glanced back, his tail high, his golden eyes mesmerizing. *Come with me,* he seemed to be saying. *Come with me.*

Beyond him she saw Stripes; the pups must have been left in a new den. And then the other members of the pack appeared like wraiths out of the thinning forest depths, standing to either side like an honor guard...or a gauntlet. As she advanced, they moved before her, always delineating the path, but never letting her get too close to them.

She could hear Merle behind her; he was hurrying to catch up, and the sound of his swift strides caused her to walk faster, too. Finally she broke into a run, her lungs straining painfully in the thin air.

The boiling clouds seemed to turn even blacker, and sparklers of blue lightning zipped through them. Stepping out into the open was going to turn her into a lightning rod, Mercy thought. She ought to stop right now....

No. Run, Tomorrow Woman. Run.

She ran, as fast as she could go, trusting the wind. Trusting the wind. The realization settled over her even as fear and worry propelled her. She was trusting the wind, the same wind that Gray Cloud spoke with. *Tate.*

A fork of lightning speared the ground ahead of her, but she kept running, urged on by the wolves and the whispers of the wind. Behind her, Merle shouted something.

Stop. Stop here....

She halted, nearly collapsing as her body shrieked for oxygen. Her legs trembled wildly, her lungs burned like fire, and every muscle screamed.

Merle shouted again. Mercy was leaning forward, hands braced just above her knees, gasping for air, but she turned her head and looked back.

Eyebrows came dashing back toward her, and when he reached her, he set himself between her and Merle, who came running up with Vince and three other men behind him. When the men approached, Eyebrows crouched and growled. One of the men leveled a gun at the wolf, but Mercy jumped in front of the animal, shielding it with her body. The man lowered his rifle.

"Damn it, Mercy, why did you run?" Merle said angrily. He approached but stopped a respectful distance back, eyeing the wolf warily.

"I don't know," she said. And honestly she didn't. "The wind told me to."

For an instant Merle was deprived of speech. He simply gaped at her before he finally said, "Honey, are you okay?"

"I'm just fine!"

"Then what do you mean, the wind told you to? The wind doesn't talk."

"Oh, yes, it does! And it told me to run. And you tell that friend of yours not to hurt any of these wolves! They're an endangered species, and this is the only known pack in Wyoming, and I'll make big trouble for anyone who hurts one of them!"

The change in Merle was astonishing. In an instant he went from concerned friend to angry enemy. She'd pushed too far, she realized. He wasn't going to try to cajole her over to his way of thinking on the subject.

"You won't be making trouble for anyone, Mercy. You won't be getting off this mountain alive."

Mercy opened her mouth to argue, then realized it wouldn't do any good. Merle had gotten her where he wanted her, and the gloves were off. She was about to die.

"Neither will you, Stockton."

At the sound of Gray Cloud's familiar voice, Mercy whirled around and saw him standing at the edge of the forest, blending closely with the dark shadows of a day turned almost into night.

Merle laughed quietly. "Thanks for turning up, Gray Cloud. I was sure you'd show your face once we got Mercy."

Mercy gasped, understanding. She had been everyone's bait. Now they could kill her *and* Gray Cloud, and take care of the wolves, leaving no loose ends behind.

But that was without reckoning on the mountain.

Eyebrows suddenly tilted his head back and gave a long, loud howl. He was answered immediately by the rest of the pack in their incredible harmony. Mercy instinctively looked around and cried out at what she saw.

She froze in shock and terror.

A crack was spreading along the ground toward Merle and Vince and the three other men who had joined them. Another crack was snaking steadily toward Mercy.

Jump back...

She obeyed immediately, without even thinking about it, jumping backward a foot. Merle looked at her oddly, then turned his head and saw the cracks that were creeping along the ground toward them. "What the hell...?"

"Thunder Mountain speaks," Gray Cloud said, his voice carrying steadily across the thunder, the wind and the sound of rupturing earth. "You have dared to threaten that which the mountain protects. You tried to kill the wolves. You want to kill the trees and countless small animals for your personal gain. The mountain will not allow it."

"The mountain doesn't have a damn thing to say about it," Merle snarled, but he didn't take his eyes from the cracks that were steadily approaching. Faster now, Mercy thought. As if the mountain had mastered the method, the cracks began to hurry toward them, gaining speed.

Eyebrows nudged at Mercy's knees, pushing her backward. She stumbled a little, but backed up, unable to tear her gaze from the accelerating cracks. Was the mountain going to try to swallow them? God, her worst nightmare!

The cracks weren't following a straight line, making it impossible to tell where they would intersect with the people...or which way she should go to avoid them. But they weren't big cracks, either, and when they arrived she would only have to step aside....

"Surrender now, Stockton," Gray Cloud called. "Tell your men to drop their guns and leave this mountain. You can still get off alive."

Merle snorted. "No way, Gray Cloud. You think a couple of cracks scare me?"

"You'll never timber this mountain," Gray Cloud said with flat certainty. Thunder rumbled in the boiling black clouds above, an angry, impatient sound. Lightning flickered faintly, almost as if it were waiting for some cue.

A restless flicker, Mercy thought. She dared a glance at Gray Cloud, then looked at the approaching cracks. They had almost reached them, she realized with an unpleasant start in the pit of her stomach. They didn't look deadly or even dangerous, but she knew the mountain better than to believe the cracks were innocent.

Step back.

She was long past wondering at the whispers in her head, long past ignoring them. She stepped back at once, just in time, it seemed, as a crack snaked in front of her, separating her from Merle. An innocuous little crack in the ground. Staggering only because of what it said about this mountain, what it revealed of the powers that dwelt here.

Another crack snaked between her and the men, right in front of Merle. He looked down at it and laughed.

Eyebrows nudged Mercy again, whining softly and pushing her away from the crack. She stepped back even farther.

"This is your last chance, Stockton," Gray Cloud said.

Another crack zipped along the ground, this time at a right angle to the one directly in front of Merle. It joined with another crack that had spread across the ground behind Merle and his men.

Mercy's heart seemed to stop. Didn't Merle see? Another crack, this one on the other side of the group. Sealing the square. Surrounding Merle and his men.

"Merle!" Mercy couldn't stand by and let this happen. Her conscience wouldn't allow it, much as she despised everything Merle was trying to do here. "Merle, for the love of God, get out of that square. Just step over here!"

Thunder roared suddenly, a furious explosion of sound, and lightning forked downward, stabbing at the ground nearby. Merle's henchmen were starting to look uneasy, but no one stepped out of the square the mountain had carved around them.

"Merle, please," Mercy begged. "Money isn't worth dying for!"

"The only people who are going to die are you and that redskin friend of yours," Merle snapped. "I'm bored with this crap. Shoot 'em!"

One of Merle's men leveled a rifle at Mercy; another pointed one in Gray Cloud's direction. But before either of them could pull the trigger, Eyebrows leapt, knocking the rifle from one man's hands and knocking the other man to one side. Immediately a third man fired at Eyebrows, but missed him.

As if the gunshots were a cue, the earth began to shake violently. As Mercy stared in horror, the cracks in the ground widened rapidly, in mere seconds becoming deep crevices, almost too wide to leap.

And from the depths of the crevices, flames shot upward. Suddenly a wall of fire stood between Mercy and Merle.

"Run, Mercy, run!" Gray Cloud shouted.

But horror held her frozen as she looked across a wall of flame at Merle. He and his men were surrounded now.

"Jump!" she shouted to him. "Jump across!"

"Mercy! Mercy, run!"

"Merle, jump! Jump!"

But the fire evidently terrified him too much, and he remained where he was, on the far side of a growing wall of flame.

"Mercy!"

Run...run, Tomorrow Woman! Before it's too late!

That was when Mercy became aware that another crack was zig zagging toward her, this one already a river of flame as it approached. Everywhere...everywhere she looked more fire-filled cracks were crisscrossing the ground.

"Mercy! Mercy!"

Eyebrows was suddenly there again, and this time he grabbed the sleeve of her jacket and tugged. As if released from a nightmare, she turned toward Gray Cloud....

And found he was on the far side of a wall of flame. She, too, was cut off, just as Merle and his men were. A scream came from one of Merle's men, but she didn't look. She was trapped by fire.

Jump through the fire.... Now!

But she couldn't. Fire terrified her, as it terrified most people. The heat of the flames felt as if it were singeing her skin without even touching her. Every instinct cried out to recoil...but there was no place to recoil to. She was trapped. Trapped.

A shriek from one of the men. Oh, God, how awful.... The bloodcurdling sound seemed to encase her in ice.

"Mercy!" Through the flames leapt Gray Cloud, appearing like some mythic warrior summoned by a wizard's spell. And suddenly he was there, holding her, squeezing her so tightly she thought a rib was going to pop.

"We have to jump," he told her. "We have to."

Some corner of her mind recognized the truth of it, but another part of her couldn't face the flames. She would be burned, and when it came to choices, she would rather be buried alive.

"Mercy, if we don't jump we're going to burn. Hold my hand. We'll jump together, and I'll make sure you don't get hurt."

She tilted her head back and looked up at him, thinking what a magnificent man he was. He had tied his hair down with a bandanna, which was the only way to keep it from catching fire, and he looked as much like a pirate right now as an Indian warrior.

"Mercy, we have to jump!"

Another scream from Merle's direction, but this one penetrated the fog that seemed to have paralyzed her mind. Yes, they had to jump. Refusing to look and see what was happening to the others, Mercy took Gray Cloud's offered hand.

"On the count of three," he said.

She nodded her understanding and tightened her grip on his hand.

"One…"

She reached inside her for the calm that helped her on the side of a cliff when she was rock climbing and there suddenly seemed to be no handholds above, no way to go.

"Two…"

When they got to the other side, the thing to do would be to roll on the ground, not wait to see if anything had caught fire, just roll to make sure that if anything *had* ignited it was put out. Focusing on the practical problem calmed her even more.

"Three!"

Somehow she was running straight toward that wall of flame as if it were an illusion to be ignored.

Jump, Tomorrow Woman. Jump!

She closed her eyes and jumped. Heat seared her skin, tightening it so that it felt it would peel off. Almost as soon as the blast furnace hit her, cool air replaced it. She opened her eyes just as the ground rushed up to meet her.

"Roll!"

She heard Gray Cloud shout the command, but she was already rolling, over and over, toward the woods. Toward what she hoped was sanctuary.

"Up!"

Hands pulled at her, lifting her to her feet, dragging her to the woods. Oh, God! Another wall of flame was zigzagging toward them. The mountain wasn't going to be denied.

"Keep running," Gray Cloud shouted. "Just keep running...."

Eyebrows suddenly appeared ahead of her and seemed to be beckoning. She ran. Hand in hand with Gray Cloud, she ran for the woods. Behind them, the screams stopped. Merle and his men were dead.

And the mountain had no intention of letting her and Gray Cloud escape. Another wall of fire zipped toward them, seeming to race along the ground like a burning fuse. When Mercy stumbled, Gray Cloud scooped her up, flung her over his shoulder and kept running. Mercy lifted her head and looked behind them. The entire clearing seemed to be on fire now.

And then they were in the trees. Little rivers of fire followed them for a bit, chasing and then stopping, as if the mountain were reluctant to set the forest ablaze.

A little deeper in the forest, Gray Cloud set Mercy on her feet and then wrapped her in his powerful arms, hugging her so tightly that she was surprised her ribs didn't crack.

"God," he whispered, "I thought I'd lost you!"

"Why did you leave me?" Struggling against his hold, she demanded an answer. "The mountain tried to kill me! It tipped up that table of rock and tried to dump me in a pit! Merle is the only reason I'm still alive!"

"I know. I saw." He shuddered. "I thought you'd be safe there. I really did. And when I came back and saw..." He shook his head and squeezed her harder. "I tracked you. I was so afraid Stockton would kill you before I could get to you."

"I thought—I thought you'd left me there to die."

He stiffened. In an instant he became as unyielding as rock. A moment later he released her and stepped back. "I see." He turned away.

"Well, what the hell was I supposed to think?" she demanded, torn between anger and tears. "You went off and didn't come back, and the mountain started trying to kill me, and Merle showed up and— Damn it, Gray Cloud, why were you gone so long?"

"I needed to locate all of Stockton's men so there wouldn't be any unpleasant surprises. They were scattered all over the place and—" He broke off abruptly. "What does it matter? Let's get out of here before something else happens."

The boiling black clouds overhead were as dark as night, and lightning speared through them threateningly. Nor had Thunder Mountain quieted. Beneath their feet the ground shook and heaved, but no fire spewed forth. The forest was safe from that, at least.

"The wolves," Mercy said. "I want to know if the wolves are okay."

"They're okay."

"How can you be sure? Eyebrows is the only one I've seen—"

"Eyebrows?" He interrupted her. "Who's Eyebrows?"

She was past caring whether she sounded stupid. All that mattered was that the wolves were okay and that she get off this mountain and never come back. "The alpha male. Because his eyebrows are different colors."

"Oh." He took several more long strides before replying. "I like it."

"Well, I want to know if they're all right, and I'm not going to settle for wondering. They helped me. All of them helped me right before Merle…got nasty. I'm not going to forget about them."

Gray Cloud halted abruptly and faced her. "All right," he said. "All right. I'll call them."

"Call them! You can't possibly—"

But he tilted back his head and let forth a perfect howl that caused the hair on Mercy's neck to stand on end. Chills ran down her spine as she listened to a sound she had never before heard issue from a human throat so perfectly.

Moments later another howl joined Gray Cloud's. Then another. Mercy couldn't tell how many wolves answered because of the deceptive harmonics, but in the end it didn't matter. In the end she was able to turn in a slow circle and make out pairs of golden eyes staring back from the forest's depths. They were all here, answering Gray Cloud's call, harmonizing beautifully with each other and the man.

Gray Cloud fell silent, while around them the wolves continued their full-throated song. "You see?" he said quietly. "They're fine."

Mercy nodded slowly, reluctant to let go of the moment, of the perfect beauty of the wolf pack's song, but she was aware that Thunder Mountain might attack again at any moment. Much as she hated to go, she had to. She had to get off this mountain before she died.

"Let's go," Gray Cloud said. "I have to calm the mountain."

The clouds remained so black and dense that it was impossible to gauge the time of day. Lightning continued to flicker, but it didn't seem threatening. The treetops swayed in the ceaseless wind, a constant rush of sound joined by the creak of bending tree trunks. From time to time an icy splatter of rain would fall.

Finally she was sure it must be sunset or later. Fatigue was making her stumble over her own feet, and the wind had developed a chilly bite. Even the black clouds seemed blacker. Just when she was beginning to think she couldn't take another step without collapsing, they emerged from the forest into the great bowl of the glacial cirque.

Mercy forgot her fatigue as she looked up at the peak of Thunder Mountain, bare and unadorned, the view unobstructed for once by the ever-present clouds. Tall and forbidding, a wall of gray granite rising to a peak as imposing as the Matterhorn. And down its side, from the glacier on its shoulder, ran a dazzling waterfall that plunged into the bowl of the cirque below.

Mercy understood instantly why this ground was sacred. Its beauty was breathtaking, but so was the bottom of the bowl, with its crazy tumble of boulders in shapes evocative of warriors frozen in stone, tall granite sentinels rising from a bed of the greenest grass and most dazzling wildflowers. Columbine and paintbrush vied for preeminence. And everywhere one looked there was a tall staff trailing a streamer of cloth—white and red, mostly, but some yellow, as well—left by someone who had come to pray.

It looked, Mercy thought, as if an army had been frozen in granite with their pennants still flying.

Gray Cloud began to chant, and Mercy turned to find him positioning three exquisite stones in a triangle, using his forearm as a measure of the distance between them. From a medicine bundle he took several other items and placed them in the center of the triangle. In the failing light she couldn't make them out, but it didn't matter. What mattered was the blue light that suddenly arced between the corners of the triangle, a dancing, flashing exhibition of vitality.

What mattered was Gray Cloud, standing over the triangle with his arms extended, palms uplifted. What mattered was that for the first time in days the mountain grew perfectly still and quiet.

Thunder Mountain listened.

The world grew silent, and even the clouds seemed to hold their breath. And a few minutes later, when Gray Cloud finished his prayer and bent to gather up all the items and wrap them securely in his prayer bundle, the world remained calm.

"It is finished," he told Mercy. "You'll be safe now."

"Just like that?"

"Just like that." He set the bundle down on the grass and sat cross-legged beside it. "We'll need to spend the night here. I'll take you down in the morning."

"I don't even have my pack anymore. No blankets."

"I'll keep you warm."

The offer drew her, and she settled beside him, nearly sighing when his arm wrapped around her shoulders.

After a while he spoke again. "I'll build a fire to keep us warm."

She watched, admiring his skill and economy of movement. He was a man comfortable in himself and in his world...and he wouldn't fit anywhere else. The thought filled her with sadness, haunting her with the awareness that their lives were worlds apart.

When the fire was burning brightly, driving back the

darkness and casting warmth over them, Gray Cloud again settled beside her and drew her to his side.

"We need to get the Conard County sheriff and the rangers up here," he said.

Mercy was suddenly struck by a terrible thought. "Gray Cloud! What if they're not dead? What if one of them is only hurt?"

"They're dead." He said it flatly, with conviction.

"How can you possibly know?"

"The life force is gone from them. I felt it when they died. They're all gone, Mercy."

She ought to feel sad, she told herself. She ought to feel some kind of grief or compassion, but all she could feel was a horror at the terrible way they had died. It seemed like an awfully high cost for a mountain and some timber, yet it had been Merle and his men who had put that price tag on Thunder Mountain. They had been prepared to kill to get what they wanted. In the end, it seemed the mountain had played by their rules.

"Has the mountain decided I'm not a threat?" she asked him.

"The wolves like you."

She suspected that non sequitur was the only answer she was going to get. Thinking about it now, she got goose bumps remembering how the wolves had helped her more than once. Odd behavior from wild animals. "The wolves here are unusual."

Gray Cloud shook his head. "No. Wolves are extremely intelligent. Man has just been too blind to see."

"White men, you mean."

He turned his head and looked at her. "Not all."

There was something she needed to say, so she looked into the fire, squared her shoulders and said it. "I'm sorry I thought you wanted me dead."

"I never wanted that, Mercy. Never. But sometimes I

wasn't sure I was going to be able to save you. The mountain sensed your connection with Merle. And I'm sorry I didn't believe you when you said it was over and done. I was jealous—not thinking clearly.''

Jealous. The word hit her hard, depriving her of both speech and breath. *Jealous.* Could he really care enough about her to be jealous? Oh, but it could never work!

Could it?

Still not daring to breathe, she tilted her head so she could look at him. Firelight played in strange patterns over his face, making him look like a warrior out of time. Beyond him, the dark shadows of the granite warriors seemed to keep guard.

"I, uh, didn't want to admit I'd come to care so much about you," he said.

"Care?" She barely breathed the word, needing more, so much more.

He moved his head a little, looking very much like a man facing an unpleasant task. "Yes," he said finally. "Care. As in love. I love you."

She felt as if she had cartwheeled off the edge of the planet into a place of brilliant light and joy. But, oh, how afraid she was to believe it could be. That it could come to anything. Their lives were poles apart.

Listen, whispered the wind. *Listen to your heart.*

She listened. And what she heard was a love so shining and bright that it could not be contained. "I love you, too," she whispered softly. "I love you."

He turned, gathering her into his arms, onto his lap, cradling her as if she were the most precious thing in the world.

And he kissed her. Kissed her with love and passion and a need so strong that she felt it to her toes. It was cold, and without blankets he didn't want to expose her to the chill of the night air, so his hands slipped within her clothes to claim her, gentle touches that painted fire on every exquisite nerve ending. She felt so incredibly possessed and loved, and it seemed only natural when her body exploded into a climax so intense that she felt as if the mountain had erupted beneath her.

And then she was lying on her side with her back to the fire's warmth, with Gray Cloud's warmth sheltering her front, as he held her and gently stroked her, as he whispered soft words of love and yearning.

For a little while she simply basked in the glow of dreams come true, but she wasn't one to hide her head in the sand. There was no way their lives could be combined in any way that would make a satisfactory relationship. So when she walked down this mountain tomorrow, she would be walking away from Gray Cloud.

A long sigh escaped her as she realized she was going to lose what she had only just found, that she was going to have to sacrifice either the man she loved or the job she loved, because she could never have both at the same time. Unshed tears clogged her throat and made it hurt. She wanted to grab him and hold on to him and never let him go. But she couldn't give up everything she had worked so hard for to become a hermit on the side of a mountain.

Gray Cloud stirred a little. "I have fulfilled my vision."

For an instant what he was saying didn't connect. When she finally comprehended it, Mercy felt her heart stop. "What—what do you mean?"

"I've fulfilled my vision. What happened today—the rivers of fire—that was my vision. I saw myself needing to be there to aid the mountain against those who would harm it. I had to be there to save the wolf pups from those who would harm them. To save you from the fire."

Mercy caught her breath sharply. "You... You saw that?"

He nodded. "It was my vision, and it has come to pass. My vision is complete."

"So...what happens now? I thought you were going to protect this mountain forever?"

"I will. But not in the same way. I no longer need to live here all the time. Stockton was the threat I saw so long ago in my vision, and he's gone. I see no other threats in the immediate future. You'll tell the world of the wolves, and the mountain will be protected. Later—years from now, perhaps—there will be other threats. If I'm needed, I'll come."

Hope was beginning to grow in her, a beautiful hope that hardly dared to unfurl its petals and bloom. "And in the meantime?"

He drew his head back and looked straight into her eyes. "In the meantime I can make my shields and create ceremonial regalia anywhere. I would like to come here and stay on the mountain in the summers, but for the rest of the year...I can rest my head wherever you are."

She drew a long, shaky breath and closed her eyes, hardly daring to believe.

Believe, whispered the wind. *Believe.*

"Will you be my tomorrow?" he asked.

She opened her eyes and let forth a laugh of sheer joy, understanding at last the name the wind had given her.

And she dared to believe.

* * * * *

SILHOUETTE *Romance*

Escape to a place where a kiss is still a kiss...
Feel the breathless connection...
Fall in love as though it were
the very first time...
Experience the power of love!

Come to where favorite authors——such as
Diana Palmer, Stella Bagwell,
Marie Ferrarella and many more——
deliver heart-warming romance and genuine
emotion, time after time after time....

Silhouette Romance——
stories straight from the heart!

Silhouette®
Where love comes alive™

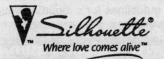

Silhouette —

where love comes alive—online...

eHARLEQUIN.com

shop eHarlequin

♥ Find all the new Silhouette releases at everyday great discounts.

♥ Try before you buy! Read an excerpt from the latest Silhouette novels.

♥ Write an online review and share your thoughts with others.

reading room

♥ Read our internet exclusive daily and weekly online serials, or vote in our interactive novel.

♥ Talk to other readers about your favorite novels in our Reading Groups.

♥ Take our Choose-a-Book quiz to find the series that matches you!

authors' alcove

♥ Find out interesting tidbits and details about your favorite authors' lives, interests and writing habits.

♥ Ever dreamed of being an author? Enter our Writing Round Robin. The Winning Chapter will be published online! Or review our writing guidelines for submitting your novel.

All this and more available at
www.eHarlequin.com
on Women.com Networks